Hope you
all enjoy

Mickey Maux
Muddles a Murder

Mickey Maux Muddles a Murder

AND SOLVES ADLER'S PROBLEM

Philip Emma

To order additional copies of this book, contact:
Xlibris
1-888-795-4274
www.Xlibris.com
Orders@Xlibris.com
760764

Contents

Day 1

I Stumble onto a Murder Scene

The big guy was dead to begin with.

I went to the main shopping mall to get a haircut, and then I crossed the traffic intersection to get to the strip mall across the street so that I could pick up some items at the supermarket before leaving in my usual way. I was making dinner that evening, and I needed a couple of things.

Mitch is the guy that I always get to cut my hair. He's usually there, and I always ask for him. Mitch is a short guy who probably can't see the top of my head when I'm sitting in the barber chair, and he probably doesn't give me the best haircut that I could get. But outside of "Hi, good to see you," he doesn't talk my ear off. That's why I like Mitch. Mitch was there that afternoon, and he cut my hair.

"Hi, good to see you," Mitch said.

"You too," I replied. He gave me the usual haircut, and I gave him the usual tip. "Thanks, Mitch," I said, and I left the barbershop. He and I liked to keep things to the point.

It was sometime after one o'clock, probably a quarter after one - not that I knew it at the time, but when I added up the parts subsequently, looking at the day in retrospect, it must have been

1

about a quarter after one. So I know that Mitch was at the hair salon as late as 1:15 on the day of the murder, because that's about when Mitch and I had said our goodbyes and I left.

To get out of the mall with my new haircut, I waited at the intolerably long traffic light to cross the intersection to the strip mall to get a couple of things at the grocery store. The strip mall contains the grocery store at which I usually shop, a fancy looking gymnasium, a large garden center, and about half a dozen smaller shops.

And to cross from the main shopping mall where I get my haircut to the strip mall where I buy my groceries is always a test of my patience. When the light's red, no one moves. And when the light turns green, again no one moves. I hate this intersection, and I try to avoid it. It always seems like I need to use my foghorn a lot just to get through it, so I always try to avoid this light if I can.

In part, this light is what motivated me to make the Shit-Ninnies.

I sat there patiently and eventually made it through the light, made it to the strip mall, parked, went into the grocery store, got what I came to get, and then started to leave by my usual way - avoiding the light, since I didn't need to go back through it to get home. Instead, I take a rear exit that isn't really an exit unless you know about it. Technically, it's not an exit at all, but I always use it anyway. To get to the rear exit - which really isn't an exit - from the strip mall, I drive around the strip mall to the back of the supermarket, and then around the garbage Dumpsters that are there.

I had gone to the supermarket after my haircut to buy a few cans of imported San Gennaro plum tomatoes, and some fresh fennel. I was making dinner tonight because my wife Carol was able to get some fresh seafood from the tip of Long Island, and I have my own autumn-special that I make when we get fresh seafood - but only when it includes shellfish - once the fall kicks in. And the fall was in the process of kicking in.

As I've said, I leave the strip mall by driving behind the supermarket, because there's a small alley there after you pass the garbage Dumpsters that circumvents the main exit. While I do have to drive over a small curb to get out into the alleyway - which leads to a cul-de-sac, which leads to a side-street - I always leave this way because I have no patience with traffic, and no patience with waiting in long lines at traffic lights.

And of course, when I say that "this trail behind the store and past the Dumpster eventually leads to a side street," I'm talking about side streets in Connecticut, which are narrow and rocky and hilly.

Side streets never form a grid here, but seem to randomly feed into each other. If you know the neighborhood - which I did - it's fine. But if you're from out of town, you'd have a hard time getting out of the labyrinth comprising any neighborhood. You'd likely go in circles. You should never rob a house here unless you're sure how to get out of the neighborhood.

It was early autumn, and the leaves were a week or two away from their prime colors. While there were still lots of green leaves blowing in the trees, there was also an entire panoply of reds, yellows, tans, and browns. Looking at the hillside about a half a mile away made a beautiful panorama if you didn't try too hard to focus - not that you really could anyway on things as tiny as leaves. And that panorama would take your breath away if you didn't allow yourself to be distracted by the machinations of the shopping center.

In addition to the beautiful colors, this week brought with it an autumnal smell as the summer heat faded and the temperature became milder. While not tangibly identifiable, the beginnings of the cooling weather - a welcome relief after a hot summer - gives a palpable substance to the smell that goes with the changing colors of the leaves. They faintly scent the air. It was fall.

I could also smell a wood fire coming from the chimney of a house in the adjoining neighborhood. While that's a stronger smell, it's also an evanescent one, as it comes and goes with shifts in the autumn breeze. It was seasoned oak that I smelled burning. Oak has a distinctive aroma that awakens my sense of the fall after a long hot summer.

The four seasons parody the life-death cycles of our abundance on earth, and I always felt that those living where it's perpetually hot and sunny are deprived of the personal introspections brought about by the changes in the four seasons. Perhaps that's why people from areas like that always struck me as too laid back. But the two most beautiful changes in this cycle are the raw innocence of spring blooms which have the clean and nascent scent of a newborn infant, and the waxing scent of the beauty that accompanies the fall colors as the leaves turn, like that of a lovely woman who's no longer a shapely teen, but who instead hits an elegant maturity that's inimitable by youths before the earth goes back to sleep.

I had gone to the store to get a few items to make cioppino, arguably a Californian dish, which I'd be reluctant point out to my Connecticut neighbors; not that neighbors in Connecticut talk to each other much. While cioppino is certainly a San Francisco

specialty, it's not much different than many of the Italian zuppa that
are improvised around the world. While Californians might think
that fennel gives it a distinctive California touch, I would argue that
it's only distinctive in the sense that California fennel is mild relative
to its Italian cousin, finnochio, although coupling it with fish is more
of a Sicilian custom than a mainland practice. But what California
has over Italy is the shellfish: the shellfish in California are much
more impressive. While seafood in general is a summer thing, the
shellfish hit their most robust size in the fall, and the fennel lends an
autumnal taste to it all.

My wife Carol has a close friend that just drove back from
Amagansett yesterday (a short drive for Californians, but not
necessarily for Easterners - especially the way that Route 27 can crawl
until you clear the Hamptons) with some lobsters and shellfish and
cod, so Carol had sent me out to get the basics for one of our autumn
standards. While I feel that shellfish are best raw, and wouldn't
debate California versus Long Island in a cooked dish, I think that
the Northeastern lobsters are special, and much better than the
Dungeness crabs of the West. And lobsters need the cold water to
develop their real flavor.

So I had come to the store to get some fennel and plum tomatoes.
And as is my custom, I did not leave by the main entrance, but
instead drove around to the back of the store past the garbage
Dumpsters. And that's where I saw the car parked at a strange angle
with the engine still running and the driver's door wide open. The
left turn signal was flashing, as if it was signaling a turn into one of
the Dumpsters. And he was sitting there in the driver's seat with his
mouth wide open. He was dead.

His car had been hit by a paintball, no doubt fired by one of
the Shit-Ninnies that patrols the roads. But it looked like it was just
a random hit over the trunk - it's hard to say that the Shit-Ninnies
had actually targeted him, since the paint spot wouldn't obscure his
vision much. The Shit-Ninnies usually don't target you unless you're
a crappy driver. And they do try to obscure your view, but they aren't
great shots. They might have been shooting at someone else for all
I know.

I parked my car next to his, and got out to have a look. He was a
big man, and he looked like he hit the gym - regularly. His head was
nearly touching the roof of his car as he sat there, dead.

He had a bullet hole in his right temple, and the blood had nearly
dried, which was a little curious as he couldn't have been there long

without having been noticed - although admittedly, I didn't climb into the car to examine the wound. There wasn't a lot of blood, but enough to make it clear that he'd been shot cleanly with a small caliber round that killed him instantly. It was a good shot, and it was obviously done by a pro.

The gunshot was not the work of the Shit-Ninny that had hit his car with a paintball, but the work of someone that knew him. And that someone must have been in the passenger's seat. After all, the bullet hole was in his right temple, and he was in the driver's seat with all the windows closed, so I left them that way.

The dead man was wearing black pleated slacks, and a grey tattersall tweed jacket. He was well dressed and had a very strong build, which explained the pleated slacks. While these may not look good on tall men in general, if a man has muscular legs, the pleated lines will make the cut of the slacks flow better; even for a tall man, who generally doesn't need this. And this guy looked like he hit the iron big time.

Except for the dead man, the car was empty. That is, other than an old gym-bag lying on the back seat. While the man was dressed well and his clothes looked relatively new - not surprising given the change in seasons and the tattersall tweed, the gym-bag was well worn. Besides his build, this is another sign of a serious gym rat.

His bag was obviously a real gym bag for carrying his gym equipment. It was not a fashionable bag used to accentuate his outfit. I'm sure it had the stuff of a serious lifter: some chalk, some knee and wrist wraps, some lifting straps, a lifting belt, fingerless gloves, and lots of odds and ends. Maybe he used the gym next door to the supermarket in the plaza here, although wearing a tweed jacket in there would be a little odd despite the autumn.

And his car was missing its license plates.

Normally, I'd assume that no sane person without license plates would pull over behind a Dumpster to talk to a stranger behind a supermarket. And I'd also think it unlikely that he just so happened to have a chance encounter behind the Dumpster with an old friend that shot him. Besides, no one leaves the parking lot this way except for me. Others have patience and don't drive over curbs to get alleyways to get to cul-de-sacs. They don't know what they're missing. I do: the traffic lights.

Of course I knew better than to touch anything. The last thing I needed was my fingerprints at the crime scene. While I sometimes do detective work for the right client and the right stakes, I don't talk to

the cops, and don't appreciate them hauling me in. I've been there
and done that, and we share a mutual mistrust. While I mistrust
everyone, that goes double for the cops.

Except for my old friend Danny.

Danny and I had been good friends when we were kids, growing
up. I'm not sure why. We didn't have much in common except for
having deep streaks of honesty missing in many, and we seemed to
get along. He and I spoke the same language at a basic level, and I
trusted him. We both did juvenile pranks and got into minor trouble
a few times. That was lots of fun when we were kids, but we've almost
both grown up. Sort of.

In High School, Danny wasn't one for the books. He graduated,
and became a cop. I guess he's never moved beyond juvenile
delinquency, which is why I figured that I still liked him after not
seeing him for many years.

But unlike Danny, I was always drawn to reading books and
solving equations, and did very well in school. I went away for a long
time and spent years in the Midwest, in California, and in Boston,
studying my butt off, and enjoying the hell out of it. I was a Professor
for a while back in California, and then down in Austin, where I came
into some money and retired young. Why I moved back here I'm not
sure. Maybe it was the rocks and the seasons. The Midwest doesn't
have rocks, and California doesn't have seasons. And neither has real
barbecue. For that, you need to go to Texas.

And like Danny, deep down at basic level I'm still a juvenile too;
I never outgrew it. I tinker a lot, and I invent things. Most of those
things are great. But like all great things, great things are double-
edged swords. A prime example is the Shit-Ninnies, who hit me every
so often despite the fact that I take my driving pretty seriously. And
because I take my driving seriously, I made The Fingers for my car,
and I use my foghorn a lot despite the fact that I don't like noise.

And also like Danny, sometimes I do detective work for the right
client and the right stakes. But I don't talk to the cops; at least I try
not to - except for Danny, who I talk to now and then. As I've said,
despite the fact that he's a cop, I trust Danny. At a very basic level,
the thing that pulled us together in High School is that we were both
honest. I've always known him to tell the basic truth, although he's
not beyond pulling the occasional fast-one.

But because this was obviously a murder, and because it didn't
involve me, I called Detective Danny on his private cell, and told

him that there was a dead guy in a car by the Dumpsters behind the supermarket. And I told him that I didn't do it.

You could tell that I didn't do it because there was nothing funny about this hit. The guy was just sitting in his car dead. If I had done it, it would have been a little more distinctive depending on who the guy was. But this guy was just dead. At least he sure looked it.

I will hit people if the price is right and the person has it coming. But I don't hit strangers, and not like this. Behind a Dumpster behind a supermarket? What would be the point? And why would I tell Detective Danny about it if I had?

So leaving the car with the Shit-Ninny's paintball on it and the dead guy with his gym bag in it, I drove over the curb and up the alley into the cul-de-sac, and then into the little neighborhood of side streets. This avoided the traffic light at the main intersection that crosses over to the shopping mall. And I always want to try to avoid that light because people always block that intersection going both ways.

Whenever I do go that way, I have to use The Fingers and my foghorn a lot, so I try to avoid it. While I don't see The Fingers because they're on my roof, as I've said, the noise from the foghorn is deafening, and can bother me. Today I drove home mostly on back streets, and only needed to give The Fingers to a few other drivers. And I didn't need my foghorn much at all.

Except for the dead guy, today was a beautiful day. I wondered who he was.

Day 2

Detective Danny, Detective Dorian, and my False Deposition

The next morning in my upstairs lab, I was working on a new idea involving the use of sunlight. The idea was to bring shimmer to certain kinds of surfaces that could then receive remote projections. This is why I was in my upstairs lab; I needed the sunlight.

I was having success with the projections, but having lots of trouble with their distortions. Unless surfaces are perfectly flat - which they seldom are if they're not especially made to be, projected images would always distort on them. Glass is actually a liquid, so it moves, however slowly. And it's amorphous. It's not a crystal, so there's very little that's regular about it, although it looks that way to the human eye - which is why we make windows out of it.

I had added this lab to our house a few years ago after receiving compensation from some work that I had done for the spooks in Washington having to do with mood-sensing. This basically allows the spooks to know what you're thinking, even if you don't think so, and even if you're not thinking. At least they seemed to think that it allows them to think that they know what you think. Ergo, it works. That is, I think that it works.

The lab itself wasn't a big expense, although some of the equipment in it was rather extravagant. The main costly renovation in putting this lab in was the kitchen under it. I had worked with a local architect on fitting both the lab and the kitchen in as augmentations to our house subject to the local zoning rules.

Zoning rules tend to make many renovations a little more complicated than you'd think, although sometimes it's for good reasons. In this case, because the house - like most up in the hills where it's difficult to pitch long runs of pipe - had a septic tank for which zoning has very definite "keep out" rules when building around it or near it. Those rules are there for real reasons. So to me, it just made the design more of a challenge.

We had wanted to double the size of the kitchen and to put in a vaulted ceiling so that we could grow fresh herbs in one corner of the room, while having a very large center island at which I could sit and work when I wanted some indoor sun. While I like the outdoors, the ambient noise and motion from birds and other animals - including neighbors - breaks my concentration. While I like the bird's sounds (except for the blue jays), the neighbor's sounds I can live without; especially their lawn mowers.

So our kitchen now extends about twenty feet further out into the back yard, which gives us a better view of the pool when you're standing at the sink looking out the window. But I did have to move most of the deck around the corner of the house to allow this, since the pool is slightly downhill from the kitchen. We are on a heavily wooded lot, so the back yard is surrounded by forest, which gives us lots of privacy. And I like privacy.

I'd been in the lab working longer than I'd thought - sometimes time flies when I'm focused on the mathematics of a problem - when I was snapped out of my reverie by my wife Carol, who was shouting for me from the downstairs foyer.

"Hey Mickey," I heard her shout. "Your buddy Danny is here. Can you talk now?"

Carol is terrific that way. She doesn't assume that I'll drop whatever I'm doing to talk to whomever calls or drops by.

"Yes, dear," I shouted down. "Tell him I'll be down in a minute or two, thanks."

Carol and I had met by chance. I had usually had my head in the books, but couldn't help but to notice Carol when I dropped by a legal office to get advice on prior-art on some patents I was examining in light of a new class of inventions. The first thing that I had noticed about Carol was that she had long beautiful hair, which grabbed my attention.

But what I hadn't expected was that when she brushed her lovely hair aside, her features were gorgeous too. Had she had short hair, I likely would have been even more taken by her classical features. Of course, when I had first met her, she was sitting behind a desk, and was wearing business attire. While the colors were neutral, the blouse she had on had a very feminine lacy trim. And she'd been wearing subdued decorous jewelry - a line of pearls, and a delicate gold chain. The jewelry didn't jump out at me. It simply complemented her overall look without drawing attention to itself.

While her jewelry made an understatement, this was entirely appropriate in her case, since her features and her hair had me hooked. In our first meeting, I had never seen her stand, and had hoped that I when I saw her stand, I'd have reasons to forget her. While I've always thought that women were terrific, they'd mostly been distractions in my life, and none of my relationships had ever blossomed.

Carol struck me as very bright and very business-like, but also very open and very normal. While beautiful, I didn't get the impression that she doted on it. She was more interested in everyday things. And her conversational style, while professional, wasn't inflated.

The next time I came to the patent office I saw her standing up, and then I really noticed her. She was stunning. Her proportions were athletic, while slightly overemphasizing her female parts. That view was hard to forget. Then one conversation led to another, which led to another, which led to another. We were dating, and then we were married. And I've never looked back.

I shut my notebook, and flung it on the pile on my desk.

I'll admit that my desk is a mess. The mess makes it feel much more like it's my personal space. People who are anal about their desks spend most of their time organizing them, and not as much time working for real. I find the act of deliberately organizing creative thoughts to be debilitating to those thoughts if done prematurely or too rigorously. But that's just me.

While I'd had a few ideas about how to crack the particular problem that I'd been working on - the projection of images on glass, none of those ideas were breaking yet. I've found that frequently, the way to break a problem is to work hard on it, and then to put it away and forget about it. The trick is to throw it onto the mess on my desk, and leave it there.

I've found that if you don't think about a problem for a while, the next time you see it, sometimes the answer leaps out at you. And sometimes it doesn't. That's guaranteed, either way.

I went downstairs and saw Detective Danny, who was standing in the foyer wearing his police uniform. I've always asked Detective Danny not to come here in his police uniform. It makes me think that I'm going to be arrested.

In High School, Danny had run track. And in High School, he also smoked. Lots of us did. That includes me, but I didn't run track. Of course Danny ran the short events: the 50-meter, the 100-meter, and the 200-meter sprints. He didn't have the raw power to dominate the 50-meter, and the 200-meter was at the upper end of his wind ability given the smoking. But Danny excelled at the 100-meter sprint. He was quick, but he smoked.

Back then, lots of High School kids smoked because most of their parents smoked. It looked sophisticated. When you went to the movies, all the movie stars smoked - especially the real men and the real women. And back then, you could even smoke at the movies if you sat up in the balcony. And all the rock stars smoked - and here, believe it or not, I'm talking about cigarettes. And when I went to college, all of the professors smoked. In fact, students were allowed to smoke in class, and I did at first.

Lots of people smoked, but not many who smoked ran track. Danny did both. I eventually quit smoking, as did Danny, and both of us now do various things to keep basically fit. Times have changed. Men used to have martinis and steaks for business luncheons. Now they have bottled spring water and salads. While this latter trend is definitely healthier, I'd hardly call it macho. Bottled water and a salad? Seriously?

Danny had been naturally athletic despite smoking, and had managed to stay relatively trim in his middle age. He usually dressed very casually: jeans and a button-down sports-shirt, with sneakers or boat shoes. You wouldn't notice him if you passed him on the street, and wouldn't guess that he was a cop. But today he was wearing his police uniform.

"Why are you wearing your police uniform?" I asked. "You know I don't want cops coming to my house. My neighbors will wonder what the hell I've done this time. Besides, it makes me want to give you the finger."

He said "I'm on business, Mick. Apparently, people in the neighborhood behind the supermarket saw you jump the curb in your car and leave the scene of the crime. I was told by the chief to ask you what you were doing there - at the scene of the crime."

"Wait a minute," I said. "I told you that I was there. I called you and told you about the car and the dead guy. I went to the supermarket to buy some tomatoes and fennel. So what? Lots of people go to the supermarket to buy tomatoes and fennel. There were lots of people there. Why would they connect this to me in particular?"

"Because everyone else who goes to the supermarket waits at the light to get out of the parking lot. And most of them don't buy fennel. What the hell is fennel, anyway? It was only you who drove to the back of the store - to the murder scene - and drove over the curb to escape into the alley behind the store. Why did you go back there and leave the murder scene by jumping the curb?"

"I 'escaped into the alley?' What's that mean? I use the alley because I don't like traffic lights." I said. "Anyway, how do you know that it was me who went behind the store and up the alley? I'll bet that other people go out that way too. How would anyone in that neighborhood know who was in the car that came out of the alley? True, it was me, but it could have been anyone's car. How would anyone know that it was my car? It's just a car."

"Your car, just a car?" he asked.

"Yes," I replied. "It's just a car."

"You mean the car with The Fingers? Four big middle fingers on its roof? A middle finger on the back, a middle finger on the front, and a middle finger on each side? Big motorized middle fingers that flip-off other drivers? That car?" he asked. "Not to mention that you're always blowing your foghorn. It's hard for people in any neighborhood to not notice you."

"So I put some four-foot middle fingers - 'The Fingers' as I call them - on the roof of my car so that I can flip-off other drivers in any direction. I can't know ahead of time who drives like an idiot, otherwise I wouldn't have needed four of them. People who drive like assholes could be on any side of me. Sometimes they completely surround me - I should have put on eight Fingers instead of four. And The Fingers are only four-feet high because I don't want to worry about overpasses, otherwise I'd have made them bigger. Are you saying that I shouldn't flip-off people that drive like assholes? That's what The Fingers are for."

"No," he said. "All I'm saying is that your car is different in that way, and that people recognize it as your car when you drive through neighborhoods and flip people off. And you're hard to not notice, because you're always blowing your freaking foghorn."

"Shit!" I said. "You know I didn't think of that when I put The Fingers on my car. I need to invent something that lets me flip people off more discretely. And I don't like using my foghorn because it hurts my ears, but I have to. So many people drive like idiots."

"So I have to ask you some questions officially," Detective Danny said. "And I'll have to do it downtown. The chief said so."

"Shit!" I said. "Downtown? Maybe 'The Big Chief' just wants more wampum, and is just shaking me down. I hope the Shit-Ninnies get him."

"Get who?" asked Detective Danny.

"Exactly," I said.

So Detective Danny and I went downtown. Tonya was the clerk there. She's the first eyeful that you get when you walk in. And she's an eyeful.

"Name?" asked Tonya, checking me in.

"Mickey," I answered, checking her out.

It was hard not to check her out. She was young, pretty, and shapely. She lacked the innate beauty that I had first seen in Carol, but unlike Carol, she worked at showing it off, so it was hard to ignore. She had elaborate sweeps of hair that must have taken hours to sculpt in her particular way, and the sweeps were highlighted with greens and purples. While this can look comical, on her it actually looked pretty good, because she would have been fairly striking even without it.

Of course she had a nose ring, which I never understood. How do these women blow their noses? Maybe they don't. Ever. And she had seven or eight earrings on her left ear. I didn't know if that meant that she was Lebanese or something, or whether it's just a random look. Her makeup was overdone - more appropriate for night-clubbing than for work. But lots of young women don't seem to know the difference.

She did look fairly fit, like she hit a gym regularly, but not too hard. She was wearing tights and ankle boots with high heels. This does tend to accentuate a woman's legs, but I don't know how some of them actually walk around in those on a daily basis. They look great when you're going out to dinner and won't be doing much walking. But I never understood how some women wear them regularly.

Tonya had on a chiffon top that drooped around the shoulders and flared out below the waist, making the tights seem a little more business-like. The top was in a tiger-print, and she had a braided belt that held it firmly around her waist, and that made sure that the thin print went tightly around her breasts, which made them hard to not notice. I'm sure that this wasn't an accident, so I noticed them.

"OK, Mickey," she said. "What's your last name?"

"Maux," I said.

"You mean you're Mickey Mouse?" she asked.

"No. Maux," I said. "Spelled M-A-U-X, although it sounds like 'Mouse.' And although my name's Mickey, I go by Mick. It's Mick Maux. In France, I'm baaaad."

"Sounds baaaad," she said. "Sounds baaaad even in Connecticut."

"*Oui*," I said. "*Tres maux.*[1] Even in Connecticut."

"Mow? I thought you said Mick." she stated. "And what's France have to do with anything?"

"*Je ne sais quoi*[2]" I said, checking her out again. "Mickey Maux. I'm baaaad."

She rolled her eyes. "Weird!" she said faintly, under her breath.

That being done - checking me in, while I was checking her out ("Weird!") - Danny and I went to his desk so that I could give him a formal deposition. Again, I wondered whether she was a Lebanese.

A young detective that I had never seen before joined us, and introduced himself: "Detective Dorian," he said.

Detective Dorian was tall and thin, and had a scar along his jawline. It looked like a knife wound, but it's hard to say. Detective Dorian had short hair and kept it carefully trimmed and neatly combed. He moved in a precise way - almost like a military person. Or maybe he just had a stick up his ass.

Detective Dorian was wearing a suit and its accoutrements, as if exemplifying business savvy, although those accoutrements made it clear that he lacked a basic knowledge of what was appropriate, and that he was devoid of taste. While it was a dark blue pinstriped suit, he wore it with an also-blue plaid tie, and had a pocket handkerchief that matched the tie exactly. He wore light brown shoes and pink socks. Had he been a mob hit-guy, I would have overlooked all of

---

[1]   French for "very bad."

[2]   French for "I do not know what."

these mistakes, but as a police detective, he should have left his suit at home if he didn't know how to accessorize it.

And I don't think a mob hit-guy would wear pink socks with a dark blue suit. It would make him much too conspicuous. Speaking of which, he was wearing a silver watch with a green watch strap.

"I'd like you to meet Detective Dorian," said Detective Danny. "He'll be joining us for your deposition. Detective Dorian, this is Mick. He's an old friend of mine."

"Mick Maux," I said, and shook hands with Detective Dorian.

"Mickey Mouse? Are you screwing with me?" Detective Dorian asked.

"No," I said, "and I usually go by 'Mick.' My last name's spelled 'M-a-u-x.' Good to meet you, Detective Dorian. Are you a big fan of Mickey Mouse, dipshit?"

"Are you a wise-ass? Would you like a bust in the mouth?" he asked.

"Maybe if it's Tonya's," I said. "Why?"

"Tonya's my girlfriend!" he said. "Do you want me to kick your ass?"

"Do I want you to kiss my what?" I asked.

Danny interjected: "Detective Dorian, my friend Mick is hard of hearing. He frequently misunderstands what you're saying. You'll have to be patient with him; he meant no offense."

Detective Dorian and I shook hands - again. "Good to meet you, Detective Dorian." I said, and I made a "toot" noise. "Detective Danny and Detective Dorian; you guys sound like twins."

"What time was it when you saw the murder?" asked Detective Dorian.

"I didn't see the murder. I saw the dead guy in the car when I was leaving the lot. It was about a quarter to two. I know that because the clock in the store said twenty-of when I checked out, and it couldn't have taken more than a few minutes to pay, go to my car, and leave. That's when I saw the dead guy. I'm guessing it was a quarter to two."

"What were you doing behind the store?"

"Leaving."

"Behind the store? The exit is at the other end of the parking lot at the traffic light out in front of the store. You can either turn onto the main street there, or you can go straight through to the shopping mall."

"Exactly," I said. "That's why I don't leave that way. I always drive over the curb out behind the Dumpsters, and go down that alley into that little neighborhood. There aren't any traffic lights that way, and I don't have to give many people The Fingers. I hate traffic lights."

"Don't you mean give them the finger?" he asked. "So what did you see when you were leaving?"

"No, I didn't mean 'give them the finger,'" I said, giving him the finger. "I give people 'The Fingers.' But back to the car. The car was angled in a strange way. The driver's door was open, the left directional was flashing, and the dead guy was in the car with a bullet in his head."

"How did you know that there was a dead guy in the car?" he asked.

"Like I said, the driver's door was open, and there he was."

"There who was?" he asked.

"The dead guy, Einstein."

"The dead guy's name is Einstein? How do you know that?"

"I don't know the dead guy's name."

"You just said it was Einstein. How do you know that?" he asked.

"I don't know who the dead guy was. I thought *you* were Einstein."

"I'm Detective Dorian," he said, "I'm not Einstein."

"Exactly," I said. "You're not Einstein. And I don't know who the dead guy was."

"But how did you know that there was a dead guy in the car?" he asked.

"Because the door was open, Einstein," I answered.

"I'm not Einstein!" he exclaimed.

"Exactly," I repeated.

"But how did you know that there was a dead guy lying in the back seat just because the front door was open?" he asked. "Surely, you couldn't see the little dead guy lying flat in the back seat from your car. And how did you know that he had been shot in the right temple? He was lying on his right side. There's no way you'd have seen that he'd been shot in the temple without moving the body."

"A little dead guy in the back seat? There was no little dead guy in the back seat," I said. "The dead guy I saw was sitting in the driver's seat. And he was a very big guy. There's no way that he could lie down in the back seat. The only thing lying in the back seat was an old gym bag. I assumed that it belonged to the dead guy, but I don't know."

Detective Dorian was rubbing me the wrong way. An oleaginous cop if I ever saw one. And he dressed like a real twiddlepoop, while feigning machismo. Call me coprophobic, but Detective Dorian was a rancorous SOB; he was a real fart-warbler. And I didn't trust him.

So Detective Danny filled out a deposition for me.

It said that I saw the car there when I was driving past the Dumpsters. The reason that I was driving past the Dumpsters was because although I live around here, I was lost, so I drove behind the store instead of out to the exit because I wasn't sure where the exit was, because I'm a numbskull, and I'd thought that maybe the exit was behind the store next to the garbage Dumpsters. And when I saw the car it looked empty - like no one was in it. That's why I parked my car and got out to look at it. Why would I do that? Oh that's right! Because I'm a numbskull. And that's when I saw the little dead guy lying in the back seat.

This is why Detective Danny fills these things out, and I don't. I'm not stupid enough.

And again, none of what he wrote was why I was there, or what I saw, or how I saw it. But Detective Danny said he could check me out if I signed it, so I did. That's what the cops are for.

And then Detective Danny drove me home. He drives like an idiot, so he really shouldn't have bothered. I was worried that the Shit-Ninnies would get him. And it's fine with me if the Shit-Ninnies get him, but not while I'm in the car with him.

"Sorry if Detective Dorian was a little overbearing," Danny said. "Sometimes he can come across like a really crude SOB, despite trying to look sophisticated by wearing a suit."

"Don't worry about it," I responded. "I pegged him as a real '*travone*[3],' as we'd say down in the Bronx. Especially with that suit."

"Huh?" said Detective Danny. "His name's not Travone."

"Really?" I asked. "A blue pinstriped suit with pink socks? He looked like a real '*travone*.'"

"Well he's not," said Detective Danny.

"You ought to know," I responded. "At least I can tell he's not a Lebanese."

On the way home, and because Detective Danny drives like an idiot, a Shit-Ninny coming from the other direction blasted his windshield with a paintball, and he had to swerve and pull over. He turned on the wipers and the rinser until the windshield was clean enough for us to drive again, and then he merged back into traffic.

"Why did you build those fucking Shit-Ninnies?" he asked me. "And isn't there a way to disable them?"

---

[3]   An Italian slang term for a homosexual man.

"I knew that was likely to happen. Why do you drive like an idiot?" I replied. "Oh, that's right. So that you can remind me why I first built the Shit-Ninnies. Every so often I think about taking them down, but then I see people that drive like you do, and it reminds me to let them keep running."

My idea for the Shit-Ninnies came from being frustrated with the way lots of people drive. The concept was a car that runs entirely on solar power so that it never needs gas. Its job is to autonomously patrol the streets and highways, and to bomb people that drive like idiots with paintballs. The hope was that it would make people drive more carefully. And to step on it when the light turns green, instead of sitting there glued to the road like a bunch of queef-boogers.

While the Shit-Ninny cars are self-driving, I put human-looking Shit-Ninny dolls in the driver's seats so that from a distance, the Shit-Ninny looks like any other car being driven by a dumb person. Up close, it's obvious that the Shit-Ninny person isn't real. It's even dumber than a dumb person; it's a Shit-Ninny doll.

The Shit-Ninny dolls look like they're dumb as stumps, which they are (and in this way, they do look like lots of other drivers). The Shit-Ninny dolls are always making chewing motions with their mouths - as if chewing tobacco, and their eyes are perpetually rolling. Sometimes the head rotates all the way around. If you saw the Shit-Ninny up close, you'd know that the driver wasn't real because their heads can rotate all the way around. Real peoples' heads don't rotate all the way around, even when they're chewing tobacco. But the Shit-Ninnies don't talk, so they don't sound nearly as stupid as many other drivers.

When a Shit-Ninny is running low on power, it finds a nice place to park in the sun, and it waits for the batteries to build enough charge to drive some more. When parked, the Shit-Ninny doll recedes down into the floor so that it just looks like a parked car. You'd never know that the car was a Shit-Ninny unless you were me.

While driving around and patrolling the streets at random, the Shit-Ninnies shoot paintballs at other cars. Originally, I had wanted the Shit-Ninnies to just shoot paintballs at cars that were doing really stupid things, but it turned out that so many people do stupid things that the Shit-Ninnies shoot paintballs at nearly everyone. And once in a rare while they seem to shoot paintballs at other cars for - more or less - random reasons, although that's unusual.

So while it's possible to get shot with a paintball by a Shit-Ninny by mistake, if a driver does something really stupid, the Shit-Ninny might blast them with more than one paintball. On rare occasions on busy streets, there can be multiple Shit-Ninnies at the same intersection. People have been hit by multiple paintballs from several Shit-Ninnies all at once for doing stupid things at major intersections. While this is rare, when it happens it's warranted.

This is why people should keep some water in their car if they like to drive like idiots. And you really need to wash the paint off your car soon, or you'll need a paint-job. Also, this is why I use my foghorn a lot: because lots of people drive like idiots.

I built up the Shit-Ninny fleet slowly, but now there are so many of them driving around that it would be a major project for me to find them all and disable them. Besides, I'm too busy doing other things now, so I make it a point to drive carefully. And you should too. I do have a control program running on a computer at my house that allows me to send group commands to the Shit-Ninny fleet. So far, I've not disabled that fleet because I think that the Shit-Ninnies make the roads safer in general.

Most people think that the Shit-Ninnies were put on the streets by the government to make people drive more carefully. That would have been too good an idea. Much too good an idea for the government to have done it.

I told Danny that he should just think of the Shit-Ninnies as facts of life. I explained that the Shit-Ninnies are why I always carry some water in my car - to at least clean the windshield in an emergency, and that he should too. I told him that if he doesn't want to use some common sense and water, and if he wants to persist at driving like an idiot, then Eff-him.

We pulled into my driveway, and I turned on the garden hose so that Danny could wash the paint off of his car. After it was nice and clean, we went inside for some espresso where we could review the facts of this case as I knew them.

We went into the kitchen and over to the coffee bar so I could pull a couple of shots. I've got a nice old FAEMA espresso machine that I leave on during the day so that I don't have to wait for the group to warm up when I want an espresso. Because it's got an E61 group, it would take a good twenty minutes to warm up after turning it on, and I'm not that patient. I always fresh-grind the coffee for espresso, otherwise the grounds dry out and lose lots of their flavor. While this isn't noticeable in regular coffee, I can taste the difference in espresso.

Espresso shouldn't be bitter when you do it like this, so you shouldn't need sugar. Many who grew up with stove-top espresso pots are used to a bitter brew, and take for granted that espresso needs sugar. That's because extraction on the stove is done at much higher temperature than an espresso machine uses, so it comes out bitter. Sure, I know lots of people grew up thinking that espresso should taste like that - which is why lots of restaurants serve espresso with slice of lemon peel, but I've never understood this, and have moved on.

So I made us each a *doppio*[4], hoped that Detective Danny wouldn't ask for sugar or a freaking lemon peel, and then continued recounting what I had seen.

Once again, I told him that when I had seen the car behind the Dumpster, the driver's door was open and the left directional was on. And the dead guy was big. He was sitting in the driver's seat, and had been shot in the right temple. I said that the shooter must have been in the passenger's seat, or had had the passenger door open because the windows were closed. And that it looked like a professional shot with a small caliber round, since there wasn't that much blood, and it had dried quickly, meaning that death had happened very fast.

Either way, the shooter would have had to open the passenger door to make this hit, because had he been outside the car, the window was closed, and had he been inside the car, he would have had to open the door to leave on the passenger side. The big guy was too big to move, and then put back, and I didn't think that anyone would try to climb over him. No one but a midget could have fit. And why would they bother?

And then I posed some questions to Detective Danny. Who was the smaller guy that the cops found in the back seat? And what happened to the big guy that had been in the front seat? And what happened to his gym bag? The big guy and his gym bag were gone, and a little guy - shot the same way - was lying where the big guy's gym bag had been. And both had been shot in the right temple. I wondered whether this was a coincidence. Why didn't the car have license plates on it? And why was it parked behind the Dumpsters?

Detective Danny confirmed my account that when the police got to the crime scene the driver's door was open, and the left directional was flashing. But everything else was different. Notably, the dead guy was different. It made no sense.

---

[4]   A large shot of espresso, a.k.a., a "double."

He asked me again how I was so sure that the guy who I had seen was big. I told him that he was sitting upright, and that his head was almost touching the ceiling.

"He looked big, rugged, and solidly built," I explained. "He looked like a serious lifter, and I wasn't surprised that he was carrying a gym bag. I was a little surprised that he was driving a yellow car. It didn't match his image."

"A yellow car?" asked Danny. "The car we found at the scene was black. Are you sure you're not mistaken?"

"A yellow car? Mistaken? Hardly," I said.

When Danny and I had first walked into the kitchen to make espresso, I saw my wife Carol in the family room on the phone with one of her friends. When Danny left, Carol finished her phone call and joined me in the kitchen.

"How's your friend Danny?" she asked.

"About the same. Who were you talking to?" I asked.

"Dottie," she said. "You know, Dottie across the street."

"Are you friends with her?" I asked. "I thought she was just a busybody. No wonder she's not married, and I never see any men over there. Do you think she's a Lebanese?"

"You've got it right that she's a busybody," Carol said. "Dottie wanted to know why the police were here. I told her I had no idea. Why were the police here?" she asked. "And what makes you think she's Lebanese?"

"The police weren't here. That was Danny. I went to the store before. When I left, I saw a car with a dead guy in it behind the store the way I usually go out. So I told Detective Danny about it. That's his business. And I meant that maybe Dottie likes other girls."

"Why do you leave the store that way?" she asked. "Why can't you wait at the light like everyone else? Dottie told me that she saw you at the store buying canned tomatoes. Did you say a dead guy was back there? And the word is 'lesbian;' not 'Lebanese.'"

"Dottie is very observant. I was buying canned tomatoes: she can be my alibi. Yes, there was a dead guy back there, but I didn't do it because I was buying canned tomatoes. And fennel. And I thought 'Lesbian' was a country in the Mideast."

"Who was it? I mean who was the dead guy?" she asked.

"I didn't get his name. I asked him, but he was dead. So I called Detective Danny and told him about it. I figured that the cops would want to know."

"Dottie said that she saw you at the store checking out at a quarter to two. She said that you were buying canned tomatoes."

"Buying canned tomatoes again? Your honor, I confess. Dottie witnessed the whole thing. I was buying canned tomatoes at a quarter to two. And don't forget about the fennel."

I told Carol what had happened - that while leaving the store in my usual back-of-the-store way, I saw a brightly colored car that had been hit by one of the Shit-Ninnies with a huge dead guy in the front seat, and no plates. And I told her that Detective Danny claimed that it was a black car with a tiny dead guy in the back seat, and no plates.

"Who's right?" she asked.

"Exactly!" I exclaimed. "But don't tell Dottie!"

Part of Dottie's problem is that she's way too honest and way too nosey. She loves gossip, and is a stickler for whatever she thinks are "the facts." Why did she bother to notice what the hell I was buying in the supermarket? That's not normal. Her honesty gets her in trouble with people, because they correctly interpret most of it as insulting. Maybe that's why men avoid her. Maybe she's not a Lebanese; I don't know, and don't really care.

I told Carol that I had gone down to the station with Detective Danny and met another detective named Detective Dorian. I told her that unlike Detective Danny, Detective Dorian was overbearing and obnoxious, and that he dressed like a little bitch. I told her Detective Danny and Detective Dorian made a great "good-cop, bad-cop" set of twins, and that I had given my story to the cop twins, who changed it for their report.

After that, I explained that Detective Danny had me sign a deposition that stated the police's version of the story. I told her that the police's version of the story was complete nonsense, but that Detective Danny told me that it would be a lot easier if I went with it, so I did. After all, the real story has too many mysteries. So they made the story about a single murder - it's the one that I didn't actually see, so it's the one that I know absolutely nothing about. But I'm their only witness.

"That's really strange," she said.

"Yes," I agreed. "But the cops think that a person who didn't see something makes the best witness. They told me that that's how the courts work. I hope that the police figure it out. And I hope that they do it without me."

"You really shouldn't drive over that curb behind the store," she said. "It's not good for the car."

"I know. But I really can't stand traffic lights. They turn red, and nobody moves. Then they turn green, and again nobody moves. I was getting tennis elbow from using the foghorn too much. And the foghorn bothers my ears. Sometimes I wish I'd made more of those Shit-Ninnies."

"What are you going to do with those tomatoes, anyway?" she asked.

"What tomatoes?" I said, puzzled.

"The ones you bought at the store," she said.

"Oh, right. Tomatoes and fennel. I was going to make a cioppino tonight with the lobsters, and clams, and cod that you brought home."

In the summer, clams can hold lots of sand, which is why I'm reluctant to cook them without opening them first. I prefer them on the half-shell when they're fresh. But in the fall, when the water gets cold, the clams drop most of their sand. You can cook with them whole and unopened; they'll open when cooking without getting any sand in the broth.

And I'm hardly a purist. While some people add oily fish - like salmon - to a broth, I don't believe in it: it overpowers the broth, although if you're simply poaching the salmon then fine. But with pure white fish, I like to add a touch of saffron - admittedly diverging from San Francisco while adding a touch of Marseilles to the dish.

"Cioppino?" she asked. "Great. And I especially like it when you put saffron in it."

I'll admit that I'm not always a purist.

That evening after dinner, Carol and I went to the mall to do some shopping. This happens every so often for many of the wrong reasons, one of which is that sometimes I'm a poor communicator. Ironically, while I was single and dating, I had deliberately cultivated a talent for communicating poorly, which made many women think that I was a great communicator.

I know that this sounds a little backwards, but not if you understand that the main action needed to manifest good communication skills is keeping your mouth shut. This works for two reasons, one of which I had been taught in a communications class that I took.

The class was called "Management Technique," or something like that. I took the class several jobs back when I worked for a paycheck. And I'd learned that it was especially true when dating, since men can be clueless when it comes to understanding women.

Suppose that you are the boss, and a hurt and disgruntled employee comes into your office and complains bitterly and somewhat unintelligibly about a situation. What I was taught is that the right thing to do as the "boss figure" is to repeat everything that he or she says exactly. There are two reasons for this.

First, all people see things a little differently. If you paraphrase what you think the employee is telling you, you're bound to get some of what they're saying a little bit wrong. This will get them even angrier and make them feel even more misunderstood. If you simply parrot what they're saying, this can't happen.

And second, if you simply parrot what they're saying, you don't even have to be listening to them. You can be thinking about completely different things: half of your brain listens to the sounds being made, and sends the right impulses to your mouth to make the same sounds, meanwhile the other half of your brain can be focused on other problems. It's a secret management technique that allows you to completely ignore the employee.

The employee feels understood, and you didn't need to get yourself worked up by thinking, analyzing, or empathizing. It was simply part of the job. That's one of many things that I learned about management technique. Admittedly, I've bifurcated my first point about communicating.

But there is an actual second point when it came to dating. I'd learned that frequently, I had no clue what women were talking about when they shopped.

They'd use the names of colors that I'd never heard of, notice differences between identical things (for example, two shoes) that I couldn't discern, take exception to the attitudes of sales people who weren't talking to us (so I hadn't been paying any attention to them), and many things like this.

I learned that in situations like this, when I said things like "um," it was usually interpreted as empathetic agreement. When I was younger, I would ask genuine questions, which I learned were usually interpreted as disagreement.

The result is that my wife thinks that I'm "fun" to go shopping with. She thinks that I enjoy it, and I always seem agreeable. Like I said, sometimes I don't communicate well.

So after dinner - our cioppino - which I did enjoy, we went shopping at the mall. As I've said, Carol thinks that I enjoy it. At night the mall is darker; rather, the most considerable sources of light during the day are the ceiling's windows. At night, those don't bring in daylight, so the light within the mall is all electrical. I noticed that window displays look starker at night, since spotlights are used to highlight what they want you to notice. This is useful for men who are out on dates, and don't know what they are supposed to notice in a display.

The shopping mall is a different place at night. I actually find it slightly eerie with the glass ceiling admitting nothing but the dark night. There were several terrific zombie movies shot in shopping malls at night. There's a certain congruence between the two, especially since the slow shuffle that most shoppers move with appears naturally zombie-like.

Aside from shoppers, there are sometimes groups of teenagers with nowhere else to go. They don't seem to be there to enjoy the mall, rather they're in the mall because none of them can disagree on it; it's neutral. And it's blah. Again, it's zombies.

I thought of the invention that I was working on that was meant for this context. The concept was commercial advertisements projected on glass windows at the mall. At night with the lighting the way it is, the projections would be apparent, which really isn't the main idea. The main idea had more to do with projections on glass in broad daylight, where the application would be subliminal, which is a new idea. Unfortunately, I'd need to do projections at night first, so that they would be apparent, so that I could sell them on the idea.

We wound up wandering into Macy's, and looking at clothing. I noticed that the main mannequin outside the men's department had a new seasonal outfit on display. The mannequin was wearing a grey tattersall tweed jacket with black pleated slacks, and there was a sign saying that this combo was now on sale.

The outfit looked very familiar. It was exactly what the dead man that I saw yesterday was wearing. It was hard for me to look at the mannequin without thinking of the dead man, so I decided to take a pass on this particular sale.

Day 3

Dottie Plants some Flowers

In the morning, I was back in the upstairs lab. Perhaps it had been helpful to wander around the mall last night, since I had been paying more attention to the glass surfaces and the sales displays. I was working on projecting images, and it's always helpful to look at where they'll go, and try to envision the application more clearly.

I had decided to pre-distort the images using functions of the distortions that were observed to undo themselves. That is, given a distortion, I would pre-distort the image by a function that was the inverse of the observed distortion. When the original distortion is applied to the pre-distorted image, what projects is the original image.

It was actually pretty obvious, now that I had figured it out. This is the gist of Jacobian transformations, which are commutative: the Jacobian of the inverse of a linear system is the inverse of its Jacobian. And in this case, it worked beautifully for images. The main work was obtaining the original distortion functions, and these would likely be unique to the surfaces on which the images were projected.

Fortunately, I'd be able to take precise contours of those surfaces, since they were relatively static, so I could tailor the pre-distortion functions accordingly. And the color range for these images was small, so I didn't think that the phase-shifting of colors would be a problem for the dimensions or the colors that I was thinking about. And after all, glass is amorphous, so it's hardly a filter in that sense of the word. Glass? This is hardly rocket-science.

Of course, the surfaces I was considering were the large plate-glass windows inside the shopping mall, which is why I'm glad that I had wandered around looking at them last night. These are static surfaces, and the temperature is well regulated. And the images were nude pictures: flesh tones. While no one had asked me to do this, I figured that it would spice up the mall a little. At least some of the people would enjoy it, and all would be sure to notice it. This is how inventions come to fruition: first some pizzazz, and then a real application.

And just like the Shit-Ninnies, the power source would be sunlight. So I packed up some imaging equipment that would measure the specific distortions of each of the specific plate glass panels on which I would project images, and I headed out to the mall to take all of the measurements.

Pulling out of my driveway, I saw Dottie out in her yard next to her driveway, so I gave her the obligatory wave, and she pretended not to notice me. I thought about using the foghorn and a Finger, and decided not to. While I'm honest like Dottie, I try to be sensitive - sometimes.

Dottie was about my age, but looked like a shrew. That's what happens when you're honest. She was walking around in her housecoat, and had her hair up in curlers. Whenever I see her walking around outside, she's always wearing her housecoat, and usually has her hair up in curlers. She wears a perpetually stern look on her face, although I've no idea what it is that she's stern about. Her curlers maybe? They matched her scowl.

Or maybe it was a smile. Dottie is the type that has to think about manifesting a smile on cue, because it doesn't come naturally to her. Unfortunately, and for this reason, it tends to look a lot more like a scowl. So I had to remind myself that Dottie was smiling, and I smiled back.

And as usual, she had her moccasins on. A housecoat with moccasins. Maybe she's an Indian. I wondered whether she knew The Chief, Detective Danny's boss, the one who makes heap-big wampum for a cop - especially from the bribes.

Dottie had a bunch of potted flowers that she was arranging. And I was surprised to see her car parked out in the street. She always parks her car in the garage. I couldn't imagine why she had parked it out in the street, unless it had something to do with the flowers that she was going to plant. I couldn't imagine her walking all the way down to the street in her moccasins if she didn't have to. Especially with her hair up in curlers, while scowling - I mean smiling.

I stopped and rolled down my window. "Hi Dottie," I waved again and tooted my foghorn. It was impossible for her to pretend not to see me, so she looked up scowled, and waved back. Again, I thought about flipping her one of The Fingers, and decided not to.

"Planting some flowers?" I asked.

"Yes," she answered. "I'm planting some flowers."

(Is there an echo in here?) "Isn't that a lot of work?" I asked. "And why is your car out on the street? I've never seen you park out on the street before."

Dottie explained. "Actually, my cousin brought the flowers over, and is going to plant them for me. His car got hit by a Shit-Ninny, and he wanted to use my garage to clean it up. He didn't get the paint off in time, so he needs to use tools and some fresh paint, and wants to keep it in my garage until the work is done. By way of thanks, he brought some flowers and plants over for me, and says that he'll plant them for me if I lay them out as I want them positioned."

"That's very nice of you to let him use your garage. And it's nice of him to do a little landscaping for you. I like the flowers," I said.

"Aren't those Shit-Ninnies a nuisance? My cousin is pretty upset that they hit his car" she said. "I wonder why the government has those Shit-Ninnies driving around all the time?"

"That's the government for you," I said. "Anything to improve the quality of life. They say that it makes the roads safer. Maybe they're right."

Very few people know that I'm the one that created the Shit-Ninnies, and instead assume that this was something that the government did to improve traffic flow. How does this improve traffic flow? I couldn't tell you. But it does make some people think twice before doing anything too stupid in crowded intersections.

On second thought, maybe it does improve traffic flow. How come the government didn't think of that?

"I didn't know that you had a cousin that lived around here. I'd like to meet him sometime. Does he do landscaping? We are thinking of adding some shrubs," I said.

"No, he's not in the landscaping business; he's just doing this small plot for me to thank me for letting him use my garage. He almost never comes over here, but he needed to use my garage," she explained.

"I see," I said, not fully understanding. It did seem odd that a cousin that has minimal interaction with Dottie would be tying up her garage - let alone that she would let him do this, or that he would bother buying plants and be willing to do landscaping for Dottie all of the sudden. Or that Dottie would park her car out on the street, and would walk down to the street with her hair in curlers while wearing a housecoat, freaking moccasins, and a big scowl. People that keep their relationships with cousins remote don't do things like this. It just struck me as odd.

"I thought I saw the cops over at your house before," Dottie said. "Is everything OK?"

"That wasn't really 'the cops.' That was a friend of mine named Danny. Yes, he's a cop, but that's not why he was here. He was just dropping by to say 'Hello,'" I explained.

"Well I'm relieved," she said. "These days, you never know what the story is with some people, and you never know what can happen."

"The cop's name is Danny. He and I went to High School together and he's an old friend. I'll have to introduce you sometime," I said.

"Yes, I'd like to meet him; it can't hurt," she said. "My cousin has a friend that's a detective down at the station. I wonder whether they know each other."

"Well have a good day," I said. "I'll be looking forward to seeing what your cousin does with the flowers, and I'm sure that you're looking forward to getting your garage back. By the way, do you know what time it is?" I asked.

She checked her watch. "It's ten after two," she said.

"Thanks. My watch has been running a little slow. Mine said five after, and I thought it was more like what you've got. I'm headed out to the mall," I said; "in case you were wondering."

"Yes," she said; "I was going to ask."

I'm not surprised. I waved and left for the mall to take some measurements. I tooted the foghorn "goodbye," and thought about flipping her one of The Fingers, but didn't. While I like honesty, I've learned that sometimes it's best to keep it in check. Besides, she might grimace.

Dottie went back into the house to get an iced tea. She wasn't used to working outside, and was thirsty. She probably worked up a real sweat in that housecoat. While standing in the driveway looking at some plants was hardly working, for Dottie it was, since she seldom spent time outdoors.

Her cousin Dagwood was sitting at her kitchen table drinking a soda while taking a break from working on his car. He was wearing jeans and a tee-shirt, both now dirty from sweat, and the paint flakes that stuck to it while he'd been sanding. Dottie didn't like him sitting in the kitchen with dirty clothes on.

At least he was wearing sneakers, and not moccasins.

"That paint from the Shit-Ninny has really set in. I should have gone to the car wash when it happened, but was too busy with other things. I'm sanding the paint spot down, and will need to repaint the car," Dagwood said.

"The whole car?" she asked. "Can't you just repaint the panel that was hit?"

"The paintball hit the top of the trunk, right where it angles. Because of where it hit - right at the fold, the paint splattered onto the roof, and also put droplets onto the side panels. I need to paint nearly half of the car to fix this the right way. So I might as well just paint the entire car, so that the paint matches exactly. Once I'm painting half of the car, it's not that much more trouble to paint the whole car," he explained.

"I see" she said, not really following, because she had tuned out the long explanation. "By the way, I put the plants and flowers exactly where I want them. When do you think you're going to plant them?" she asked.

"My friend Stu, who runs the garden center by the mall has a backhoe," he said. "Stu said he'd bring it over first thing tomorrow morning, and we can excavate that little area and prep the soil."

"You're going to dig it out that whole plot with a backhoe?" she asked, surprised. "I thought you just needed to dig little holes where the plants will go."

"That's what lots of people do, and sometimes the plants die. The problem here is that there's lots of clay in this soil, and it doesn't take water very well. The right way to do this is to dig the soil and the clay out to a depth of four or five feet, and to put real dirt in the flower bed. That way, you'll get much healthier growth. The plants will really thrive, especially if I add a special kind of fertilizer," he explained.

She replied, "I had no idea you were going to go to all this trouble just because I'm letting you use my garage for a few days. The guy across the street thought you were a professional landscaper. I'm wondering whether he's right. Do you really have to dig up the ground? I didn't expect you to do anything this complicated."

"It's not that big of a deal," he said. "Stu's a pro and a friend of mine. He has a backhoe and said he'd bring it over. That actually makes less work for me. The plot is only about ten feet by four feet. A backhoe can dig that out in about fifteen minutes. It would take me a couple of hours to dig individual holes by hand. This way, after Stu is done I can put the plants into loose soil. It makes them easier to plant. It's actually a lot less work for me if I do it this way."

"And you're also putting in fertilizer?" she asked.

"Yes," he said. "It's a very special kind of fertilizer. It came from the other side of the country; from California."

"That sounds like lots of trouble" she said. "But it sounds like you'll probably have the whole garden in by tomorrow afternoon. I can't wait until it's done."

"Actually, no," Dagwood said. "I had said that this was a very special kind of fertilizer that came from California. I can't put it in the hole in broad daylight, because I don't want people to see exactly what it is, and because the sun might damage it. I'll have to put the fertilizer in the hole at night, after the sun goes down. Then I can fill in the hole and put the plants in the following morning."

"I see," she said, not really seeing. Lots of what Dagwood said sounded contrived. Dottie never trusted him, but was looking forward to the new garden. Dagwood always seemed to be up to strange deals, and Dottie was just as happy not to listen too hard to his bullshit.

"When is this fertilizer from California going to be delivered?" she asked.

"I brought it with me," Dagwood said. "It's in the trunk of my car."

"Bullshit," she thought, without saying so. And bullshit makes good fertilizer.

While Dottie and Dagwood were discussing her garden and his car, I drove to the mall.

As is my practice, I always take the backroads and try to avoid the traffic lights. That way I don't have to use my foghorn as much, and I'm less likely to get hit with paintballs.

Just as I have a way to get to the strip mall on backroads, I have another way to get to the main shopping center on backroads as well. While the strip mall and the main shopping center are across the street from each other, I try to avoid going through the intersection that connects them, because the traffic always backs up at that intersection.

There's a small dirt road that crosses some railroad tracks. That road has been blocked off with a small barricade and a "Do Not Enter" sign which is just past an underpass that crosses under the highway on the one side, and a small barricade and a "Do Not Enter" sign that is at the back of a secondary parking lot at the mall. They didn't make the barricades quite wide enough, so I can drive around them if I'm careful, and I can cross the railroad tracks if no trains are coming.

I came into the mall this way today, and was able to avoid most of the traffic. But now that I was in the main parking lot at the mall, I was using The Fingers a lot. Many drivers don't seem to pay attention to what they're doing when they're parking. That's why there are so many fender-benders in parking lots.

I had pulled up an aisle to where it was close to the main entrance because it looked like there was a parking spot. When I got to it, I saw that someone had parked their new car in a way that it took two spaces so that no one could park exactly next to them. Fortunately, a Shit-Ninny had seen this parking job, and had blasted the car. And fortunately, since no one could park exactly next to them, no paint got on any other cars. I'd love to compliment the car's owner on how considerate it was of him to park that way so that other cars weren't hit.

Shit-Ninnies do patrol the mall every so often, and do launch paintballs at people that can't park correctly. Also, if you get in your car and start it, and then sit there to make other people wait, a Shit-Ninny might hit you. The idea here was to make people a little more considerate.

I stopped wasting time looking for a great parking spot, and instead, I simply parked.

I took my imaging equipment, which is compact, and walked into the mall. I walked along the same concourses I had walked with Carol last night. It looked very different in daylight. I walked the entire circuit of the mall, and selected my windows. I chose the ones that were the largest and that had the largest fields of view.

I walked a second circuit of the mall, and used my imaging equipment to photograph the glass contours for these windows. I did it all with infrared imaging, so the ambient light didn't effect things, and no one saw me taking strange photos.

I walked out with my measurements, found my car, and left. I drove back around the "Do Not Enter" sign, over the railroad tracks, and then merged onto the highway underpass.

It was an easy drive home, although I'd had to use the foghorn a lot to first clear the underpass. I was looking forward to going up to my lab and monitoring the golf course that's near our house. I'd finished another invention that I wanted to use today.

It was late in the afternoon, and I wanted to use my new golf invention. Late in the afternoon is when golf games tend to get the tensest because people are getting tired, and because some of them have been drinking too much. So I went to my upstairs lab to experiment with my new Golf-Ball Mortar. I call it the "GBM" for short.

Our house is about a block over from the local golf course. And when I say "about a block," remember that in Connecticut, blocks are topological concepts without direct physical interpretations: the roads meander.

I wanted to use the GBM as a new way to liven up the game of golf. Rather, I viewed the GBM as a new way to stimulate interaction between golfers, who seldom talk enough. I was trying to fix this, and the GBM was likely a splendid tool for doing it.

I had put in some ranging equipment on the roof of our house that can measure points on the golf course. The equipment can pick up these ground points - which I established by discretely sinking rebar on the course in the early spring, before they had opened. This way, I can make an accurate topographical map of the two holes on the golf course that are closest to our house. Both holes have wide water hazards, so people occasionally lose their golf balls.

With the cameras on the roof, I can see exactly where the people are who are playing the holes. What the GBM allows me to do is to fire golf balls - quite accurately - onto anyplace on the course for these two holes. The GBM can synchronize the ball launcher to a player's swing, taking distances into account, to make the player - or at least some of his friends - think that the ball sent over could be his. Granted, sometimes it's not the same kind of ball, but by the time they figure this out the argument is usually in full swing.

The GBM is a useful tool for studying human interaction. And it puts a little more randomness into the game of golf, which can make it more fun - more like miniature golf. True, there is the occasional fist-fight. But who says that golf shouldn't be an action sport?

So I was upstairs in the lab, playing with the GBM, and launching the occasional golf ball. That's when the phone rang. It was my friend, the new High School science teacher, Pete Fletcher. I occasionally go to the High School to show interesting things to the science students in the advanced class, because they are actually interested. That's where I struck up my friendship with Pete Fletcher, the science teacher.

I stopped using the GMB to shoot balls so that I could talk to Pete, but I kept watching the action on the golf course. "Hi Pete, how's school?"

Pete said, "Great. One of the students came in with an interesting logic puzzle today, and I wanted to know if you could solve it."

"I'm always interested," I confessed.

So Pete posed the problem: "There are two brothers. They're identical, so you don't know which is which, but one always lies and the other always tells the truth."

"Those are the Tweedle brothers," I said. "This is a Louie Carroll puzzle."

"The Tweedle brothers?" asked Pete. "I never heard of them. And who's Louie Carroll?"

"Dee and Dumb are the Tweedle brothers. Sometimes they're just called 'The Tweedles,'" I explained. "Louie Carroll is the guy that made this problem up. They wrote a song about him called 'Louie, Louie.' Maybe you've heard it? It's a good tune to dance to - especially if you've had too much to drink. But sometimes it's hard to remember all the words."

"What kind of a dumb name is Dumb Tweedle?" asked Pete.

"Dumb Tweedle is the one that always lies," I said. "That's why he's called Dumb."

"But how do you know which of the brothers is Dumb?" asked Pete. "They look the same."

"You know because Dumb's the one that's always lying," I explained.

"But how would you know whether he's lying?" asked Pete.

"If Dumb Tweedle is doin' the talking, he's lyin'. This is one of those trick problems where Louie Carroll gives you the answer in the very statement of the problem," I explained. "Lots of people don't realize it because they think that mathematics is supposed to be hard. So sometimes with math problems, they try to trick you this way."

"I think I get it now," said Pete. "If he's lying, he's Dumb Tweedle."

"Exactly," I said, "you've got it. Take that back to your students, and I'm sure you'll impress 'em."

"Thanks Mick. I knew you probably already knew this one. That's why I called you," said Pete.

"Nice talking to you. I'll come to the school soon. Bye," I said, and hung up the phone.

I went back to playing with the GBM - which I'd been watching - and launched the occasional ball. I wondered how long it would take Pete to... the phone rang again, so I picked it up. It was Pete. I had been expecting him to call again.

"OK, we know that Dumb Tweedle is lying. But how do we know which one is Dumb? The student that came in with this told us the answer, but I'm not sure that it makes sense, so I wanted your opinion," said Pete.

"What does he say that the answer is?" I asked.

"He said: 'Suppose that two roads, X and Y, leave town, and that one of them goes to the city and the other goes to the beach, but we don't know which is which.'"

"Two roads leave town?" I asked. "What's that got to do with who's lying? Why have two roads leaving town? Why not just have the two Tweedles leave town?"

"Well this is part of the solution," explained Pete. "You ask one of the Tweedles - let's forget Dee and Dumb for a minute, because we already know that Dumb lies - we'll call the Tweedles 'A' and 'B.' So you choose a Tweedle, say we choose A, you ask him: 'A, what road would your brother B say went to the city? Would your brother B say that it was road X or road Y that went to the city?'"

"OK, but suppose he said that his brother would say that road X went to the city. We don't know which road goes to the city, so what good does that do?" I asked.

"Well if he says that X goes to the city, then we take road X. If it goes to the city then he was telling the truth. See?" asked Pete.

"Who was telling the truth?" I asked.

"Brother A was telling the truth," concluded Pete. "You see? If road X went to the city, then brother A told the truth."

"Which one was A again?" I asked.

"We don't know," said Pete. "We said that we were going to call them 'A' and 'B.' So we now know that A was telling the truth, but we don't know which one is A."

"A is obviously Dee. We've already established that Dumb lies. So if A was telling the truth, then A is Dee. Make sense?" I asked.

"Yeah, that's right, that was the answer. That's a clever problem, don't you think?" asked Pete.

"Yes, that's a classic," I said. "That's Louie Carroll for you."

I went back to playing with the GBM. I wondered how long it would be before Pete worked his way through my non-argument, and called again.

For dinner, Carol and I decided to take a short drive over to Westport to a very casual place called the Black Duck Cafe. It's a combination bar and eatery on the Saugatuck River, which runs down to the Long Island Sound. It sits nearly under the Interstate 95 overpass, and when the cars cross the Saugatuck, the overpass makes a banging sound. The bar is on the river side, and when the weather's nice, they open most of the wall to the river, so the drinking crowd can watch the boats pass.

They feature whole-belly clams, which most restaurants do not have, and their standard preparation of most of the seafood is deep-fried, although it's not at all oily, so they've perfected this art. And as signs inside boast, on Fridays, they offer a special "Friday Clam Jam." Typically, the way a jam is made is by combining the main ingredient - clams in this case - with close to an equal volume of sugar, and boiling it down with a little lemon juice. My understanding is that the clam jam goes well on nearly anything, so I was looking forward to trying it.

We sat up at the bar where it's livelier, and had a nice view of the river. With some bloody Marys, fresh rolls with clam-jam, and the lively atmosphere, it's hard to beat. It was pretty clear that lots of people at the bar were regulars, although the staff has a way of making you feel like you're one of them.

At the bar it was easy to run through the facts of the case with Carol without letting the mood turn morose. That had more to do with the atmosphere of the Black Duck Cafe and the merriment of the other customers than with the facts of the case.

I mentioned that the victim that I saw in the car was wearing what looked like a new outfit, and that it was the same outfit that we had seen on sale at Macy's when we were there last night. I wondered whether he had just bought that outfit at Macy's, and decided that they likely did not have his size in stock. I wondered whether someone at Macy's had seen him in the outfit, and that was where they got the idea to feature it, or whether this was just one of the new outfits that a man would be likely to buy anywhere.

I went through my trip to the police station, and told her that I didn't like it when Detective Danny came to the house with his uniform on, but he had said that they'd gotten my description because I was using The Fingers after leaving the scene. This is why I always let Carol drive when we go out. She doesn't like it when I use the foghorn and The Fingers, so I make it a point to be patient at traffic lights when she's driving. I try to take back-ways where there aren't lights.

And then I described the detective that I had met named "Detective Dorian," who was working the case with Danny. I explained that I didn't trust Detective Dorian because of something about his manner. I also told her about Tanya who I had met at the station who checked me in, that she was young, pretty, and fashionable, and that Detective Dorian told me that he was her boyfriend, although I'd a hunch that he was a closet snot-diddler.

We went through the murder scene that I had witnessed, and the one that I didn't witness that the detectives told me about, which they described on the affidavit that I'd signed. I hadn't seen the second murder, and that was the main surprise in this case. I wondered why both cars were in the same positions with the same doors opened and the same flashers flashing, and why both victims were shot in the same way, but the one I found was big, and was sitting in the front seat, and the one that the cops found was small, and was lying in the back seat.

I also found it curious that Dottie had taken the trouble to notice me in the store, as well as having taken the trouble to notice what time it was when she noticed me.

We talked about Dottie a little, and both wondered what her situation was. She seemed reclusive, and neither of us were aware of her ever having people over until today. And today, I found it curious that a cousin of her's had emerged to use her garage to repaint his car, and that he was going to put a small garden in for her by way of thanks. Both seemed un-natural.

I thought Dottie would do better for herself if she got rid of that old bathrobe and those moccasins that she always wears. And she always seemed to be scowling, and I wondered why.

We finished a hearty dinner at the bar, and Carol drove home without using her horn once. I don't know how she does it.

Day 4

Stu's Garden Center, and the Backhoe

Very early in the morning, Dottie's cousin Dagwood showed up with his friend Stu, from Stu's Garden Center, which is in the same plaza as the supermarket where I shop; the same plaza in which the murder was committed. And Stu had brought a backhoe with him.

Stu was stocky and portly. He liked to do landscaping early in the morning before the sun was fully out. There's less sweat that way, although Stu was wearing a sweatshirt - just in case.

Stu dug a nice hole where the new garden would go, dredging out the hole to a depth of about five feet. Sure enough, there was a lot of clay in the soil down to about three feet, but after that it was just nice loose soil. Stu took the backhoe out back to the woods, and brought a load of fresh soil to the side of the hole that he had dug. He then took most of the clay out back to the woods and dumped it in the hole he had made out in the woods.

Dagwood thanked Stu for his help and explained about the fertilizer that he'd brought: that it would need to go in at night, and that he'd take care of it. As a landscaper, Stu never heard of anything like this, and assumed that it was just some of Dagwood's standard bullshit. And standard bullshit makes good fertilizer.

Dagwood told Stu that he should come back the following morning to help fill the hole in. He let Stu know that he appreciated all the help, and that he owed him one. While Stu didn't trust Dagwood, he had learned not to ask too many questions. Dagwood usually made things worth Stu's while, and was lots of fun when the guys occasionally went out for some beer at night.

Dagwood was usually full of shit, but could be funny as hell, and had the gift of being able to 'put the rap' on good looking women that wandered by. Stu wished he could be like that.

Dagwood spent the rest of the morning in the garage, sanding the paint off of his car.

When I went up my driveway across from Dottie's to take my mid-morning run, I saw the big hole and the big pile of fresh dirt. I could hear the sanding machine running in the garage, even though the garage door was closed. I thought that the pile of dirt looked like too huge a pile of dirt for planting a few flowers and shrubs. But some people overdo small things. Dottie was strange, and I didn't think that this was too out-of-character for her.

So I went for my run.

When I got back about an hour later, a car was coming down Dottie's driveway. I stopped at the curb and waited for the car to get to the street, squinting a little to see if I could tell who was driving. Dottie's car was still parked on the street, so I was sure that the driver wasn't Dottie. At a distance, the driver looked vaguely familiar. When it pulled up next to me, I recognized Detective Dorian, from the police station the other day. There was also a passenger, who I'd never seen before.

"Detective Dorian!" I exclaimed. "What brings you to my neighborhood? Are you arresting anyone? How's Tonya?" I asked.

"Oh, no, it's the wiseass," Detective Dorian said. "I should ask what are you're doing here."

"I live here," I said. "But what are you doing here?" I repeated. "And who's your friend? Is he under arrest?" I asked.

Detective Dorian said "This is my friend Dagwood. He's working on his car here, and I came to pick him up because he can't drive it yet. It was in some kind of accident, and the lady who lives here is letting him use her garage for a few days. Why? Don't ask me."

Then Detective Dorian introduced me. "Dagwood, this asshole is Mickey Mouse."

"Mick," I said. I reached into the car to shake hands with Dagwood. "Your cousin Dottie told me that you knew one of the detectives downtown. I didn't realize it was this moron. He works with an old friend of mine that I've known since High School."

I continued: "Dottie said you got hit by one of those Shit-Ninnies the other day. You weren't driving like this asshole Dorian, were you?" I asked. "She said you're repainting your car because you didn't get the paint off soon enough," I said.

"Yeah," he said. "I didn't wash the car soon enough because it was a very busy day when I was hit. The result is that I need to repaint the car. Dottie is a distant cousin of mine, but she's letting me use her garage to do the work. Those Shit-Ninnies are pains in the ass, but I guess the government put them out there to make the roads safer," he said.

"Yes, they make the roads safer," I parroted. Maybe they do.

"Dottie told me that you're putting in a small garden for her to thank her for the use of her garage," I said. "That's really thoughtful of you."

"No problem," he said. "Since she's letting me use her garage for a few days, I figure the least I can do is to do a little work and give her a new garden."

"That's some hole you dug," I observed.

"I have a friend with a landscaping business and a backhoe, and it just took him a few minutes. Maybe you've seen his place over at the plaza across from the mall? It's called 'Stu's Garden Center' - it's named after him; his name's 'Stu.' Having Stu do this with his backhoe is actually easier and much quicker than having me dig holes for each plant. It's not a big deal," he said.

"But did it have to be that deep?" I asked. "That's really impressive. And how did Stu come up with 'Stu's Garden Center' for the name of his garden shop? That's really impressive too."

"The soil here has lots of clay in it," he said. "I wanted to dig through the clay so that the ground can absorb water and can drain. And I don't know how Stu thought of that name. Maybe he's a genius."

"Makes sense," I said. "Still, I'm impressed." It sounds like bullshit.

"Don't be," Dagwood said. "Nice to meet you Mick."

We waved to each other, and they drove off. What a pair of slimes. At least a Shit-Ninny got one of them.

I went in and took another shower. I never understood people who don't shower after workouts. They stink like hell. When I got out of the shower, the phone was ringing. It was Detective Danny.

"Are you sitting down?" he asked.

"Uhhh, no. Should I be sitting down?" I asked, and sat down.

"No, not really; it's just an expression," he said. "You can stand."

"But I just sat down," I said. "Now you want me to stand up? Is this 'Simon Says?'" I asked.

"Never mind," he said. "Stand or sit. We found out who the dead guy was."

"What dead guy?" I asked.

"The dead guy in the car," he replied.

"Do you mean the big dead guy in the yellow car, or the little dead guy in the black car?" I asked.

"There was no big dead guy in a yellow car" he said. "The only dead guy was a little dead guy in a black car."

"Oh, you mean the one that I didn't see?" I said. "So why are you calling me? I didn't see the dead guy, remember?"

"Because you know this dead guy," he said. "In fact, I'm wondering whether you're the one that killed him."

"Why would I have called you - the cops - if I had killed him?" I asked.

"That's what I'm trying to figure out," he said. "Why would you kill this guy, and then make up a bullshit story about a different dead guy in a different car? It doesn't make sense. Do you really expect us to believe that there was a big dead guy in a yellow car that was in the same place at the same time as a little dead guy in a black car? I know how you like to twist logic, and I'm trying to figure it out. I think you're shitting us," he said.

"You said that I know the dead guy. Who is he?" I asked.

"His name's Mitch Goldberg," he said.

"Who's that?" I asked. "I don't know anyone named Mitch Goldberg."

"That's the guy who cuts your hair at the mall. You described him to me once, and said that you always ask for that guy 'Mitch' when you go to the hair salon."

"Oh, you mean Mitch the stylist. I didn't know his last name. So why would I want to kill him?" I asked. "Especially if I always ask for him when I get a haircut?"

"Because you look like shit," he said.

"But I have to work at it," I pointed out. "I wasn't born that way, like you. And I didn't kill my hair stylist. While I'll admit that he does a mediocre job cutting my hair, at least he shuts the hell up while he's doing it. You could have learned something from him," I said. "And speaking of looking like shit, how's your good buddy Dorian *Travone?*" I asked.

"You mean Detective Dorian?" he asked.

"Isn't that the same guy? Sometimes I have a hard time with names," I said. "I didn't kill Mitch Goldberg. Make sure that Dorian *Travone* understands this. He gives me the creeps."

"Are you talking about Detective Dorian?" he asked? "His name's not '*Travone.*'"

"It's the same guy," I said. "So why would anyone kill Mitch Goldberg? He was a hair-stylist; a barber. Was he in the mob, or something like that? And again, why are you telling me?"

"We don't really know whether Mitch Goldberg had ties to anyone bad. And I'm telling you because this one is a real puzzler. You're good at puzzles, and I was hoping you could help us," he said.

"Sorry Danny, but I don't work for the cops," I replied.

"I hope your next hair-stylist talks your ear off," he said, and hung up.

I finished drying off, and got dressed.

I went downstairs, and Carol was in the family room reading a book. "Hi dear," she said. "Who was that on the phone?" she asked.

"That was Detective Danny," I said.

"Why was he calling you?" she asked.

"Exactly dear," I said. "I couldn't agree more."

"But he was here yesterday. Was he calling about that?" she asked.

"Yes," I said. "Apparently, they've figured out who the second murder victim - the little guy in the second car - was. It was one of the stylists at the salon at the mall."

"So why is he calling you?" she asked.

"Exactly," I said.

"Do they know who the first murder victim - the big one - was?" she asked.

"They're not even talking about that. They never found that victim, and are pretending that it never happened. I'm the only one that saw that victim, and the cops aren't sure that they believe me.

They're acting like I was hallucinating. I guess it makes their job simpler that way," I said.

"Then why is he calling you?" she asked again.

"Is there an echo in here?" I asked. "Actually, that's a great question. It sounds like they've cleaned-up the case. The first murder never happened, and they know who the victim of the second murder was. All that they have to do is talk to people and see if they can figure out who killed him and why. I've no idea what they think I could do for them on this case. And I'm not interested. I've other things that I'm working on, and I don't work for the cops."

"Then why are they calling you? That makes no sense," she said.

"It makes no sense," I agreed.

"Were you up there talking to Dottie when you finished your run before?" she asked. "I thought I saw you up at the top of the drive, but you didn't come down for a while."

"No, it wasn't Dottie," I told her. "It was her cousin and a friend of his. She's letting him use her garage for a few days, and he's going to put in some flowers for her by way of thanks. Interestingly, his friend is a police detective that I met the other day named Dorian. He works with Danny. I don't trust Detective Dorian. There's something about him that makes me think he's not on the level. It's interesting that he's good friends with Dottie's cousin."

"Dottie's letting her cousin use her garage?" she asked. "That's weird. For what? And why is he driving around with a police detective?"

"Dottie's cousin is named Dagwood. Apparently, his car was hit by a Shit-Ninny, and he didn't wash it off in time. So now he needs to repaint it. She's letting him keep it there to do that so that the paint can dry without getting rained on, and all the other things that can happen to wet paint when you let it dry outside."

"That's nice of her," she said.

"Yes. That's why Dagwood is putting in a small garden for her," I said. "But to me, it looks like he's overdoing it."

"Overdoing it?" she asked. "How?"

"Well Dagwood had a friend come over early this morning with a backhoe. His friend is Stu. Stu is a professional landscaper; he runs 'Stu's Garden Center' over by the mall. This morning, Stu excavated a hole that seems to be far deeper than you'd need to plant some flowers. Dagwood told me some nonsense about wanting to get through the layer of clay that we have around here, so they used the backhoe to dig out about five feet of dirt - and clay."

"But how does that get rid of the clay?" she asked.

"It doesn't. He took the backhoe out back to the woods, and dug up a load of topsoil. He dumped that where the garden's going, and took most of the clay content back to the woods to fill in the hole he made from where he took the topsoil."

"That makes a lot of sense," she said. "Maybe we should do that the next time we plant anything."

"It makes a lot of sense," I said, "but it's a lot of trouble to go through just to plant a small flower bed at a distant cousin's house. I'm even surprised that he had his friend bring over a backhoe. That's the kind of thing you'd use for a major project, but not to put a few flowers in."

"I'd like to go up and see Dottie, take a look at her flowers, and see what this hole looks like," she said.

"A hole is a hole. What's to see?"

"You never know. Planting some flowers seems to have become a big production. I'm interested in how she's doing it with a backhoe, and I'd like to see what flowers she chose."

———————————

Carol went up Dottie's drive and stopped to take a look at the big hole that had been excavated. She saw Dottie's choice of flowers and plants sitting next to the hole, as well as the pile of fresh dirt that they brought over from back in the woods.

Carol continued up to the front door. "Ding-dong!" Carol rang the bell at Dottie's.

She had brought up some pastry, hoping that Dottie would let her in and serve some coffee. She had never seen any men at Dottie's, and assumed that she was a widow - or had never married. But if she'd never married, Dottie must have gotten money from somewhere to buy the house, because as far as she knew, she never saw Dottie leave for work.

Dottie came to the door.

"Hello Dottie," Carol said. "Mick said you were putting in an impressive garden, and I wanted to come over and see it. And I brought you some pastries."

"That's very nice of you. Please come in," said Dottie, taking the plate of pastries, and grimacing in her version of a smile. "Let's go out to the kitchen. I've already made coffee," she said.

They passed the living room, and it was pretty much what Carol expected. Neat as a pin, and decorated with lots of prints and frilly lace. There were a few magazines on the coffee table, but they were fanned-out like another decoration, and not merely thrown into a pile the way they'd be in most living rooms. She probably didn't actually read them.

Dottie and Carol went into the kitchen, and Carol took a seat at the island that was opposite the cooking area. There was a coffee maker at the island, and the pot was half full. Dottie passed her a cup and asked "cream or sugar?"

"Just a little milk, thanks," Carol said.

Dottie opened a mini-fridge on the side of the island, and passed her a small container of milk.

Like the living room, Dottie's kitchen was also too neat. Carol's guess was that Dottie didn't actually cook much. If she did, the kitchen wouldn't be nearly as neat. The only thing that was out of place was an old gym bag that was lying on the floor next to a doorway. From the layout of the house, Carol guessed that the doorway was the exit to the garage. Dottie had a nice picture window in her kitchen, and it looked out into the woods, where there was a nice outcropping of natural rock.

Dottie saw her looking at the gym bag, and was momentarily embarrassed. "Pardon that old bag," she said. "I'm letting my brother-in-law use the garage to refinish his car, and that's his gym bag," she explained. "He dumped it in here probably because he doesn't want paint and dust to get on it - although it does look like an old bag, so I don't know why he'd care. He isn't neat about anything else."

"Your bother-in-law is refinishing his car? What for?" Carol asked.

"He was hit by one of the Shit-Ninnies. He didn't wash it off in time, so he needs to repaint his car," Dottie explained.

"Oh," Carol said. "What a pain!"

"Yes," said Dottie. "But at least I'm getting a small garden out of it," and she chuckled.

"Can I take a look?" Carol asked.

"At what?" Dottie asked back.

"The car," said Carol. "And the new garden."

"I don't know why you'd want to see the car," said Dottie. "The garage is a mess. Dagwood was out there sanding all morning. And the garden isn't in yet, so there's nothing to see. So far, it's just a big hole. I'm not sure why Dagwood dug it out that deep."

"Who is Dagwood?" asked Carol. "Mick mentioned him this morning. I guess they ran into each other when Mick was coming back from his run."

"Dagwood's my cousin. It's his car that was hit by one of the Shit-Ninnies," said Dottie. "You can open the door and take a look at the spot he was sanding, but don't go walking around out there because I'm afraid you'd track too much paint dust back in with you."

Carol got up, walked over to the door, and opened it to see the car. Looking into the garage from the kitchen, she could see the back of the car where Dagwood had been sanding. She saw that while Dagwood had sanded lots of the trunk, that paint had splattered the roof and both sides of the car as well. "Wow," she said. "That paintball hit in the worst possible place. It splattered over most of the back of the car, including the roof."

"That's why Dagwood's talking about repainting the whole car," said Dottie. "He said that since he needs to repaint about half of the panels, he might as well do them all so that the paint matches exactly."

"Dagwood seems to be a perfectionist," observed Carol. "He dug a huge deep hole out front for your garden, which is the right way to do it - but lots of work, and he's painting the entire car to get the panels to match exactly. Is he always such a perfectionist?"

"Hardly," said Dottie. "He dresses pretty messily. That beat-up gym bag reminds me of him, but as far as I know, he doesn't go to a gym."

"Well, some men are like that about their cars," Carol said. "But I'm surprised that he's also like that when it comes to your garden. That's pretty unusual. You're lucky!"

As Carol walked back down her own driveway, a limousine was coming up. She tried to see inside, but the windows of the passenger compartment were darkly tinted. While she could easily see the driver, she couldn't see inside the passenger compartment.

Mick was in the living room listening to some music. "Who was in the limo?" Carol asked. "Was he lost?"

"No," I said. "He was looking for me. That was a well-known senator from the other side of the country - Senator Adler from California. I'm sure you've heard of him. He didn't want it known that he was looking for me. Apparently, someone that works for him - a special bodyguard - came out here to visit a relative, and disappeared. The senator had been told that perhaps I could help him, so he wanted to know if I could investigate. He wants to see if I can figure out what happened to his man."

"How would you know?" she asked. "Did Senator Adler give you a description of the man?"

"Not much. But he told me that anyone would notice him in a crowd. He said that this bodyguard is a big guy - about six-foot four, and muscular. He said that when his man travels, he always takes his gym bag with him because he never wants to miss workouts. He goes to local gyms wherever he is."

"Isn't there a fancy gym in that plaza where you went to the supermarket the other day? The plaza where you saw a big guy shot dead in a car behind the supermarket - next to a Dumpster?"

"You mean the big guy who wasn't there?" I asked. "Senator Adler's people asked the cops, and the cops told him that no one of that description was seen around these parts. The senator said that the cops didn't seem to know anything, but one of them - I'm guessing it was Danny - suggested that he come see me."

"So what are you going to do?" she asked. "Are you taking this case?"

"I'm thinking about it," I said. "Maybe I'll go over to that gym and ask a few questions."

"Did Senator Adler know who the relative was that his man came out here to see?" she asked.

"No. He does know that his man was out here - he had the airline tickets checked, and they were used, and one of the stewardesses said that a man in first-class fit his description. But after his man disappeared, he had his own people check to see who the man's relatives out here are. He doesn't have any relatives that live out here. So the man was not out here to see relatives, as he told his boss. He was out here to see someone else. But who? And why? The senator claims that he has no idea, but he wants to know."

"Why would a senator care about this at such a personal level as to come out here himself to look for his bodyguard?" she asked. "Wouldn't he just replace him, and forget about it? Maybe the guy quit and moved. I'm surprised that a senator from California would travel out here personally to follow up on something like this."

"I thought that was a little strange too. I'm sure that there are things that the senator isn't telling me. That's one of the reasons that I'm reluctant to get involved, but at the same time, intrigued. I'm not sure that I want to know all of details," I said, "but I'm interested in some of them."

"Maybe it's best if you steer clear of this case," she said.

"You're right, of course" I said. "But there's something about this case that I find compelling. As you've pointed out, why would a senator get personally involved with this? And why would the police insist on pretending that this never happened? And why would a second, nearly identical murder take place in the same location at nearly the same time? There are too many strange things about this, so I'm very intrigued. I think I'll - at least - scratch the surface of this case, and see if anything turns up."

I went back up to the lab to think.

Later that afternoon, I drove back over to the strip mall where I had seen the dead guy. I thought that I'd check out the gym to see whether Senator Adler's bodyguard - who I'm guessing was the dead guy that I saw - had been there.

This time, I got to the strip mall by going through the little neighborhood behind it to the cul-de-sac, up the alley, and over the curb. In addition to missing the lights, the chances of getting hit by Shit-Ninnies were much smaller. And I didn't pass any cars along the way. I didn't need to use The Fingers at all. Or the foghorn.

I parked in front of the gym that was next to the supermarket, and I and went inside. There was a desk inside the front door, and an older looking guy behind the desk asked if he could help me. He was wearing a pullover with the gym's logo on it.

"I was thinking of joining," I said. "Mind if I have a look around?"

"Not at all," he said. "We've got the aerobic equipment over on the side by the windows, and there are TVs there so that you can watch the news or whatever show you like while you're training. Up front here are all of the automatic weight machines. They're all easy to use. You just stick the pins into the weight stacks and use the machines in the obvious ways; there are diagrams on the side of each machine showing how they work, in case it's not obvious."

"What about free weights?" I asked.

"The free weights are in the back of the gym where the mats are," he said. "There are four power racks and various benches. You'll see Olympic bars both lying around and on the power racks, and there are fixed-size sets of dumbbells going up to 100 pounds each. Also sets of EZ-curl bars with plates already attached. Kettle-bells too, but we don't recommend playing with the big ones unless you know what you're doing."

"I'll take a look around," I said.

"Be my guest," he answered.

I walked through the automatic weight machines. This area was well populated. I've noticed that most people like the machines because you don't need to do anything to use them. You just stick the pin in, and go. Also, there's no way you can drop the weight on yourself. And if it's too heavy, there's no problem: you just won't be able to move it. But because these are simple to use, the area was crowded.

Also, the free-weight area tends to have some real metal-heads in it in most gyms, and normal people can feel a little intimidated walking in there to use what are (relative to these guys) small weights. While the serious metal-heads are more easygoing than the business types in the other areas of the gym (when did anyone ever get nasty with people that look like them?), sometimes people who aren't serious lifters don't feel comfortable there. There were only three lifters in there working out, and I didn't disturb them because I know that it takes focus.

In the aerobic equipment area, there were stair-masters, treadmills, rowing machines, and all of the usual things. About half of the machines were empty, and lots of the people had earphones on - listening to music or watching one of the many TVs. No one looked like they were working too hard, since very few of them were sweating: especially the few young women who were wearing nice tight leotards and who were all made up. You don't put on make-up to do a serious workout.

Speaking of which, I recognized Tonya - Detective Dorian's girlfriend - on one of the machines. She had her hair up in an elaborate set of braids, and was chewing gum. Chewing gum is OK if you know you'll not be breathing too hard, otherwise you might swallow it. I could see Tonya's eyes repeatedly dart around all the mirrors so that she'd have a good view of whoever walked into the gym.

So I walked over to her, and said "Hi Tonya."

She gave me a vacuous smile, and said "Hi!" Then after a minute, "Do I know you?"

"I'm Mickey Maux," I said.

"That's right!" she replied. "You're baaad!" she said, laughing, while still looking vacuous.

"Is Detective Dorian here?" I asked.

"Who?" she asked.

"Detective Dorian. You know, Detective Dorian, your boyfriend," I responded.

"My boyfriend?" she asked. "Who told you that?"

"Detective Dorian did," I said.

"Yeah, he wishes. I go more for the wealthy type," she told me.

"Is that why you hang around here?" I asked.

She laughed and looked vacuous.

"Good to see you Tonya, take care," I said, waving and walking away.

"Bye," she said, waving and looking around in all the mirrors.

I went back to the main desk, and the same guy was still there.

"Did you like what you saw? Thinking of joining?" he asked.

"Yes," I said. "It's a nice gym. Especially the serious part. Many gyms today don't have much by way of real weights, but I can tell that you guys are more serious."

He smiled proudly.

"Actually, I have a gym at home," I explained, "but have been thinking of joining a gym so that I can get spotters on occasion. But the real reason that I came in today is to see whether you remember a really big guy who might have been in here two days ago. He was about six-foot four, and looked like he lifted seriously."

"We get a number of serious lifters in here," he said, "but I know most of them, and none of them are that tall. I remember a guy who was about that big who came in the other day who I had never seen before or since. He paid cash to use the gym since he wasn't a member, and didn't talk like a local, although he didn't talk much at all. All he did was work out."

"Do you remember anything else about him?" I asked. "How did he get here? Did he just walk in with his gym bag?"

"He was driving a big car," he said. "He parked it right out front. I noticed it because I didn't think that it looked like his type of car, so it struck me as funny when I saw a guy his size get out of it."

"What do you mean that it struck you as funny?" I asked.

"It was a big yellow car. Somehow, he didn't look like the type of guy to drive a yellow car," he said.

"Anything else?" I asked.

A man from the back who obviously worked here had come out to join us. He was carrying a toolbox, and obviously fixed things.

The new man said, "He asked me if he could borrow a screwdriver. He said that his license plate was loose, and he wanted to tighten it. I lent him a screwdriver."

"Is that it?" I asked.

"Yes, that's about it," they both said.

At home that night after dinner, we were sitting in the family room, watching a detective movie on TV. Those always get me: the plots are contrived, and the solutions are always too easy. Nonetheless, I always enjoy watching how the detective character acts - if you call that acting.

Our family room is reached by walking out of the kitchen through a double-door on the right side of the room. The broad side-window of the family room faces North, but there are a set of windows along the narrow western wall that look up the hill toward the street. We've set the TV up in the Southwest corner of the room, so that you can see it anywhere from the semicircular sofa that lies along the Eastern and Northern walls.

At about 10:00, when it was pitch dark outside, I saw the house lights come on way up the hill at Dottie's house. The double garage door opened, and a car with the headlights on drove out. It must have been backed into the garage, which fits with the position of the car that Carol had seen in the garage that day. I was surprised to see the car drive out, because I had thought that Dagwood was still doing body work on it. That's why the car had been shut up inside the garage, with the garage door closed.

While I couldn't see the car itself, I saw the headlights. Whomever was driving must have had the brights on. In fact, whomever it was wasn't going to drive around town, since they stopped the car right by the new mound of dirt about halfway down the driveway, where Dagwood and Stu had dug the hole that morning. I wondered why whomever it was would drive Dagwood's car to the hole at night.

It seemed that the car sat there with the lights on for about twenty minutes. Then it backed back up the driveway into the garage, and the garage door closed. Then the house lights went out - pretty damn odd.

We finished watching the detective movie, and the star got the villain to contradict himself several times by asking some obvious questions. The villain finally fell apart, admitted to the crime, and begged for mercy. This always cracks me up. I wish it were that easy in real life.

As I was getting up to shut the TV off and go to bed, I saw another car come around the corner and go up Dottie's driveway. It parked up at the house. I wondered who could be visiting Dottie at this hour of the night. I had just assumed that she usually went to bed before I did, although I'm not sure why I assumed this.

I went upstairs and got ready for bed. I made some notes about the events and conversations that I had had that day, and again wondered why a senator from the other coast would be out here looking for a particular bodyguard. It made no sense.

When I got in bed, as I lay facing the western window, I saw the car come down Dottie's driveway, and go back the way it came. Curious. I wondered whether he was picking someone up, or dropping someone off.

Day 5

Mitch Goldberg and Senator Adler

The next day, mid-morning when I went out for a run, Dagwood was up Dottie's driveway planting the flowers. I stopped and waved.

"Looks good," I yelled up.

"Thanks," he yelled back.

"When did you manage to fill the hole in?" I asked.

"I did that early this morning. My friend Stu - the one with the backhoe - was here early, and we filled it in. Right now, I'm just finishing up by planting the flowers," he answered.

"I saw a car up here late last night, and wondered whether everything was OK," I yelled.

"Car here last night?" he asked.

"Yeah, it was about when I was going to bed. It came and left."

"Are you sure it was this house, and not the one next door?" he asked.

"Yeah, I'm pretty sure it was this house, but maybe I was mistaken. I was pretty tired last night."

"Well it wasn't me, because I wasn't here. And it wasn't my car, because my car's in there" - he pointed up at the garage. "Maybe Dottie has a boyfriend," he laughed.

"You never know," I responded, then waved goodbye and started my run.

When I got to the next block, about half a mile into my run, I became aware that a car was following me - very slowly. I wasn't sure what to do, so stopped and squatted down as if to tie my shoe.

The car sped up slightly, and drove past me with the driver's window rolling up. It was a pure white limo, and the driver was staring straight ahead as if he didn't see me. Talk about bad actors. He could have been in the detective movie last night. Although I tried to get a good look at him, he went by a little too quickly. While I wouldn't be able to pick him out of a lineup, I was pretty sure that I'd never seen him before. But I did use my phone snap a quick shot of the back of the car in case I wanted to know the plates.

And I continued my run.

About a mile later I saw the white limo again, this time headed towards me, but again, driving a little too slowly for the neighborhood. I pretended not to notice, and kept my pace up.

When he was about fifty feet ahead of me, he hit the gas all at once and headed right for me. I bolted through a row of hedges, and cut through the yard over to the next block. I heard him tap the brakes as he kept his car under control, and he kept going. I could see between two houses that he took a right, and left the neighborhood.

Since I was standing at the corner of a house, looking around it, a man with a rake - presumably the man who lived there - asked me what the hell I was doing in his yard hanging onto his house.

I told him that a crazy driver on the next block had tried to run me over.

He looked at me like I was crazy. I could tell that he didn't see how this could happen in his neighborhood, and that he wondered whether I was a lunatic, and if so, whether I was safe to talk to.

"You mean the bad crazy man in his car tried to run you over?" he asked.

"Yes, exactly," I told him.

"Well he was obviously a bad crazy man," he said. "Are you OK, and do you know where you live?" he asked.

"Yes, I'm OK now," I said. "Thank you for saving me!"

He looked at me like I was nuts. He looked nuts.

"Then have a nice day!" he said. He was nuts.

"You too," I said, and started running down the street. I was pretty sure than the man in the car had left the neighborhood. At least for now.

But I did wire the shot of his plates to the Shit-Ninny controller with a code telling the Shit-Ninnies to look for him. And to target him with extreme prejudice.

When I got home, Detective Danny was waiting for me. At least he was out of uniform. "Hi Danny," I said. "What brings you around? Thanks for not wearing your uniform."

"We got a lead on the Goldberg case," he said.

"Who's Goldberg?" I asked.

"The dead guy in the car," he said.

"You mean Mitch. So it sounds like it's all wrapped up. Good for you! Why are you telling me about it?" I asked.

"Goldberg was tied in with the mob," he said.

"Aha!" I said. "I knew you'd solve it."

"I didn't say that we've solved it yet" replied Danny.

"Then good luck Danny! Hey, it was good seeing you!" I said, and I started to wave at him.

"We need your help," he said.

"But I don't know anything about it. Mitch used to cut my hair. He didn't talk much. I liked that. That's all I know," I said.

"We think the mob he was tied up with is run by people on the West coast - in California," he said. "And we think that the senator from California is tied into that mob, somehow. Did you meet him?"

"Who?" I asked.

"The senator," he replied.

"What senator?" I asked.

"I referred him to you. I thought maybe he'd pay you a visit."

"Oh, that senator," I said. "You mean Senator Adler. Yes, I met him the other day. He never mentioned Mitch Goldberg. I'm surprised. He needed a haircut."

"Where'd you meet him?" Detective Danny asked.

"He dropped by here," I said. "He didn't mention Mitch Goldberg, but he mentioned the big dead guy that I saw. The one that you guys think doesn't exist. He said that the big dead guy worked for him."

"He had a dead guy working for him? I'll bet he was the life of the party," Detective Danny said.

"No, he was paid muscle," I told him. "And he wasn't dead then."

"What makes him think that his guy was even here?" he asked.

"They traced his flight, and the stewardess remembers him. Apparently, he was the kind of guy you'd tend to notice: big, built, and he looked tough," I said.

"But why would a senator come all the way out here to look for one of his bodyguards?" he asked.

"He wouldn't," I said. "That doesn't make much sense to me."

"And what was the dosey-doe that was done with the cars - assuming that it ever happened?" he asked.

"I can't imagine," I said. "The timing was too perfect. It's almost like they were trying to pull me into this thing, but I can't imagine why. I can't imagine that the senator even knew who I was. And even if he'd heard of me, what do I have to do with him? Nothing! It makes no sense."

"But what about Goldberg?" said Detective Danny.

"Who?" I asked.

"Mitch Goldberg," he said, "your barber."

"Oh, you mean Mitch. What about Mitch Goldberg?" I asked. "How does he tie into this?"

"Apparently, Mitch Goldberg was running pretty large quantities of drugs in from the West coast. We think those drugs came from the mob that was tied to the senator," he explained.

"But Mitch Goldberg was a hair-stylist," I said. "Why would he be running large quantities of drugs in? Rather, if he was doing that, then why was he a hair-stylist? That's hard work - standing there all day."

"Because as a hair-stylist, he had lots of contacts," Detective Danny explained. "We think that the mall was a central place for dealing large quantities of drugs, and we think that Mitch Goldberg was running that operation."

"Very interesting. And all this time, I thought Mitch was just a nice quiet barber. I never would have guessed that he was a drug kingpin," I said.

Then it occurred to me to tell Danny about Detective Dorian, and about the fact that he seemed to know my neighbor's cousin who was across the street digging a garden for her.

"I just came home from my morning run, and was about to head over to the mall," I began, and then thought about how to explain lots of little things that were sure to sound like a confusing jumble.

"But I thought you'd be interested to know that yesterday I bumped into your buddy Detective Dorian who was coming down my neighbor's driveway," I said, and paused.

Then I continued: "My neighbor is a single woman who I seldom see outside, and her cousin was over there digging a large hole for her to put in a garden in exchange for letting him use her garage to paint his car. Apparently, he was hit by a Shit-Ninny, so he's doing a paint job on his car. Yesterday I was up on the street after my run, and I see Detective Dorian coming down her driveway with her cousin Dagwood in the passenger seat. So I thought you'd like to know that Detective Dorian has a good friend who's my neighbor's cousin. Small world?"

"That's a little confusing," Detective Danny said. "Detective Dorian came over here to give this guy a ride? And he's your neighbor's cousin?"

"Apparently so," I replied. "I've never noticed her cousin over here before, and I didn't get the impression that they were at all close, but she's letting him use her garage, and he's putting in a garden for her. And he's friends with Detective Dorian. So I thought that it would be interesting if we went up and said 'hello' to see if my neighbor looks at all familiar to you. Her name's Dottie."

"Dottie?" he asked. "That's a funny name. Sure, let's drop in on Dottie on your way out."

We both drove up my driveway, and then up Dottie's driveway. We parked, got out, and rang the doorbell. Dottie answered the door.

"Hello?" she said, trying to smile, cracking her face.

"Hi Dottie," I said. "You mentioned that the police were at my house the other day, and I just wanted to reassure you. This is my friend Danny, and he was the one that came to my house. It was just a social call, but he happened to be in his uniform. You mentioned that your cousin's friend Detective Dorian is a detective. Well so is Detective Danny, and it turns out that Danny knows Dorian, because they're in the same department, and they sometimes work together. They're both detectives."

Danny had been looking at Dottie, and when I was done with the monologue, Dannie said, "Pleased to meet you ma'am. I'm a friend of Mick's, and I just wanted to say 'Hi.'"

Danny smiled at her, and her face broke. Rather, I saw her facial muscles relax, and she made what looked like a real smile. Lots of the lines went away, and she wasn't at all bad looking when she relaxed like that.

"Hi Danny," she said. "I'm pleased to meet you," and she put out her hand to shake hands with Danny.

They shook hands, and I cut in: "Well I just wanted to reassure you that everything was OK, so I wanted you to meet Danny. Now that you've both said 'Hello,' we need to go."

Danny gave her a funny look, and she smiled again. "Pleased to meet you," she said again.

"Me too," he said, and waved.

I took Danny by the shoulder and motioned him off the stairs and back to the cars. I wondered why Danny was acting strange, but I had a few more questions for him, which I asked while getting into my car.

"So if Mitch Goldberg was running the operation," I asked, "why would they kill him?"

"That's what we need to figure out," Danny said.

"Have you gone to his house or apartment and had a look around?" I asked.

"Yes we did, but we didn't find anything incriminating. By the way, the black car at the scene of the murder was Mitch Goldberg's. I've no idea why he took the plates off of it," Danny said. "We also found a little booklet in his kitchen. It looks like a list of names, but it's all written in code. We're trying to decipher it now."

"Who's working on the cipher?" I asked.

"His name is Moe," Danny said. "I don't think you know him."

"I might," I said. "Is his brother named Larry?"

"Who?" he asked.

"Larry," I said. "And I think he has another brother named Curly."

"Not this Moe. But I'm having poker night at my house tomorrow, and Moe's coming. Maybe you'd like to come over, play some cards, and talk to him." Danny invited me.

"Maybe I'll drop by. I'm not much for cards, but I'd like to talk to him. What time do you guys start?" I asked.

"At about 8:30," Danny said.

After leaving Dottie's house, I drove to the mall with all of the surface distortion data that I had taken the other day, and a dozen mini-projectors that could project nude pictures on a dozen of the large interior glass surfaces that covered several of the largest stores.

As usual, people drove badly, and I had to use The Fingers a lot. I'd put a small panel in my car to flip The Fingers in the right directions. I found that between The Fingers and the foghorn, I could usually get people to step it up a little.

The Finger panel had four buttons: DF and PF for the Driver's side (left) and Passenger's side (right) Fingers, and FF and BF for the Front and Back Fingers. Traffic was a mess, and I was using all of The Fingers, and plenty of foghorn.

DF, DF, FF, toot-toot, FF, RF, toot-toot-toooooot! And BF, BF for those of you who don't like the toots. Nothing was moving. There was obviously some kind of hazard ahead at Main and Broad, which was the busiest intersection in town.

So I cut through a back lot, and I took a trail that went through the woods to some side streets. At least you don't need to give anyone The Fingers out in the woods.

I couldn't imagine why the main road was such a mess, or why I'd tried to take it. I should have gone as I did the other day: the small dirt road that crosses the railroad tracks, albeit you need to sidle around two "Do Not Enter" signs, and look out for trains.

The mall is a long, two-storied structure with large department stores at each end, and lots of smaller stores along the two-storied promenade. The upper level walkway is open in the middle so that people on the second level can look down onto the first level, and vice versa. This allows strollers to see what stores are on both levels, which is helpful if you're not sure exactly what you're looking for.

The ceiling of the structure is angled glass, so that daylight shines in and illuminates the entire plaza. The department stores at the two ends have large glass facades which allow them to showcase whatever styles they're pushing. All in all, there are lots of glass surfaces, and lots of railings. I had measured the glass contours the other day, and had entered the corresponding calibration data into the mini-projectors that I had brought with me.

At the mall, I positioned the mini-projectors underneath the railings in the center promenade on the second level, where they would not be visible. Since it was still daylight, I couldn't make out the images too clearly, but since I knew what I was looking for, I saw plenty of nice, albeit faint - in daylight - nude photos being projected on the windows. This was the effect that I was looking for - images that were not clearly visible during the day, but that stimulated the subliminal functioning of the brain.

I was sure that when sunset got underway, some of the people would enjoy the show. Others wouldn't. I had set the projection timings to be random and intermittent so that security (or whomever would do this) would have less of an idea what was happening. Of course, projection at night was not the real application, but I felt that it was needed to showcase the equipment like this, so that the stores would appreciate the general capability of this technology.

While today it was nude pictures, I was sure that once people saw them, some of the stores would be interested in buying the projection technology to broadcast advertisements. The idea is to first grab their attention, and then give them the application. This is part of how I became successful. And FF if you don't like it. Of course, subliminal advertising was the real target, but people can't picture that until you show them some real projected images.

So I left the projectors running, and I headed home. There was a large cargo train going through, so I couldn't take my usual exit. Unlike on the way over, the roads were pretty clear, but I could see that there had been a real mess at Main and Broad that I'm glad I had missed. There was paint all over the intersection. It was deep, hence still fluid, and it had all colors. It looked like there had been a massive Shit-Ninny attack, and I hoped that they'd nailed the guy that tried to nail me.

While I didn't get hit with any paint going through the residual mess, I did have to drive through it, so my tires picked lots of the paint up which painted the street ahead of me for a few blocks; not that you'd notice, because hundreds of cars before me had done the same thing. I wondered what had happened, and hoped that they'd got the right guy.

I gave my friend Detective Danny a call. "Hey Danny, what's the big mess out on Main and Broad? I just drove through it, and it wasn't pretty."

Detective Danny explained: "There was a massive Shit-Ninny attack on a car that was stuck at the light."

"He should have run it; I always do," I said.

"This guy couldn't. The Shit-Ninnies had blocked him into the intersection. They were around him on all sides, and he had nowhere to go. They kept unloading paint bombs on him, and he couldn't move. The paint completely covered his limo, windows and all," Detective Danny said.

"Did you say it was a limo?" I asked, just to be sure. "And was it white?"

"Yes. It was a solid white limo, but I doubt it will ever be solid white again. And the driver should have stayed in the car. He tried to get out and make a run for it, but the Shit-Ninnies pelted him with paint bombs. He was practically stuck to the pavement when we got there. He must have been an out-of-towner, because he should have known not to get out of his car. And how did you know that the limo was white?"

"What a mess. I saw the aftermath. And I didn't know it was white; that was just a guess. What happened to the driver?" I asked.

"They took him to the hospital. He's going to need his head shaved and his skin cleaned. He got paint in his eyes, in his nose, and in his mouth. They just need to clean him up and make sure that he's OK," said Detective Danny. "He probably swallowed a lot of it."

"Do you know where he is in the hospital?" I asked. "I think I might like to ask him a few questions. I might have seen him driving around town when I was out for my run this morning."

"Is that how you knew it was a white limo?" Danny asked.

"No, that was just a guess. It matches the color of a limo that nearly ran me down this morning, and I thought that maybe the Shit-Ninnies would go after him if he always drove that recklessly," I explained. "Again, do you know who the driver was, and where they put him in the hospital? I wanted to ask him what made him drive so recklessly."

Detective Danny told me where he was.

"By the way, are you coming to the card game tomorrow night?" he asked.

"I'll drop by, but I likely won't play. I'm not good at gambling. I always calculate odds, and wonder why I'm betting. But I'll drop by. See you then," I replied, and hung up.

When I got home, I saw the new flower bed across the street. It looked very nice indeed. And I wondered what had happened to the big guy in the yellow car that no one saw - or seemed to care about - no one but Senator Adler. And Dottie's car was finally gone from the street. I assumed that her cousin Dagwood had finished painting his car and had left.

Carol and I had dinner, and I told her about the day's events to see whether she had any insights. Tonight, neither of us had cooked, so we got Chinese take-out at our favorite Chinese take-out restaurant, named "Jeffrie's." It's a place where the portions are large and everything is always delicious.

Over our dinner, I told Carol about the paint mess on Main Street at the corner of Broad, and that Danny had told me that a white limo had been creamed by the Shit-Ninnies, and that the driver was in the hospital. "He said that the white limo would never be white again."

"I wonder who the poor guy was that got paint-bombed," she observed, "and whether he'll be OK. Isn't that unusual for the Shit-Ninnies to all gang-up on one car?"

"Very," I said. "Downtown the roads were a mess."

"They finished that garden across the street," she said. "It looks really nice. I'm still surprised that her cousin did all that work for her. And I saw him leave this afternoon."

"Really? That must be why her car's not out on the street anymore. She must have put it back in the garage," I said.

"Yes, I saw him drive out, and he waved. His car looks like new. He did a great job with the painting," she said. "Baby-blue isn't for everyone, but I thought his car looked great. Maybe I should go get hit by a Shit-Ninny, and you could put a fresh coat of paint my car for me."

"You don't need a new paint job," I said. "You just need to use your horn a little. And besides, I wouldn't know how to paint a car the right way. We'd have to hire Dottie's cousin for that. He seems to be a jack of all trades."

I told her that I thought that the guy who had been hit by the Shit-Ninnies had tried to run me down this morning when I was out for my run.

"How do you know it was that car?" she asked.

"I don't," I said, "but it sounds like the same kind of car. And I did get a shot of his plates, and sent them to the Shit-Ninny controller. Danny said that the driver is in the hospital, and I'm going to go over there in the morning to talk to him."

I also told Carol that Danny was going to have a poker game at his house tomorrow, and that I'd been invited.

"But you don't play poker," she said. "Are you going?"

"I'm probably not going to play cards. I'm no good at bluffing. But Danny said that the police have a booklet that they picked up at the murder victim's house that's written in some kind of code. The man who is trying to decrypt it will be there, and I wanted to talk to him. His name is Moe. I don't want to play cards with him; he'd probably take my wallet."

"What time is the card game?" she asked.

"He said it's at 8:30. But like I said, I doubt that I'll stay for poker. If I have to play a few hands, I will, but other than that all I want to do is talk to Moe for a bit. And I'll try to leave as soon as I've done that."

"Why do you want to talk to Moe?" she asked.

"I want to know if he's had an opportunity to look at the code yet, and whether he has any clues. As I had said, there are lots of loose-ends in this case, and a few of them point toward me. I can't imagine why, and I'd like to figure it out. We have a dead bodyguard that no one but me saw, and that no one but Senator Adler - from the other side of the country, from California - is interested in. And we have a dead barber - my barber - who they think was running drugs for the senator. And the senator comes to talk to me. I'm not sure why, but I think that I might have to figure it out before the police do. If I let them figure it out, they'll decide that I'm the one that did it."

"Does that mean that you're taking this case?" she asked.

"Well outside of Senator Adler - who wants to know what happened to his bodyguard, and outside of Detective Danny - who wants to pin the murder of my barber on me, no one has offered me the case. But it has been suggested - by both - that perhaps I should figure it out. Detective Danny doesn't have any money, and the senator does. So maybe I should work for the senator and try to pin it on Detective Danny," I said.

I told Carol that I had taken Danny across the street to meet Dottie. I said that since I had seen Dottie's cousin driving out the other morning with Detective Dorian, and since Danny worked with Detective Dorian, I thought it appropriate that Danny meet Dottie, just to see whether she looked familiar to him.

"And how did that go?" asked Carol.

"It was a little strange," I said. "Dottie's face relaxed, and I realized that she's actually pretty nice looking when she's not scowling. I had the feeling that she liked Danny. And Danny was acting a little weird too, but I wouldn't read anything into it. I doubt she's his type."

Carol smiled, knowingly. We had finished our dinner, so we opened our fortune cookies.

The fortune that I got stated an inarguable truth: "Man who eat photo of father soon be spitting image of him." Now who could argue with that one?

Day 6

John Rogers at the Hospital

In the morning, I went over to the hospital. The hospital is nearly always impossible to figure out the first time you go to see someone there. There are different street entrances for cars depending on which wing you think you're going to, since each wing has a different parking facility, and most of the parking facilities have signs that say "No Parking."

I've learned that you need to know how to read the "No Parking" signs correctly. Whether you're allowed to park in a certain zone depends on what disease you think you're suffering from, and the disease that you're suffering from will determine the wing to which you are assigned.

I'm not sure how the parking attendants determine this. Presumably, they wear different kinds of hazmat suits when they patrol different areas of the garage. But then the garage attendants would have to assume that when sick people drive to the hospital, they already know what disease they have, and that the only reason that they're coming to the hospital is to fill out the correct papers for whatever insurance company is billing them.

But if you're a visitor, then the presumption is that you know the disease of the person that you're visiting. Either that, or the presumption is that if you're a guest, then you're carrying some kind of disease, but you just don't know it yet. But this makes it hard for you to decide which wing you should park in, the point being that they can issue you a parking ticket if you choose the wrong disease. But if you get a parking ticket for this, the trick is to send it to your insurance company, and tell them that the hospital coded it wrong.

So I parked my car and walked around several ramps and into the hospital, being careful not to touch anything. Unlike the parking attendants, I wasn't wearing a hazmat suit. However, I was careful to cough a lot. This way, other people who were visiting the hospital were careful to accord me a wide berth.

I went up to a nurse's station and told the woman who was sitting at the computer that I was looking for a particular patient. She stopped typing as if she was annoyed, pulled her glasses down her nose somewhat, and gave me a wide-eyed stare over the top of her glasses. She had a scary-looking "perm" that her nurse's cap couldn't cover sufficiently, and was wearing all the right kinds of jewelry for working in a diner.

"Are you a Doctor?" she asked.

"Yes, I am," I replied, honestly.

"And what's the name of your patient?" she asked.

"Well he's not exactly my patient - yet," I explained. "He's some dipship that got hit with lots of paint, and I think I know how to help him make sure that it doesn't happen again."

"Oh," she said. "You're talking about that Roberts guy who was brought in yesterday. I've never seen anything like it. He was totally covered. We had to shave his head. You're in the wrong wing. You've got to go to the E wing."

"Yes, I know that," I said, and I pulled out a piece of paper that I had written the room number on that Danny had given me. "I'm looking for E8-39," I said.

"You don't know where E wing is? And you're sure that you're a doctor?" she asked again.

"Yes," I replied, "although I'm still a student. All I've learned is A, B, C, and D so far. I think we're going to learn about E next semester."

She told me how to get there. So I went up the elevator, down the corridor, took a left, and into the E wing. I took another elevator to the 8th floor, and then I walked around in a circle until I found room 39. Assuming that this was John Rogers, he was sitting up in bed, watching TV.

"John Rogers?" I asked. "Were you looking for me?"

He did a double-take. "What do you mean? And how do you know my name?" he asked.

His head had been shaved, but his skin - all of his face and the parts of his body that I could see - were stained with paint. The hospital was running tests to make sure that he'd be alright after all of the paint he'd ingested.

"Yesterday morning I took a run," I said, "and I had the feeling that someone in a large white limo was following me. It was you, wasn't it, Rogers?" I asked.

"I don't even know you," he said. "Why would I follow you?"

"Because someone paid you to, and because you don't know any better," I said.

"What's that supposed to mean?" he asked.

"Do you know who runs the Shit-Ninnies?" I asked. "It's not the government; it's me. They've got your number now. What I need you to do is explain to me who sent you after me and why, or I'll make sure that the Shit-Ninnies keep your number, and do this to you forever, and from now on. You probably couldn't even make it out of town unless I told them to let you go."

He looked scared, and gave a shudder.

"Are you working for Adler?" I asked him.

"Who's Adler?" he replied.

"You don't know who that is?" I asked.

"No," he said.

"Then who are you working for?"

"His name is Jack Holdt," he said. "He told me to find you, and to follow you."

"Why?" I asked.

"He wouldn't say exactly why he was interested in you," Rogers said. "But Holdt said that if he disappeared, that you caused it, and that I should make you disappear too."

"But you tried to run me down," I said. "Why? Did Holdt disappear?"

"You know the answer to that one. And you were there when he disappeared. I was following you. And you're the only one who's talking about him, and the only one that knows what happened to him. The cops don't even know that he ever existed. Once I was sure that Holdt was gone, I tried to carry out his orders."

"I don't know anyone named Jack Holdt. What did he look like?" I asked.

"He was a really big guy, about six-foot-four. Strong as hell. He lifted weights pretty seriously. He was visiting from California, and thought you'd try to hit him. I saw him dead in his car with you standing over him making sure that he was dead. Then you made him and his car disappear. I don't know how you did that, but I was told that you're one of those science guys that can make strange things happen. What did you do with Holdt?" he asked, looking scared and desperate.

"I didn't know Holdt, and I didn't do anything to him. I came upon him by accident. He was dead when I found him. Again, I had no idea who he was. I called the cops and left. When they got there, he had disappeared," I explained.

"How would he disappear?" he challenged.

"I have no idea. I'm trying to figure that out too, for some other reasons," I said. "But I didn't do anything to Holdt."

He looked like he wasn't sure whether to believe me.

"Look," I said. "I'm working on a bigger case. I can't tell you the details of that case, but the case started when I was driving home from the store and saw Jack Holdt. I had never seen him before, and I called the cops. I've no idea who killed him. Then lots of other things happened. Important people want me to figure out what those other things were about. And I'm sure that I won't be able to do that unless I figure out who Jack Holdt was, and why he was here."

"Jack Holdt came out here to get married," he said. "He met her on the internet. They've been corresponding for quite a while now, so he was coming out to marry her."

"Do you know who the lady was?" I asked. "The one he was going to marry?"

"No, I don't," he said. "But whoever she was, she had warned Holdt about you, and had advised him to be careful when he came out here."

"She warned him about me?" I asked, incredulous. I left the hospital more puzzled than when I had gone there this morning.

I went over to the High School to visit Pete Fletcher's "Advanced Science" class, and to talk to the kids about the Louie Carroll problem with the Tweedles. The High School is big: it's several wings, and up to four floors in some places. People who aren't students or teachers need to check in at the front office, where there's a police officer standing security.

I parked in a large lot in front of the visitor's entrance, and went in. I knew the drill. You go to the main office where the staff ignores you until you do a loud "Ahem!" Then they look at you like you're dirt, and they ask you to sign in. After I had done that, I told them that I was visiting Mr. Fletcher's class, and they pointed me in the right general direction.

I took an Ell, went up a couple of flights of stairs, and found Pete's science classroom. It was good to see Pete, and good to see the students. These were the top students in the school: they were interested in learning more about science, and they came to class to learn, not to goof off. While they had their textbooks, and were learning basics, I liked to come by every once in a while to expose them to thinking that they wouldn't likely see in their books.

I enjoy working with young eager minds, and sometimes miss the teaching that I used to do at universities. I stopped at the doorway and waved to Pete. Pete waved me in, and we shook hands.

"Class," he said, "today we're lucky that Professor Maux was able to join us. I was talking to him the other day about the problem that John brought in last week about the twins, where one always lies and the other always tells the truth. Professor Maux knew the problem from his studies at the university. He said that the problem was created by a mathematician named Louie Carroll, and that it's such a famous problem that a band wrote a song about him called 'Louie, Louie.'"

He continued: "The twins are known as the Tweedles, as Louie Carroll framed the problem. One is named Dee, and the other Dumb. Dee always tells the truth, and Dumb always lies. But other than that, you can't tell them apart. Now Carroll put constraints on the problem to make it more logical, and to make sure that it had a unique solution. To do this, Carroll posited exactly two roads leaving the town in which Dee and Dumb Tweedle lived. One road goes to the city, and the other to the beach."

"We'll listen to the problem again," Pete said, "as I state it more formally. We are in a town that has exactly two roads, called 'X' and 'Y,' which leave town. One road goes to the city, and the other one goes to the beach, and we don't know which is which. And the Tweedle twins live in town. They're identical twins, and we don't know which is which. But one always lies and one always tells the truth. Let's call the Tweedle brothers 'A' and 'B.'"

I decided to interrupt Mr. Fletcher just to make the discussion livelier.

"There's one thing I don't get," I said. "Why do two roads leave town? Why not three roads, or four roads, or even fifty roads? Why is it two roads?"

Very professionally, Fletcher said: "That's part of the problem. It only works if there are exactly two roads. We should note that the number two is very important to Carroll, which is why he was commemorated with the song 'Louie, Louie'. The song is not 'Louie,' and it's not 'Louie, Louie, Louie.' That's because there are two roads leaving town. Of course, 'Louie' is code-speak for either one of the roads. That's why there are two of them." (Bravo Pete! Bullshit, bullshit.)

"So you mean that the solution - which you'll get to - only works in towns that have exactly two roads leaving town? That's not a very general solution. For example, what if there were only one road leaving town? Then what would you ask him?"

"I'm not sure," Pete said. "But at any rate, let's do it for two roads. Two roads leave town: one goes to the beach, and the other goes to the city. We get to choose only one of the brothers, and we get ask him only one question. What question do we ask him?"

"Simple," I observed. "Since you only get to choose one of the brothers, choose the one that tells the truth. That's Dee. Ask Dee: 'Dee, which road goes to the city?' Dee will tell us the right road."

"Ah, but here's the trick," explained Pete. "We don't know which one is Dee. We don't know whether we're talking to Dee or to Dumb."

"Well why not ask him?" I asked.

"They'll both say that they are Dee," explained Pete.

"So then we're good," I said, "because Dee always tells the truth."

"But that's part of the problem," said Pete. "Dumb will say that he is Dee, but he'll point to the wrong road."

"So don't pick Dumb," I said.

"But we can't tell them apart. So we don't know whether we're talking to Dee or talking to Dumb," explained Pete. "Whichever one it is - and remember that we don't know - what we ask him is whether his brother would tell us that road X went to the city."

"Why ask him what his brother would say? Why not just ask his brother?" I asked.

"Because he'll say the same thing," explained Pete.

"If they both say the same thing, then how could one of them be lying, and the other be telling the truth? They'd have to say different things," I explained.

"You know, you're right!" said Pete. "I think we need to go think about this problem some more."

"That's the fascinating thing about math and science," I told the class. "Every time you solve a problem, it usually creates even more challenging problems. As an intellectual exercise, you can't beat mathematics."

I continued, "I always find it really exciting coming to Mr. Fletcher's class and talking to the people in here. You are the smart ones, and I always learn from you. I thank you all for the opportunity to discuss this famous problem, and am looking forward to my next visit."

"I'll come visit the High School again soon," I said to Pete on the way out. "I always enjoy myself when I'm here."

"I'll look forward to it," he said. "Are you looking at any other interesting problems?"

"As a matter of fact, tonight I'm going to a poker game," I said.

"You?" he laughed. "Those guys are in trouble. You know all the probabilities, and all the math."

"No, I'm in trouble," I said. "Since I know the math, I'm terrible at bluffing."

I found my way out of the High School, and went home.

That night after dinner I went to Danny's. The other detective, Detective Dorian - who I didn't trust, was there. So were two of Danny's neighbors, and so was Moe, the man that was working on Mitch Goldberg's notepad.

"Hi Detective Dorian," I said, shaking hands. And then I said to the room, while gesturing at Detective Dorian, "Detective Dorian's surely a tragomaschalian renifleur if I've ever met one."

Detective Dorian assumed that I'd said nice things, and smiled, blushing slightly. He felt sophisticated, and I fanned the air. I introduced myself to the neighbors, and to Moe. I was glad I wouldn't be playing poker with Detective Dorian, because I had a strong hunch that he cheats.

"Moe," I said, "I was wondering whether you've had a chance to look at the little book that was left by Mitch Goldberg."

"Yes," he said. "It's a straight substitution code - nothing clever. That's what I figured, since he wrote it in a little notepad. There's nothing to calculate. And since it's phone numbers and names, and things like that, the statistical frequencies are pretty obvious - most of the area codes and prefixes are known, and that makes the whole thing easy to crack. This is what most people use that jot things in notepads. I'm not even sure why they bother."

"Yeah, I guess that's not surprising," I said. "Well Danny has asked me to help a little, because I'm good with odds and ends. So I'd be curious to know if certain people show up in his book when you're done."

"Just ask Danny, and I'll pass it along," Moe said. "I can tell already that most of these phone numbers go to the West coast - to California. People are weird there. Do you know that they actually elected a creepy-looking guy named Adler to the senate? Can you imagine that? Senator Adler: he talks with a lisp, and walks funny. They're weirdos out there."

"Probably no weirder than here, just a little more flagrant about it," I said.

I then explained my ideas about the four seasons to him, and how much of California was missing them. While it's clear that I was boring him, the notion of seasons is essential to cards as I was about to explain to them all. Without the seasons, poker isn't poker.

"Wanna play some cards?" asked Detective Danny, to the whole group, gesturing at the table.

"I don't like to play Earth poker, so I won't be joining you tonight," I said.

"What's Earth poker?" asked one of his neighbors.

"It's four suits with thirteen cards in a suit," I explained. "That's too easy. And it's boring. But it illustrates why the four seasons are important. The suits are the seasons."

"How are the suits the seasons?" asked Detective Danny. "And what makes you call it 'Earth poker?' Why isn't it just 'poker?'"

"Simple." I explained: "There are 52 weeks in a year and 52 cards. There are 4 suits and 4 seasons. Each season has 13 weeks, where a week is 7 days. Where do you think 4 suits come from? And why 13 cards in a suit? It's because there are 4 seasons of 13 weeks each. These come from Earth's solar cycle."

"But that's just a coincidence, surely," suggested one of his neighbors. "There's no other kind of poker."

"Why do you think we have 7 days in a week?" I asked. "It's because of poker. The cavemen figured this out. It's because there are 52 cards in a deck that we have 7-day weeks. Do you think it's an accident that there are 364 days in a year?"

"I thought it was 365 days in a year," said Moe.

"But I'm talking about leap year," I explained. "Think of the 365th day as a Joker. Besides, the cavemen thought that every year was leap year. It wasn't until Galileo that we knew that leap year only happens every four years - that is, unless the year is divisible by 100, unless it's divisible by 400. For example, 1900 was not a leap year, and 2000 was."

"OK, but 52-card poker is the only kind of poker that there is," said Danny.

"Wrong," I said. "That's the kind of poker that Earth cavemen came up with. But what about all of the cavemen on the other planets?" I asked.

"You mean that people on the other planets play poker too?" asked Detective Dorian.

"Of course they do. And in accordance with their calendars, they created different kinds of poker," I said. "For example, Uranus has 40,796 days in a year, Saturn has 24,560 days in a year, and Jupiter has 10,615 days in a year. Note that these all factor into seasons and weeks, which led the cavemen on those planets to create different forms of poker."

"I don't get it," Danny said. "Those are big numbers. How do they have seasons and weeks?"

"For example, let's take Uranus. Uranian poker uses 124 cards. Uranus orbits the Sun every 84 Earth years, and has an 18-hour day. That's 40,796 Uranian days in a Uranian year. That gives them 4 seasons of 31 weeks per season, with 329 days in a week. Sure - it's a long week. So their deck has 4 suits of 31 cards each. That's 124 cards - it's pretty hard to shuffle that deck though. Believe me, I've tried many times. That's why they make the cards big on Uranus."

"That's Uranain poker?" they asked. "Is that what you like? Uranian poker, with 31 cards per suit?"

"Not really," I said. "It's too hard to get a straight. Or even a pair. And getting a flush is the same odds as Earth poker. So for most hands, no one wins. And how often do you see a flush when you play Earth poker?"

"So why would you play Uranian poker?" they asked.

"I wouldn't. It's even more boring than Earth poker, although the pot can really fill up, since no one wins most of the hands," I explained. "That's why they call the planet Uranus."

"What kind of poker do you play then?"

"I like Jupiterian poker and sometimes Saturnian poker if I don't want to think too hard," I said.

"What's Saturnian poker?" Moe asked.

"Saturnian poker uses 80 cards. Saturn orbits the Sun every 29.5 Earth years, and has a 10.5-hour day. That gives them 24,560 Saturnian days in a Saturnian year. So they actually have 16 seasons with 5 weeks in a season, where a week is 307 days. This gives them 16 suits with 5 cards in a suit - that's 80 cards. In Saturnian poker, there's almost never a flush - but it's also too hard to hope for flushes in Earth poker. But there are lots of 3-of-a-kinds, 4-of-a-kinds, and 5-of-a-kinds in any hand. And with 16 suits, any hand you get is very pretty to look at. It makes the game lots of fun."

"And what about Jupiterian poker?" they asked.

"Jupiterian poker uses 55 cards. Jupiter orbits the Sun in 11.9 Earth years, I explained, and it has 9.8 hours in a day. So this gives them 10,615 Jupiterian days in a Jupiterian year. That's 5 seasons of 11 weeks per season, with 193 days in a week. So they have 5 suits with 11 cards per suit. Therefore, their deck has 55 cards, which is very close to our 52-card deck. While the odd number of cards in a Jupiterian deck can screw up magic tricks, there are slightly more pairs and full houses than in Earth poker, so the game moves a little faster."

"That sounds better than Earth poker," they said.

"It is," I replied. "It's a lot more fun - unless you're doing magic tricks, in which case the fact that the number of cards is odd can screw you up. So if you're going to play Jupiterian poker some night, invite me back, and I'll play late. But I have a hard time staying awake in a game of Earth poker. So sorry gents, but I've gotta go. Nice to meet you all."

We all shook hands, and I left, all my money intact. All of my money on Earth, Jupiter, Saturn, and Uranus.

When I got home, most of the lights were out, and Carol was in the family room watching an interesting documentary asking whether we were created, or whether we'd evolved. I never really understood what the difference was. All I know is that talking about "creationism versus evolution" is sometime safer than sports or politics, but it can depend on who's in the room.

Were we "created," or did we "evolve"? I guess it all depends on your perception of time: what's the time scale of either of these? And aren't they the same, or does it depend on what "time" is?

Certainly, when I look around the world, I see so many people that are obviously Cro-magnon troglodytes that it's hard to believe that we've actually evolved.

"But those people do complicated things like drive cars!" people will tell me.

Well that's exactly how I know that most of them are troglodytes. I don't actually get to talk to most of them; all I can do is blow the foghorn and give them The Fingers. So I doubt that it's possible that we've evolved much at all. On the other hand, if you'd like to posit something like a devolution, I think you'd have something. Both are evolutionary; the only question involved is one of direction, which I'll get to shortly.

But on the other side of the argument - for the real believers, I wonder why, since so many of the people who were created are obviously Cro-Magnon troglodytes, I find it hard to believe that God created them. Lots of them are ugly too.

"God is great! And god created that troglodyte!" they'll assert. Are they joking? Why would God do that? It's kind of like pulling a rabbit out of a hat. Sure: it's a rabbit. So? At least rabbits aren't ugly.

I think the argument is that because God pulled a rabbit out of a hat, it proves that he's great. Looking back at when I was a small child and saw my first magic act, I understand the argument. Since then, I've become a skeptic: maybe Cro-Magnon troglodytes were always running around, and we just didn't know it. Maybe people were always ugly.

Actually, as I warned before, I've been able to conflate the two sides of this argument by using my theory of "devolution." I think that as troglodytes, we were always running around, but none of us were that stupid.

Only after enough of us devolved into abjectly stupid states did the remaining ones decide that "they" (which always implies "we" to whoever's speaking - since it obviously includes the person that's doing the speaking - especially when a collection plate is involved) are great. Maybe today, this is what we think of as "evolution."

It's really "devolution."

These things are all matters of perception, so I decided to watch the show with Carol to see whether I'd learn something. I was hoping that the show would help me to evolve.

What I learned was that when you choose to frame this argument in a certain way and make certain assumptions, others might assert that you're wrong. And if you assert them wrong in turn, then they might assert you both wrong and stupid. And they might want to kill you, so it probably makes sense for you to kill them too.

All in all, "sports" seems like a better bet for civil conversation than "evolution" does. Years ago, troglodytes would howl and curse and beat the ground with sticks. That was called "worship." Today it's called "golf." This is why I made the GBM.

Although even with sports, I once learned the hard way that if you're not sure about the vocabulary specific to a sport, you should simply smile, shrug, and not try to join a discussion - even if it's in agreement.

I was once in a nautical bar outside Newport, Rhode Island where there was a sailboat race on the TV. I had spent the day out on the docks learning "words" (note that I didn't say "acquiring a nautical vocabulary," because this would include learning the meanings of the words). To feel a deeper kinship with the crowd at the bar - so that I could fit in, I merely commented that the crew who took second in the race had needed to "tac their jib-boom leeward," and I almost wound up in a fist fight with a bunch of drunks without having any idea what those words meant.

At least if the argument had been about evolution, I wouldn't have been a sitting duck. And I would have known to swing first.

Day 7

The Facts as I Know Them

In the morning, I ran through what I had learned with Carol. I told her that the big guy that was dead - the guy that Senator Adler had said came out to visit relatives - was named Jack Holdt. While he worked as muscle for Adler, he hadn't come out here to visit relatives. He had come here to marry a woman that he had met on the internet. That woman had told him that I was dangerous, and that he needed to watch out for me.

So Jack Holdt brought a guy named John Rogers out with him. Rogers claims that he doesn't know who Adler is - which I find hard to believe, since Holdt worked for Adler, but he claims that Holdt had told him that if anything happened to him, that he was to try to take me out.

"Do you think that Rogers is dangerous?" she asked.

"Not anymore." I explained that Rogers was the man who had been hit by the Shit-Ninnies who I visited in the hospital. I told her that I had explained to Rogers that if anything happened to me, the Shit-Ninnies would get him again, and again, and again, and again. I was sure that Rogers didn't want any more trouble.

I also told her that they were starting to decode Mitch Golderg's book of phone numbers - again, Mitch Golberg was both the other dead guy, and my barber. And I told her that the cops thought that most of the phone numbers in Goldberg's book were to the left side of the country; to California; to Senator Adler's home state.

"Who was the woman that Jack Holdt came here to marry?" Carol asked.

"Rogers didn't know. All he knew was that Holdt had exchanged lots of email with her, and then came out here to get married. Rogers had apparently been following me, and saw me checking out Holdt dead in his car. Rogers assumed that I had killed him and made his car disappear, but he doesn't know how I was able to do that. He thinks that I'm some kind of a magician."

"But Jack Holdt disappeared. And so did his car," Carol pointed out.

"Yes," I said. "That's the puzzle. But even if I knew what happened to Jack Holdt, and what happened to his car, I'm still not sure I could make sense out of it. My first impulse would be to tie it to Senator Adler. But then if it was Adler who had him killed, why is Adler the one who's out here looking for him? It makes no sense."

"I think that Rogers knows more than he's telling you," Carol said. "I also have a feeling that somehow the cops are involved. It's puzzling that they've simply dismissed your story about Holdt, and have no interest in investigating. That doesn't sound like how the cops work. It's fishy," she said.

"You're right," I said. "Several things don't add up. I'm going to go back to the hospital to talk to Rogers again, and I'm going to have a more direct conversation with Detective Danny. He wants me to 'get involved,' but I have a hunch that the cops are hiding some details. It could be that they are trying to get me to implicate myself - or at least to stick my nose into something that would make a jury believe that I had implicated myself. I'm not sure who to trust."

"There's another strange thing I heard from one of my friends - Julie - who was at the mall last night," said Carol.

"What's that?" I asked.

"Julie said that the big department stores were displaying sexy pictures of nude women on their windows. She said that it looked like a completely new kind of image, and that no one seemed to know where the images were coming from."

"Really?" I asked.

"Yes," she said. "Julie said that for the first time, she saw clusters of teenage boys who seemed to be taking an interest in the department store windows. But she also heard that there is a religious group, and also a women's group that are both threatening to sue the department stores if they keep doing it. What do you think the stores are trying to do?"

"Actually," I confessed, "I set that up. I thought that it was a new display technology that had possibilities. I knew that those images - from the web - would draw attention. What I'm happy to hear is that the technology is drawing interest. I think that having seen this, department stores might be interested in using this technology to draw customers in to purchase certain products - not nude women, of course. But this got their attention. That's good to hear. I'll take those projectors down, and give them some time to think about it."

I called the hospital to ask about my "brother-in-law" John Rogers. They told me that he was OK, and was being discharged this morning, but that he didn't have clothes to wear. So I told them that the reason that I had called was because I was going to bring him some clothes, and that I'd give him a ride to the airport. They were relieved to hear this, and were looking forward to seeing me.

John was about my size, so I threw together some of my clothes, put them in a bag, and drove to the hospital. Traffic wasn't that bad, but I did need to use the foghorn several times, and seemed to need to use the FF button at most of the lights. The light would turn green, and no one would move. Foghorn and FF. People need to move when the light turns green.

I parked in the lot for E wing, and I took the bag up to John's room. I took the elevator up to the 8th floor, and I walked down to room 39. This time I knew where it was, so I didn't need to read all of the room tags, although I did cough along the way so that people would give me a wide berth.

John was sitting in a chair with the TV on, wearing a hospital gown. He looked surprised to see me again.

"Good morning John," I said. "They told me that they're releasing you, but that you needed some clothes, so I brought you some of mine. You look about my size. I'll also give you a ride to the airport if you're leaving town, which you should."

John said, "That's thoughtful of you. But I still have a carry-on bag in one of the hotels on the edge of town, so if you could just give me a lift to the hotel, I'll get my stuff and take the airport limo from downtown."

"OK, well here's some clothes and I'll give you a lift," I said. "But there are a few details that you told me yesterday that don't make sense. I think you tried to obfuscate in a few of your answers."

He looked uneasy. "Such as?" he asked.

"You were working for Jack Holdt. You flew out here from California - just like Holdt did. Jack Holdt worked for Senator Adler. And when I asked you who Adler was, you acted like you never heard of him. Do you think I'm stupid?" I asked.

"OK, I lied - a little. I was told never to tie the senator into any of our business. I knew that Jack Holdt was one of Senator Adler's people, but again, I was told that Adler was never to be mentioned - ever," John said.

"So you were working for Jack Holdt who worked for Senator Adler?" I asked. "Do you think that Jack Holdt needed a bodyguard or something? Take a look at Holdt and take a look at you. You are a pencil-neck. Why would Jack Holdt hire a pencil-neck like you? And do you think that Holdt was paid so much that he could afford a bodyguard? Again, do you think I'm stupid?"

"No. I've learned not to assume that. OK then, I wasn't working for Holdt. Like Jack Holdt, I worked for Senator Adler. The senator didn't believe Holdt when he said that he was coming out here to visit relatives. The senator's computer guys said that they couldn't find any relatives of Holdt that lived out here, so the senator sent me out here to keep an eye on Holdt."

"But you said that Jack Holdt had come out here to get married. How did you know that?" I asked.

"Like I said, we both worked for Senator Adler, so we knew each other. Jack Holdt had confided in me why he was coming out here, but he asked me to keep it to myself. Maybe he was worried that it wouldn't work out, because he had never actually met the woman before, so he didn't want to announce to the boss that he was getting married."

John continued, "So the boss sent me out here to keep an eye on Jack, and I figured why not? What am I supposed to do, tell the boss that Jack has a girlfriend? So I did what I was told. I came out here with Jack to keep an eye on him."

That made sense. "But you don't know who the girlfriend was?" I asked.

"Not a clue. While Jack and I got along, we didn't share stuff like that."

"But you also said that Jack Holdt's girlfriend told him that I was dangerous, and that he should worry about me. Why would she tell him that? I didn't know Holdt at all," I said.

"Again, I don't know who she is. And I didn't know who you were until I saw you standing over Holdt's body in his car. So I can't help you with that one," John said. "Did they ever find his car?" he asked.

"Still no sign of his car, and still no sign of his body," I said. "And the cops don't seem interested. This is what seems fishy to me. Senator Adler is interested enough to fly out here and ask me to investigate the disappearance of Jack Holdt, but the local cops act like this never happened. I've got to believe that the cops are tied into this somehow."

"Why would the cops kill Jack Holdt?" he asked. "He's not even from around here, and wasn't breaking any laws. He's a guy from the other coast who came out here to marry a mystery woman that he met on the internet. Why would the local cops have enough interest in him to cover it over?"

"It makes no sense," I said.

I let John Rogers get dressed, waited for them to check him out of the hospital, and then I drove him across town to his hotel. We saw the Shit-Ninnies hit a car on the way over - it was one of the cars that I had given The Fingers to (LF with the foghorn as we passed him going the other way - the guy was driving like a jerk), so good for them.

I let John out, and then went back across town to 'Holy Moly,' a coffee shop where I thought I'd find Detective Danny hanging around drinking free coffee on our dime. I thought I needed to learn a little more from him.

Detective Danny was sitting at a two-top in the coffee shop. He had a large cup of coffee and was reading the paper. I bought a large latte at the counter and walked over and sat down.

"Hi Danny," I said. "Anything new on the case? And did you win any money playing Earth poker?" I asked.

"Yes and no - you asked two questions," said Detective Danny. "Dorian took me to the cleaners playing poker, and Moe translated Mitch Goldberg's little book, and we checked his phone calling history. Needless to say, many of his calls matched the numbers in his book."

"Detective Dorian cheats. I could have told you that. I can tell by looking at him. Does anything that Moe found stand out?" I asked.

"In his last two days, Mitch made lots of calls to a number registered to a guy named Jack Holdt. We're trying to figure out who that is," Danny said.

"I've already learned who Jack Holdt was," I told him. "That was the first dead guy that I found at the scene. He was the dead guy in the yellow car, both of which have disappeared."

"We're still not sure whether you're bullshitting us, and whether there was a first dead guy in a yellow car," Danny said. "We found Mitch Goldberg dead in a black car in the exact same place where you claim Jack Holdt - the guy who Mitch Goldberg called a lot - was shot in the same way in a yellow car left in the same position as the black car - also with the driver's door open and the left directional on. The question is: 'If there was a big dead guy named Holdt who was sitting in a yellow car, then what happened to Holdt, and what happened to the yellow car?'"

"That has me stumped," I confessed. "I saw a big guy - who I now know was Jack Holdt - dead in a yellow car. So I called you, told you that, and left the scene without touching anything. You guys go over there right after I called, and you find a different car in the same position with a different dead guy - Mitch Goldberg - in it in a different position. And the yellow car with Jack Holdt in it is gone. It makes no sense. We're missing a few pieces of this puzzle."

"What's missing?" asked Detective Danny. "Besides Jack Holdt and the yellow car?"

"I don't know. When I saw Holdt in the yellow car, I called you and told you about it. Who was the cop who actually went to the scene after I called?" I asked.

"When you called, I was right in the middle of another case, so I sent Detective Dorian," he said.

"You mean the Detective Dorian that was with you when I came in for a deposition, and who was at your house for the game of Earth poker? That Detective Dorian? Tonya's boyfriend? The one that fleeced you?" I asked.

"Tonya's boyfriend? He wishes. Is there another Detective Dorian?" he asked.

"Not that I know of. Detective Dorian looks fairly young. Has he been a detective for very long? Would he screw obvious things up? I mean, besides getting a date with Tonya?" I asked.

"No. Detective Dorian's smart," Danny said, "but inexperienced. As a detective, he's often defective."

"And you're a poet and you don't know it," I observed.

"What's that? I'm not a poet. Detective Dorian went to the scene and found what we now know is Mitch Goldberg's car with Mitch Goldberg dead in the back seat. He'd been shot," said Danny.

"Yes. And the plates had been removed from his car," I said. "Why would Mitch take the plates off his car? And where are his plates, anyway?"

"I can't imagine," said Danny.

"The day of the murder, I had left the store at 1:45, put my bags in the car and drove around to the back of the store where the Dumpster was. I figure it was 1:50 when I saw Jack Holdt dead behind the wheel of a yellow car. I got out and looked around - being careful not to touch anything. I probably called you within two or three minutes. Let's say I called you at 1:55. Then I went home. What time did Detective Dorian get to the murder scene?"

"I don't know. I'll have to check the records," Detective Danny said. "But I would think it would take a while to move one car - with a big dead guy in the driver's seat, and to replace it with another car, and put another dead guy in the back seat. Whoever did this - assuming that this is what happened - would have had to move fast. And why would they? After all, the car was behind the Dumpster in the back of the store. No one ever goes back there except to dump the trash."

"I go back there," I said. "That's how I usually enter and leave that plaza."

"But that's you," Detective Danny said. "I meant no one who's normal goes back there."

"You mean no one that likes to wait at traffic lights goes back there. We need to find out what time it was when Detective Dorian got to the scene. That would at least give us a time window. I'm not sure what good that will do, but I'm not sure what else to do in the meantime."

"I'll ask him," said Danny.

Detective Danny finished his coffee and left Holy Moly. He left his newspaper. I still had half a cup of coffee, so I stayed to drink it, and started thumbing through the paper.

Then my phone rang. It was Pete Fletcher, the science teacher from the High School.

"Mick, I figured it out. If you ask the liar, Dumb Tweedle, which road his brother, Dee Tweedle, would say went to the city, Dumb will point to the wrong road. And if you ask the truth-teller, Dee Tweedle, which road his brother, Dumb Tweedle, would say went to the city, Dee will also point to the wrong road."

"So you mean that now both are lying?" I asked. "I'm a little mixed up."

"No. Dumb is lying, and Dee is telling the truth," Pete explained.

"But they're both pointing to the wrong road. It sounds like they're both lying now," I explained.

"Well that's because there's one lying and one telling the truth. As one of the computer kids explained, it flips the parity," Pete said. "So you always get the wrong answer."

"Why would you want the wrong answer?" I asked.

"It's OK if it's wrong, as long as we know it's wrong," explained Pete. "That leaves it up to us to flip the answer."

"That's way too confusing. Then we have to remember whether to believe the answer or whether to not believe the answer. It's too easy to make a mistake," I told him.

"Well this is just a logical problem," Pete said.

"There's actually a much better solution," I told Pete. "It has to do with the fact that the answer is binary."

"Binary?" asked Pete. "What's binary?"

"Binary is a system of exactly two states. We've either got Dee - who tells the truth, or we've got Dumb - who lies. We don't care which one is Dee or Dumb; we just know that one is always right and the other always wrong. That's binary. We also have two roads: one goes to the city, and one doesn't. That's binary too," I said. "The point is that it allows us to construct an answer that's either a lie about the truth, or the truth about a lie. Either way, it's the wrong answer, so you'll have to switch it, or you'll wind up at the beach - which isn't a bad idea."

"So how would we get the true answer?" asked Pete.

"Simple," I explained. "You need quadruplets. Suppose there were four identical quadruplets. And suppose that two of them always told the truth, and that two always lied."

"Isn't that much more complicated?" asked Pete. "And much rarer? I mean quadruplets? There are lots of twins, but not many quadruplets."

"Let it be quadruplets," I said. "It makes the problem simpler."

"I don't see how four is simpler than two," said Pete.

"Because it allows us to flip the parity of the problem," I said.

"What's parity?" asked Pete.

"It indicates whether the number of true states is even. And with quadruplets, the number of truth-tellers is even. That's how we're going to change the problem," I explained.

I continued: "Let's suppose that there are quadruplets. We've already got Dee Tweedle and Dumb Tweedle. Let's assume that there are two more brothers. We'll call them Duh! Tweedle, and Doo-doo Tweedle. So now we have Dee, Dumb, Duh!, and Doo-doo. To make it easy, let's call them A, B, C, and D. And remember, two always lie, and two always tell the truth."

"OK, so now we have quadruplets, and two roads," allowed Pete.

"What we do is that we take one of the quadruplets; say we take A. We ask A: 'A, which road would B say that C would say that D would say goes to the city?' His answer will point us to the correct road."

"Really?" asked Pete. "That sounds a lot more complicated."

"It does take quadruplets," I allowed, "but we don't have to remember to reverse the answer. Also, the part I don't like about Carroll's solution is that there are just two roads. We needed to fix this."

"This is Mrs. Maux's solution?" he asked.

"No, it's Carroll's," I replied.

"But isn't Carol your wife?" he asked.

"I was talking about Louie Carroll. Remember?" I reminded him.

"Who's he?" he asked.

"He's the guy that the 'Louie, Louie' song is all about. And he's the guy that came up with this problem. Let's consider the case where there are more than two roads. Suppose that there are three roads," I suggested.

"OK, let there be three roads. I don't see how that changes anything," he said. "You shouldn't need quadruplets. You just need to remember to flip the answer."

"I'll show you why it doesn't work with twins when there are more than two roads. Suppose there and three roads, and that we have twins instead of quadruplets," I said. "It's Dee and Dumb again. We don't know which twin is which, but we know in the end that whichever one we chose is pointing to one of the wrong roads."

"That's right," said Pete. "So the other road is the right one."

"But there are two other roads. All we've done is eliminated one of the wrong roads. So there are two left. Which one goes to the city?" I asked.

"Hmmm. I'll have to think about that," said Pete.

"And in fact, you don't actually need quadruplets," I said. "All you need is four people."

"But we needed twins in the original problem," said Pete.

"Actually, the fact that they're twins is immaterial," I said. "I don't care whether I can tell them apart. They could be cousins, or just friends. The point is that they know each other, and that one always lies and the other always tells the truth. The liar knows that the truth-teller tells the truth, and the truth-teller knows that the liar lies. That's the only precondition. Other than that, I don't care who the two people - or in my posited case, the four people - are."

I finished my coffee, said goodbye, and left Holy Moly singing "Louie, Louie" to myself.

————————————

On the way home, the car ahead of me was going well under the speed limit, so I was laying on the foghorn and giving him The Fingers, with a good FF. Despite this, he never sped up. But then a Shit-Ninny that was coming the other way got him right on the windshield, so he had to pull over. Who says that the Shit-Ninnies aren't worth having?

I wanted to get Carol's opinion of what I'd learned, which is why I was headed home. I found Carol in the living room reading a book.

"Have time to take a break?" I asked. "I've learned a few things, and wanted to know what you thought," I said.

"Sure," Carol said. "Why don't you wait for me in the kitchen? Make yourself a coffee; it'll just take a couple of minutes for me to finish this chapter."

So I went into the kitchen, hit the buttons, made another coffee, and sat down at the island. I had my notebook and a pen, so I started writing down the facts as I knew them.

Holdt and Rogers both worked for Senator Adler, who some people think might be running a drug ring on the West coast that does lots of business here. Holdt meets a woman on the internet, and comes out here to (maybe) get married. He lies to the boss and says that he's coming here to visit some relatives that Adler figures out don't exist, so Adler sends Rogers out to keep an eye on Holdt.

Jack Holdt takes a workout at the gym next to the big supermarket, and then drives behind the store - back by the Dumpster, where someone gets into his car - into the passenger's seat, and shoots him. After he's dead, he opens the driver's door and puts the left directional on. (This makes no sense.) Then I find him at 1:50, look the scene over, call Detective Danny at 1:53, and leave. Rogers sees me with Holdt between 1:50 and 1:55 and assumes that I killed him.

Then Detective Dorian shows up. (At what time?) When he gets there, Holdt and his car are gone, and Mitch Goldberg's car is there - also with the driver's door open and the left directional on. Mitch Goldberg is dead, lying down in the back seat of the car. He'd been shot the same way as Jack Holdt. For some reason, Goldberg had gone to the same Dumpster in the back of a supermarket that Holdt had gone to. And he'd also taken the plates off his car. Why?

The cops see no evidence of the first murder or the first car, because that evidence has disappeared. The cops are not investigating, because they don't believe me, but Rogers witnessed it. And the senator shows up to talk to me, because he hopes that I can figure out what happened to Holdt.

Carol came in and joined me. "What have you got?" she asked.

"A big mess," I said. I explained all of the facts as I knew them, and was eager to see if she had some creative ideas.

"Rogers thought you killed Holdt, because he saw you at the scene. But the senator comes to talk to you, and asks you to solve the case. Why didn't the senator assume that you killed him? Wouldn't Rogers have told him that?" she asked.

"Maybe," I said. "On the other hand, maybe Rogers hadn't told the senator about me yet, because he wanted to wrap the whole thing up by himself before telling him. Or maybe he did tell him, but the senator was smart enough to have doubts that I would have done that - he seemed to have heard of me. Either that, or the senator wanted me to get involved to implicate myself."

"Maybe you need to talk to the senator again," she suggested.

"What do you think happened to Jack Holdt's body and his car before the second killing - the killing of Mitch Goldberg?" I asked.

"What time did the second killing happen?" she asked.

"We don't know yet. I asked Danny to get that for me."

"I had a strange idea," she said. "Maybe Goldberg wasn't the second killing. Maybe he was the first killing, and you missed it. Maybe the cops had already been there and had moved Goldberg before Holdt even showed up."

"How would they even know about the killing?" I asked. "I hadn't even called them yet. And again, what happened to Holdt and his car?"

"Good questions," she said, "but I'm just turning everything upside down to see if we can come up with a scenario that makes sense. But to answer your question, maybe the cops knew about Goldberg because they were in on it. It seems odd that the cops still don't want to know anything about Holdt, and that Senator Adler thought that they were unhelpful. And why did the senator go to the local cops anyway?" she asked. "That sounds strange too."

"All of those are great points," I said.

"Finally," she asked, "who's the woman that Jack Holdt supposedly came out to meet? It's odd that no one has figured this out yet."

"Another great point," I said. The more I learn about this case, the more confusing it gets.

"I think you need to have a talk with Senator Adler to try to get a little more clarity from him, and you need to figure out who Jack Holdt's girlfriend was," she concluded.

I called the number that Senator Adler had left me with, and a staffer answered. I told them that the senator was expecting my call, so would they please tell him that I had called. About ten minutes later, Senator Adler called me on an unmarked line.

"So are you interested in taking this case?" he asked.

"Yes," I responded. "I find it very intriguing, and I'm assuming that the money you had suggested as a 'thank you' will be sent over to my bank."

"Consider it done," he said.

"Jack Holdt worked for you as a security person," I said. "Is that correct?"

"Yes, that's right," he said.

"And he came out here to visit relatives," I said. "Isn't that what he told you?"

"That's what he told me, but I didn't believe him. I have a sense for when people are lying, so I suspected that he was going to Connecticut for other reasons," he said.

"Did you investigate that?" I asked.

"No, but I sent a second man to tail him, just in case," he said.

"Who was that?" I asked.

"It was a security guy named John Rogers. He told me that he thought you'd killed Jack Holdt," Adler said.

"Why would I do that?" I asked.

"That's exactly what I thought," Adler said. "Jack Holdt kept to himself and didn't ever make any trouble. I doubted that you knew him, I doubted that you'd ever run into him, and I doubted that Holdt would ever give you a reason to kill him. I knew that it had to be something else. Rogers said that Holdt had been shot while sitting in a car behind a supermarket next to a Dumpster. That doesn't sound at all like your style."

"Actually, that's my best defense," I said. "I'm surprised I'd never thought of it."

"Rogers told me that Holdt had actually come out here to meet a woman that he'd gotten to know on the internet. I didn't know that Jack Holdt was that naive. Maybe that's why he told me some nonsense about visiting relatives: he didn't want me to think he was that stupid."

"Do you have any idea who the woman was?" I asked. "Maybe I could begin with her."

"No idea. I didn't even know he was coming out here to meet a woman. How would I know who she was?" he asked.

"Computer files?" I suggested. "Any chance you can get a hold of his computer, and figure out who he was corresponding with?"

"That's a good idea," he said. "I'll have my people look into it."

"There's one other puzzle," I opined.

"What's that?" he asked.

"With due respect, Jack Holdt was a security guard. Why are you that interested in where he goes and why, and why do you take the pains to investigate when you think he's giving you white lies? Why did you care that he was coming out here for personal reasons? And why did you bother to have him shadowed? These things strike me as odd," I said.

"I had my reasons," said the senator. "And you don't have to know what they are to solve this case. Again, I'll make sure that what I had suggested gets transferred to your bank. And if you have any other questions, don't hesitate to ask. Good bye," he said, and hung up.

Day 8

I Take the Case

In the morning, I checked my bank account and saw that a large deposit had been made. So I was now working for Senator Adler, although I hadn't promised that I could solve this, and he hadn't been entirely free with the facts. But as they say, money talks, and bullshit walks, so I was on the case.

My phone rang, and it was Detective Danny. He told me that last night he had talked to Detective Dorian about when he had gone to the murder scene. I had guessed that it had been a few minutes after 1:50 - maybe it was 1:55 - when I had called Detective Danny from the murder scene. Danny said that he had been writing a document for another case when I had called, but had called Detective Dorian within a couple of minutes of my call - it was probably at about 2:00 when Detective Danny had called Detective Dorian.

And Detective Dorian had happened to be over at the mall, just across the street from the shopping plaza where I had been with Jack Holdt, dead in his car behind the garbage Dumpster. Detective Dorian had guessed that he was able to get out of the mall, into his car, through the traffic lights, and back to the Dumpster behind the supermarket in about twenty minutes. So Detective Dorian was at the murder scene by about 2:20; maybe 2:25 knowing the traffic at that light - the one that I avoid.

Therefore, it was probably almost half an hour between the time that I had left the scene at (my guess) 1:55, and Detective Dorian arrived at 2:20-2:25. That would be plenty of time to move Holdt and his car, and to commit another murder. But who had moved the first car and committed the second murder? And why?

"Do you happen to know why Detective Dorian was at the mall?" I asked Danny.

"He said he was getting a haircut. He keeps his hair short and very neatly trimmed. I think he gets haircuts frequently," said Danny.

"Getting a haircut?" I asked. "And he can just jump out of the barber chair when he gets a call? Maybe he didn't get there in twenty minutes," I suggested. "Maybe he finished getting his haircut, and then left the mall and went to the murder scene."

So maybe it wasn't 20-25 minutes. Maybe it was more like a half an hour. That's even more time for the scene that I witnessed to have been changed. But if it was a half an hour, it's hard to believe that no one else had happened to drive behind the store and seen the murder scene.

"By the way, who cuts his hair? Was it Mitch Goldberg by any chance?"

"I don't know," said Danny. "That's a good question. But keep in mind that Mitch Goldberg was sitting there dead in his car when Detective Dorian got to the murder scene. So I doubt that he'd been cutting Detective Dorian's hair."

"Probably not. Unless he went to the murder scene with Detective Dorian, and Detective Dorian killed him," I suggested.

"But that makes no sense. If Mitch went there with Detective Dorian, why would Mitch drive his own car? And why would he take the plates off of it?" Detective Danny asked.

"Maybe Mitch isn't the one that took the plates off of his car. Maybe Detective Dorian did that. Or someone else," I said.

"But why would Detective Dorian want to kill Mitch Goldberg?" Danny asked. "I can't imagine a motive."

"Maybe Mitch was porking Detective Dorian's girlfriend Tonya. You know, the Tonya that won't go out with Detective Dorian? Maybe Detective Dorian was jealous," I said.

"Are you joking?" asked Danny. "If she wouldn't go out with Dorian, why would she go out with Mitch? Mitch was twenty years older and six inches shorter."

"Because Mitch might have been making big money. Tonya told me that she's attracted to big money. That's why she hangs out at that gym," I said.

"There are rich people at that gym?" he asked.

"No. But I don't think she's thought about that," I explained.

"That's ridiculous," said Danny. "At any rate, I doubt that Mitch was cutting Dorian's hair, and that Dorian bolted out of the barber chair and ran over here, and found Mitch dead. And that while Detective Dorian was running over here, Mitch got here first and moved the first car and body, and then got himself murdered. I'll find out whether Mitch was working that day, and if so, how late he worked so that we can rule this out. But this didn't happen."

"Mitch was working that day," I said. "He cut my hair. I left the salon at about 1:15, and he was still there. If Detective Dorian claims to have found him at around 2:20-2:30, and if I assume that it would take Mitch 15-20 minutes to get from the salon to where Detective Dorian found him, Mitch must have left the salon by 2:00 at the very latest."

"But what if he left earlier?" asked Danny. "You left the salon at 1:15. He could have left the mall right after you did."

"Well if he did, he couldn't have gone directly to the murder scene," I said.

"Why not?" asked Detective Danny.

"Because I got to the murder scene at about 1:50, and Mitch wasn't there yet," I replied. "It was a different murder scene when I was there."

"You're right Mick," said Detective Danny. "Regardless of when Mitch left the salon, and regardless of when the first murder happened, Mitch couldn't have been murdered before about 2:00 - after you left the first murder scene, and before 2:30 - the latest that Detective Dorian might have gotten there."

"So Mitch was murdered sometime between 2:00 and 2:30," I concluded.

"Yes," replied Detective Danny. "And Jack Holdt, Senator Adler's professional muscle from California, couldn't have done it, since he was already dead."

"So who killed Mitch Goldberg? And who killed Jack Holdt?" I asked. "And why?"

I went for my morning run, and no cars followed me today. When I got back, I saw Dottie out watering her garden with a hose. It was unusual for me to see Dottie doing yard work, so it didn't occur to me to honk or wave at first, and then I realized that she was waving at me. And smiling. It made me wonder what she'd planted, and whether you could smoke it.

Momentarily surprised, I waved back. "Nice garden," I shouted up her driveway.

"Thanks," she replied, "and it's a beautiful day, too."

I noticed that she wasn't wearing a housecoat or moccasins; she had on jeans with a nice top, and was wearing sneakers. And her hair was down. She'd forgotten her curlers. Marijuana, I concluded.

"Gee, you're all dressed up," I said. "What's the occasion?"

"No occasion," she replied. "I just was thinking that I should try to get out of the house a little more. I used to be more of an outdoors type, and it occurred to me that I've been spending too much time sitting around indoors. Maybe I'll come running with you someday. Do you know that I used to run track when I was in High School?" she asked.

"Really?" I asked. "I wouldn't have guessed that. I didn't do much of anything in High School but read books. I started running much later, but not seriously. I just do it to get some exercise."

"It's really good exercise," she replied.

"Do you know who else ran track in High School?" I asked. "My friend Danny - the police detective that I brought over the other day to introduce. He and I were friends in High School, and he was on the track team."

"Really?" she asked, looking pleasantly surprised. "He seemed very nice," she said. I could have sworn I saw her eyes twinkle. Marijuana, I concluded.

"Well maybe you should go running with him," I joked. "He's faster than I am."

She laughed and waved as I went down my driveway. I wanted to tell Carol about the new Dottie and her marijuana. Maybe we should start using it too.

I went in, took a shower, changed into some clean clothes, and poured myself a coffee. Carol was sitting in the living room reading a book, so I went in with my coffee and sat down. Carol put her marker in her book, closed it and put it down, and looked askance.

"How was your run?" she asked.

"Very interesting," I said. "I just saw Dottie out watering her garden, and she's different."

"Different?" Carol asked. "How?"

"I don't know," I said. "Maybe she fell and hit her head. She had her hair down, was wearing jeans and a nice top, and she waved at me first. She seemed like a different person. She was actually pleasant to talk to, even though our talk was brief."

"Ah," said Carol. "You never did understand women."

"What do you mean by that?" I asked. "I don't understand."

"As I said," said Carol. "My guess is that she met a man that she likes, and that she's now seeing the world through a different set of lenses."

"But where would she meet a man?" I asked. "She never goes out."

"I don't know," said Carol. "Didn't you say that her cousin Dagwood brought a friend of his over? A police detective named Detective Dorian? Maybe she likes Detective Dorian."

"Detective Dorian is a rebarbative jerk. I can't imagine her liking Detective Dorian. She's direct and honest - which has always been her main problem. Detective Dorian's the other way. I can't imagine her falling for him and his toploftical manner, not to mention his pink socks - the ones he wears with a blue suit," I said.

"Well, as a woman, I can tell you that that's probably what's going on," she said.

"Even with those socks? If you say so," I said.

Then I brought up the case. "I also went over some timings with Danny, and we figured out that Mitch must have been murdered sometime between 2:00 and 2:30. I left the first murder scene - the one with Holdt - at about 1:55, and Detective Dorian showed up to find the second murder scene - the one with Marty the barber - sometime between 1:55 and 2:30. This would have given whomever did this plenty of time to move the first car - with Holdt - and then to murder Marty in Marty's car."

"But again," she asked, "what happened to the first car? Who murdered Holdt and why? And who murdered Marty the barber and why? And why is Senator Adler sticking his nose into it?"

"You're very good at netting out the key questions, and stating them plainly," I said. "I told you that I'm very good at understanding women."

"I'd also like to float a different idea again," Carol said. "You said that you don't trust Detective Dorian. Maybe his account of the times is false. Suppose that Mitch left the salon right after you did - say at

1:20. Suppose that he crossed the intersection and got to the murder scene when you were in the supermarket, was murdered while you were still in the supermarket, and Detective Dorian was already there. Suppose Detective Dorian already did his police report and had Marty and his car moved while you were checking out, and then Jack Holdt showed up and was murdered too. Then you found Holdt, and then called Detective Danny who called Detective Dorian, and then Detective Dorian made Holdt and his car disappear."

"That's lots of maybe's, some very close timings, and a whole other set of 'whys?'" I said. "For example, why would Detective Dorian care about making Jack Holdt and his car disappear?"

"I can't imagine," Carol said.

"And why would he be in such a big hurry to get Marty and his car moved?" I asked. "It was a murder scene. They never move things from a murder scene this quickly. Usually they like to take lots of pictures, dust for prints, and all that kind of stuff. If Marty's murder was to be on the record, why would Detective Dorian get it all cleaned up so quickly - just in time for Jack Holdt's murder? It makes no sense. Also, why would Detective Dorian then lie about the timings? That's the kind of thing that gets found out very quickly. While he's likely a rantallion that lies about certain measurements, that doesn't necessarily mean that he's got a set of balls big enough to try this. I can't imagine that he'd be that stupid."

"Maybe things aren't exactly the way they appear," Carol said.

That's what I like about Carol. She always keeps an open mind. Sure there are hypotheses that look likely. That doesn't mean that any of them actually happened. Maybe there's yet another scenario that we're missing.

"Perhaps the reality is neither of these," I said. "Perhaps what really happened is still eluding us, and we're not seeing it because we're holding too many preconceptions. For example, I can't imagine what happened to Jack Holdt's car. It was bright yellow. Bright yellow cars are hard to hide - unless you shut them up in garages, and/or paint them - and they don't just disappear."

Carol look surprised. "Did you say Jack Holdt's car was yellow?" she asked.

"Yes," I said. "I've told you that before."

"No you didn't," Carol said. "You just said that his car was colored and that Marty's car was black. You never said that Holdt's car was yellow."

"What difference does that make?" I asked.

"Dottie's cousin Dagwood," she said, "had a yellow car."

"I thought you said that it was blue," I said.

"When he was finished painting it, it was blue," she said. "The day that I brought pastries up to Dottie's and looked in the garage, the car that Dagwood was working on was yellow."

"So one day, Jack Holdt, a guy from California, shows up in a yellow car, is murdered, and disappears," I said. "And the next day, Dottie's long-lost cousin shows up at Dottie's with a yellow car, keeps it closed up in her garage, and paints it blue. And he has his friend come over with a backhoe to dig a very large hole that he puts 'fertilizer' in - but only after the sun goes down. And it's 'a special kind of fertilizer from California,' that was in the trunk of his car that he buries in the big hole in the dead of night?"

"I think that some of the pieces are falling into place," said Carol.

"They're falling into place a little harder than pieces of puzzles like this tend to fall into place," I said. "If this was a TV detective story, I think we've solved it. But my hunch is that it can't be that easy. True, lots of these people are stupid. But that stupid? It's a little too obvious."

"Usually in real murder cases, the obvious answer is the correct answer," said Carol. "Most people don't waste their time being exceptionally clever. Ironically, the most puzzling piece - if the simple answer is correct - is why Senator Adler chose to get involved."

Again, she had a great point. And I'm good at understanding women.

Stu's garden shop is in the same plaza where the murder was. I thought I might learn something if I went there and had a look around, and maybe talked to Stu.

So I drove to the strip mall using the back way, and on the way over I made a quick call to Detective Danny. "Danny, it's Mick," I said. "Do me a favor and ask Moe a question. He had said that Mitch Goldberg had made lots of calls to Jack Holdt. I'd like to know if Holdt made lots of calls to anyone else out here. Maybe we can figure out who his girlfriend was, and talk to her."

"OK," said Danny. "I'll be at the station later, and I'll ask Moe whether he can figure that out."

"Another thing," I said. "Carol said that the car that was being painted in Dottie's garage across the street from me was originally yellow. That's the color of the car that I saw Holdt sitting in. Dottie's cousin was painting it, and he made it blue. Can you find out who the car belongs to and where it is? I saw Dottie's cousin riding out of there with Detective Dorian, who's obviously a friend of his. So don't make it too clear to Detective Dorian that I'm interested in knowing."

"OK, got it," he said.

I rang off, pulled over the curb by the Dumpsters where the murders were, and turned right this time to drive around the back of Stu's Garden Center. Stu's had stacks of bags full of fertilizer, mulch, sand, topsoil, and lots of other things stacked behind the store. I guess it's too much trouble to steal that stuff, because I doubt that he takes it all in at night.

There was also a large space where he had some commercial equipment parked, including a few backhoes; presumably including the one he used to dig the hole over at Dottie's. There were also a few parking spots back there where Stu kept his landscaping trucks.

I continued driving around the strip mall, and when I came to the front, I parked my car, went in to Stu's and pretended to browse at a rack of gardening tools. I noticed a sweaty looking portly guy in blue sweats and work boots with slightly thinning hair and thick glasses on who was walking around the store with authority, and telling some of the younger employees to neaten various areas of the store up. While I'd not met him before, I assumed that this was Stu.

"Excuse me," I interjected as he was passing. "Are you Stu?"

He said, "just a minute" holding up his hand, and he went back into his office. About a minute later he came back out, and said "what's up?"

"Again," I asked, "are you Stu?"

He looked suspicious. His eyes appeared both beady and vacuous - which is tough for a normal person to do. His eyes darted around the store, avoiding me. He looked like a real queef chortler. "Yeah, I'm Stu," he said, chortling.

"I just saw some work you did for my neighbor, and was thinking of doing something similar," I said.

Again, he looked suspicious. "Who's your neighbor?" he asked.

"Her name's Dottie," I said. "She just put in a flower bed."

His beady eyes darted around some more. I think he was thinking, but I'm not sure. That probably would have taken too much effort for him. "It doesn't ring a bell. Dottie? I never heard of her."

"Actually, she owns the house, and her cousin was putting a flower bed in for her to thank her for letting him use her garage to paint his car. It got hit by a Shit-Ninny," I said.

"Oh, you mean Dagwood," he said. "Yeah, I'm friends with Dagwood. What about Dagwood?" he asked.

"I don't care about Dagwood. But my wife was talking to Dottie, and she said that you had excavated where the flower bed was going to go down to a depth of about five feet, to get rid of the clay," I said, "and I thought that's sounded like a good idea."

"I don't think that you really need to do that, and I didn't really care about the flower bed," said Stu. "Dagwood wanted me to dig the hole so I did. He claimed that he had some special kind of fertilizer that he was going to put in the hole. That sounded like typical Dagwood bullshit, but I don't pry too much. Otherwise he talks my ear off and he gets boring. I was just doing a favor for a friend, that's all. If I were you, I wouldn't bother going to that much trouble: just plant the plants by digging a small hole for each one."

"Really?" I asked. "Dottie told my wife that Dagwood claimed it was actually a lot less trouble to do it this way, because you had dug one big hole and then brought out topsoil from the woods. This way Dagwood didn't have to do much of the work himself."

I saw a lightbulb go on in his head, and his eyes stopped darting. "That son-of-a-bitch," he said. "He had me believing his bullshit story about some kind of 'special fertilizer.' That's typical Dagwood. He was just getting me to do all the work for him."

"Didn't he pay you?" I asked.

"No, I was just doing him a favor," he said.

"So if I were to put a garden in, you wouldn't recommend doing that?" I asked.

"If you want to pay me to do that, I will," he said, chortling. "But I don't think you really need to do it."

"OK, well I'll keep it in mind. Nice meeting you, Stu," I said, chortling, and I left his store.

On the way out to my car, my phone rang. It was Detective Danny.

"Hi Mick," he said. "Moe gave me a lead on a phone number in New Jersey. It's a 201 area code, and the address is in Hoboken. It's a brownstone on 3rd Street not far from the river."

"I'll bet you that's Jack Holdt's girlfriend," I said. "Get me the address and I'll pay her a visit."

"No, it's not Jack Holdt's girlfriend," he said. "You're not gonna believe who's name is registered to that phone number."

"I don't believe it," I said.

"You don't believe what?" asked Danny.

"I don't believe who's name is registered to that phone number," I responded.

"But I didn't even tell you yet," said Danny.

"That's OK," I said. "I trust you. Who's name is registered to that phone number?" I asked.

"It's registered to Mitchell Goldberg," he said.

"I don't believe you," I said.

"That makes no sense," said Danny.

"So Jack Holdt makes lots of calls to Mitch Goldberg's cell up here in Connecticut, and he also makes lots of calls to Mitch Goldberg's cell in New Jersey. Why would Mitch have an address in New Jersey, and why would Holdt call him on both numbers?" I asked.

"Well as we've found out, Mitch Goldberg was running drugs and money from California, and we think it all ties in to Senator Adler. And we know that Jack Holdt worked as a bodyguard and also did odd jobs for Adler," Danny explained. "So it's not surprising that Holdt made lots of calls to Goldberg when he came out here."

"But why would he call him at both numbers?" I asked.

"That's a good question," Detective Danny said. "Maybe Senator Adler didn't know about the New Jersey number, so Holdt used that number to call Goldberg whenever he wanted to make sure that Adler couldn't listen in. Maybe Goldberg and Holdt were skimming some of the drugs and the money, and were running their own private business on the side."

"That sounds plausible," I said. "So I'm guessing that the New Jersey address is bogus. This is just another phone that Mitch Goldberg kept to make calls that he wanted to make sure weren't bugged. I'll go to Hoboken tomorrow to see who really lives there. My hunch is that it isn't Mitch Goldberg; he likely registered the phone to a random address down there. That's not hard to do. I think Goldberg was a lot cleverer than he acted."

"Mitch was the kind of guy that you wouldn't notice in a crowd of two," Danny said. "My bet is that he was a lot smarter than anyone thought."

"And what about the car?" I asked. "Did you find out anything about the car that was painted by Dottie's cousin, Dagwood? Dottie's cousin who also happens to be Detective Dorian's personal friend?"

"No, not yet," Danny said.

"See if he owned a yellow car. Because if he painted it blue, he's supposed to change the registration to show that," I said.

"I should know soon," Danny said. "I'm waiting to hear from the Department of Motor Vehicles."

"Well enjoy waiting," I said. "And smile."

I drove home by going around the strip mall to where the Dumpsters are located behind the grocery store - the scene of the two murders. It had been a beautiful fall day when I'd been there before. Today it was looking overcast. Some would view that as a propitious omen, but they're not always right. I view it as portending rain, but I'm not always right either. That makes two of us.

I drove over the curb and up the alley to the neighborhood behind the strip mall. I made a conscious effort to not use The Fingers. I was practicing traveling incognito. I remembered how The Fingers had gotten me fingered on this case the first day, and I try to learn from my mistakes.

Years back, traffic didn't used to bother me as much as it does today. I took it as a healthy sign of societal growth. But lots of my perspectives changed after having had brain surgery.

Apparently, they had removed a tumor that was beginning to interfere with certain functions, and by so doing, the surgery interfered with others. One way to look at it is that the surgery merely changed some of my perspectives. I had once been living partly in a paracosm in which I had two imaginary friends who would only talk to each other. Unfortunately, while they were my friends, they wouldn't talk to me. Then I realized that while some of the voices in my head were probably not real, they'd sometimes get plenty of good ideas. So I was reluctant to lose those voices, but the surgeon insisted.

To me, what had once looked like a healthy sign of societal growth now looks like an unhealthy sign of societal growth. The reality is the same, but the perspective is different. For example, before surgery, the tumor was making me a little schizophrenic, and it bothered me. After the surgery, that hadn't changed, but I figured that unlike most people, at least I could say that me, myself, and I still all had each other.

This is a lot like art. When a person that doesn't understand a painting looks at it, it's merely a picture: it has one or more subjects, one or more colors, one or more perspectives, and one or more brushstrokes. But it's merely a picture. Once the various contexts comprising these elements are known, the painting tells many different stories. And a good painting can be both fascinating and perplexing: it usually raises more questions than it answers, and it leaves you feeling enriched by pondering them.

Most invention happens by viewing the world from new and different perspectives. Given a different perspective, many inventions become obvious. The components of invention that are not obvious are those perspectives.

Unfortunately, many confuse the two. When you are able to bring new perspectives to people, they will frequently discount your inventions as having been obvious. The obvious question in this case is then: "Why didn't anyone else think of it?"

Inventions are obvious. Perspectives aren't.

I don't think I ever would have thought of the Shit-Ninnies before having had brain surgery. But after the fact, they seemed obvious. The same can be said for The Fingers, and for many other things. And I'll bet you an ear that most of us can't envision the world the way that Van Gogh was able to. To many, it's just a bunch of haystacks.

The phone rang. And this exemplifies what I was thinking: the desire to have the ability to talk to people that were anywhere was always obvious. But until there was a phone, this was fiction. Had you raised this possibility before there was a phone, people would have thought you mad. And even with one phone, you'd be mad. But when everyone has a phone, and there are millions of phones all interconnected, it's obvious.

Of course the man who invented the phone wasn't all that clever. But the one who invented the phone bill was a genius. Telephones never would have become ubiquitous without phone bills. Some would call this "greed." I call it "having a vision."

I answered the phone: "Hello?"

It was Detective Danny. "The yellow car belonged to Dottie's cousin, Dagwood. He hasn't yet re-registered it yet to show that it was painted," he said.

"So it *was* his car after all," I said. "That begs the question as to how he's tied into this."

"Actually, it raises some more questions," Danny said.

"Like what?" I asked.

"Dagwood lives in a fifty-five hundred square foot house with a six-car garage on the Long Island Sound, and he has four cars registered to him. The yellow car was his 'beater' - the car that he used for trips to the hardware store. His other three cars are actually expensive," Detective Danny told me. "He also has a forty-foot yacht."

"Then he wouldn't have bothered to paint the car unless he was hiding it," I said. "But why would he bother? If he had that kind of money, why wouldn't he simply ditch it?"

"If he ditched it, it could be found," Danny said. "And then the car could be ID'ed, and tied back to him. By simply painting it, he essentially makes the car disappear."

"That makes sense," I said. "But if he was going to paint it, why would he paint it at his cousin Dottie's? He has a six-car garage. Why wouldn't he simply paint it there? Or not paint it, and just keep it there? That's the same as making it disappear."

"The fact that he made it a point to come to Dottie's to paint it means that he was doing something else at Dottie's," Detective Danny said. "And he put in a garden. For what? It means that he wanted an excuse to dig a big hole at Dottie's, and to put something in the hole. And whatever it was that he put in the hole was something that he didn't want hidden at his house."

"Like what?" I asked. "If he dug a big hole at his house, who would know? And if he lives on the ocean, there are better ways of making things disappear than by putting them in a hole. It doesn't make any sense."

"No, it makes no sense," agreed Detective Danny.

"There's another thing that makes no sense," I said. "Why is he friends with Detective Dorian? Detective Dorian's a cop, like you are. People who live in mansions on the beach don't hang around with cops. Do you have any idea where Dagwood's money comes from?"

"No," said Detective Danny. "But if he inherited it, then he came from money, and it's unlikely that he'd know people like Detective Dorian."

"But if he made the money illegally," I said, "then it's even more unlikely that he'd hang around with a police detective. That is, unless there's something wrong with the police detective."

Day 9

A Trip to Hoboken

In the morning, I took a short drive over the border to Westchester, and caught a train into Grand Central Station. From there, it's a short walk across 42nd Street to 6th Avenue, and then down to Herald Square, where you can catch the PATH train under Macy's. It runs down the West Side to 9th Street, then heads West, with a last stop in Manhattan at Christopher Street near the river, and then it goes under the Hudson to the Hoboken terminal. It runs right between the Lincoln and Holland Tunnels, and it's a very short ride.

From the terminal in Hoboken which is right on the river, it's a three-block walk North on Sinatra Drive to 3rd Street. And a beautiful walk it is. Unlike the West Side of Manhattan, which has a panoramic view of New Jersey, Sinatra Drive has a very wide walkway along the river, and it has a panoramic view of Manhattan. Who has the better view? I'll take Hoboken any day.

I walked along the river, passed the W Hotel, and headed up 3rd Street, which is at the Southern end of a miniature park that's been built out onto the Hudson as a little island. Runners like to jog along Sinatra Drive, and then out around the mini-island, which has a circular walkway around it. I found the brownstone that Mitch

Goldberg had registered his New Jersey phone number to, and I rang the bell to see who answered.

There was no answer, so I rang it again. And again, there was no answer. So I rang it again. A woman was coming out of the brownstone next store, and she saw me ringing the bell. "Are you looking for Mitchell?" she asked.

"I was trying to find an old friend of mine named Mitch Goldberg, and I was told that he lives here," I said.

She told me "Mitchell is usually in the city at practice during the day, and his partner is probably at the gym, or he's taking a run along the Hudson. And Mitchell usually works at night, also in the city. You'll hardly ever find him here unless he's coming or going."

If that's what the neighbors think, that would explain why they don't think it's odd that he's never here. "So Mitch Goldberg does live here?" I asked, incredulously.

"I never knew that his friends called him 'Mitch,'" she said. "I've always called him Mitchell. I think he goes by 'Mitchell' professionally."

"Mitchell?" I asked. "Is he about so tall?" I gestured with my hand, showing Mitch the barber's diminutive height. "And is he on the slight side? Looks middle-aged? Maybe I've got the wrong guy."

"No, that's not Mitchell," she said. "Mitchell is your height, and he looks very athletic and graceful. He has to be."

"Why does he have to be?" I asked.

"Mitchell is a principle dancer with the American Ballet Theater," she explained. "He puts in lots of hours practicing, training, and performing. It keeps him very athletic."

This was obviously a different Mitch Goldberg. I guess it's a pretty common name. But why would Jack Holdt be calling this Mitch Goldberg too? Maybe this Mitch is also in on the drug deal, and the Mitch Goldberg in Connecticut sought him out specifically because he has the same name. This would confuse the cops - if they ever got wind of his business - just like it's confusing me.

"Well I've got the wrong Mitch Goldberg," I said. "Thanks for all your help anyway. Unfortunately, this was a dead end. Nonetheless, it was worth coming over here just for the view I got while walking along the Hudson."

She smiled and said, "well good luck finding the other Mitchell Goldberg."

"It's *Mitch* Goldberg," I said. "Thanks again."

I passed the gym on Hudson Street, and saw a really big guy in there doing squats with some serious weight, although I didn't get a good look at him because the power racks were in the back of the gym. There were several others doing work with dumbbells up front. It looked like it might be a serious gym. And it was a great place for a gym if you were going to finish your workout with a run along the Hudson.

I went over to the bar at the W Hotel, sat at the window with a nice view of the waterfront, and ordered an espresso and an anisette. And no, I didn't mix them. I was making notes in a pad that I'd brought, intermittently looking up to see the New York City skyline, and the joggers going by.

Somehow the two Mitch Goldbergs were tied together. But how? Could they be cousins? Or even father and son? I hadn't meet "Mitchell," but if he was a principle with the American Ballet Theater, he could be about the right age to be Mitch's son. I wondered whether Mitchell knew that the Mitch Goldberg up in Connecticut had gotten whacked. They obviously both knew Holdt, since he had made lots of calls to both of them.

I finished my espresso, took the PATH back to Macy's, walked over to Grand Central Station, and took the train North. It had been an interesting trip. While it hadn't solved anything, it had added yet another dimension to the problem. Maybe one of the Goldberg's always lies, and the other one always tells the truth. I was sure that if I looked at the problem correctly, I could solve this case.

When I got home, I stopped at the mailbox to pick up the mail, and I noticed a police car parked up Dottie's driveway. I wondered why the police were over there. I guess it was my turn this time, and I enacted the satire in my head: "Dottie, I saw the police over at your house, and I was wondering what the trouble was . . ." I don't think I enjoyed that game as much as Dottie did. I got my mail and continued down my driveway.

Carol was in the kitchen starting dinner, so I went in to help. I thought that perhaps I could julienne something, or do a brunoise or a batonnet with something. A carrot maybe? Or a piece of celery?

Carol didn't need that kind of help, and suggested that I simply do the dishes later. That was fine by me. And there's no chance of slicing my fingers while doing the dishes. So I poured a nice tall glass of seltzer with ice, and took a seat on the outside of the kitchen island to tell her what I found.

"It turns out that there really is another guy named Mitch Goldberg who lives in Hoboken. Jack Holdt was calling both Mitch Goldbergs. Originally, I'd thought that the New Jersey number was also owned by the Mitch Goldberg up here, and that he used that number when he wanted to make sure that no one was listening in. Apparently, it was known that the Mitch up here was working for a California drug ring, so he rightly assumed that the police might be following his Connecticut number," I said.

"The Mitch Goldberg in New Jersey is younger. I didn't meet him, but his neighbor told me that he's a professional ballet dancer who works at Lincoln Center, so I'm guessing that he's a generation younger - maybe not quite - than the Mitch Goldberg that got murdered up here. But somehow, both Mitch Goldbergs were tied into this, because Holdt was interacting with both of them. Do you think that the dancing Goldberg was part of the drug operation?" I asked.

"I've no idea," said Carol. "Maybe the Goldbergs are related?"

"Yes, that could be. In fact, it's likely. What are the chances that two unrelated guys named Mitch Goldberg are both tied to Jack Holdt from California? So much so that he talks to both of them a lot?" I pointed out.

"Almost zero," she said.

"Also, Senator Adler wasn't entirely forthcoming with me. Why did he have Holdt followed out here? The guy comes out to chase a woman. Why should Adler care? And who's the woman anyway? How come we've got no leads on her? Maybe that's not why Jack Holdt came out here. My hunch is that Senator Adler didn't have him followed; my hunch is that Adler sent him out here on an assignment. Adler came out here himself because something went very wrong, and Holdt wound up dead," I said.

"But didn't you tell me that the other security guy - the one that wound up in the hospital, I forget his name - was sent out here by Senator Adler to keep an eye on Jack Holdt precisely because the senator didn't believe that Holdt was getting married?" she asked.

"Not exactly," I explained. "The claim was that Holdt had told the senator that he was coming out here to 'visit relatives,' and that Adler suspected that this was not true. So Adler had him followed out here by John Rogers. It was Rogers that told us about Holdt's girlfriend, and that Holdt had actually come out here to marry her - maybe."

"But didn't John Rogers tell you lots of lies?" she asked.

"Yes, but then I sent the Shit-Ninnies after him, and he told me the real story," I explained.

"There's no way you'll know whether he told you the entire real story," she said. "Maybe the story about Holdt coming out here to get married was made up. Isn't it strange that we don't have phone calls or emails that would tie him to his supposed betrothed?"

"Senator Adler was going to have Holdt's computer files looked at to see if he could figure out who she is," I said. "But I also find it odd that Holdt comes out here, gets shot, disappears, and there's no woman looking for him."

"Where would she look?" Carol asked. "And how would you know about it?"

"Good point," I said. "Maybe she is out there and she doesn't know what happened to him. Or maybe they got together, decided that marriage wasn't in the cards, and they separated. And then Holdt got himself killed in some kind of crooked drug deal that people working for the senator orchestrated. She's now gone and out of the picture. And he's gone too, but she doesn't even know it."

"That's probably what happened," I continued. "I think that there are people that meet on the internet and think that they've found a good match based on a bunch of notes that they've exchanged. But then they meet each other and find that there are more dimensions to a person than the notes that they write. And if you're going to get married, you won't be communicating by writing each other notes. Lots of these romances probably don't work out when the people actually meet."

"That's probably what happened," she said, "if there even was an internet romance. Maybe the senator sent Holdt out here to do some of the senator's dirty business. After all, from the way you've described Holdt, he sounds like he was more than a security guard. Maybe Holdt gets the dirty business done, and maybe he doesn't, but somehow, he winds up dead. Then he vanishes off the face of the earth. Keep in mind that vanishing off the face of the earth is hard to do unless it's professionals making it happen. And then the senator makes a special trip out here, and hires you to figure out what happened to him. He wouldn't do that unless there are loose ends that the senator needs to tie up."

"Once again, you've opened my eyes to some more possibilities," I said. "The strange thing about this case is that the more information that I get, the more complicated it becomes. That's the exact opposite of how most cases work."

"I think you need to get more information out of Senator Adler," she said. "He could probably tie up a few of these loose ends easily without openly admitting to any fishy business. After all, some of the loose ends are likely innocuous, and just look like loose ends. If you can tie those up, at least it makes the case simpler."

"You're right," I said. "I need to ask the senator a few more questions. I'd be curious to know whether he was aware that Goldberg had a twin."

"A twin?" Carol asked.

"Not literally," I said. "I was just alluding to a problem that I've been talking to the students at the High School about. It's a logic problem involving twins. I'm sure that the Goldbergs aren't actually twins."

———————

The doorbell rang.

So I answered it. There was a police car in the driveway, and a cop in uniform was standing on my doorstep. It was Detective Danny.

"Danny," I said, "I thought I told you not to come here in your Cub Scout uniform. It makes people suspicious. Dottie across the street will ask questions. She'll wonder whether I'm committing crimes. It will start rumors. What the hell are you doing here in your uniform?"

"Good to see you too," Danny said. "Actually, I was right across the street, and thought I'd just drop by to say 'hello,' and ask you about the case."

"You were *right* across the street?" I asked. "You mean at Dottie's?"

"Yes," he replied. "She thought that there was a suspicious smell coming from her garage, and wanted someone to come check it out. She actually asked for a detective. We were just going to send a patrolman over, but when I heard who it was, I told them that I'd check it out."

"Why did you bother?" I asked.

"Because you're right across the street, and I figured it would be a good excuse to drop by," he said.

"So you came across town to see me?" I asked. "Bullshit."

He turned a very slight red. "Well I know that there were lots of activities over there in the last few days, and I just wanted to have a look myself to see if anything looked out of order. We had a big hole dug, dirt moved around, a long-lost cousin showing up to paint his car and to plant a garden. So when I heard about a strange smell, I thought I'd have a look."

"Really?" I asked. "And how's Dottie holding up?"

"She looked great," he said quickly and enthusiastically. Then he deliberately slowed his pace: "I mean, she looked OK. I went in and had a look around. I didn't smell anything funny in the garage, but who knows?"

"And that's it?" I asked. "And then you came over here?"

"Yes," he said. "Basically."

"But I saw your car over there forty-five minutes ago when I got home," I said. "It took you forty-five minutes to figure out that the garage didn't smell funny? That's some detective work."

"Actually, I checked out the garage, and didn't find anything unusual," he said. "But Dottie had made some coffee and some cookies and she wanted me to sit and talk for a few minutes."

"I see," I said. "Sounds like tough police work. I'm glad I'm not in that business. Did anything turn up?"

"Not really," he said. "But we found out that she and I have a lot in common. I like the way that she's so direct. Most women that I've gone out with talk lots of nonsense. Dottie isn't like that. And she's very logical. That's unusual in women. She also was wearing a nice perfume. I didn't notice it at first; it was very subtle. I like when women understate things like that."

"Perfume? Was she in a housecoat?" I asked.

He looked surprised. "Housecoat? No, she had on a nice pair of slacks and a flowery blouse, and she was made up. She looked very nice."

"This is 'Dottie' that you're talking about?" I asked.

"Yes, that's who we've been talking about. You should have told me you had nice neighbors like that," said Danny.

"I would have, but I didn't know it," I replied. "I get the feeling that you like Dottie."

"Yes, she's very nice," he said. "In fact, I asked her if she'd like to go out tonight. I thought it would be fun to take her out to dinner."

"Are you feeling OK?" I asked.

"Yeah, great," he said. "Thanks for asking."

"You know I had a hunch that she liked you," I said. "A smell in her garage? Did it smell like bullshit? Because it sounded that way. I think she's reeling you in."

"Dottie wouldn't do that," he said. "I can tell that she's not a manipulator."

I rolled my eyes. "Well that's great news. I'm sure you'll have a nice dinner. I'm actually glad that you dropped by. I took a trip to New Jersey today, and learned a few things. And I could use some insights, and maybe some more information from Moe."

"Why did you go to New Jersey?" Danny asked.

"We knew that Jack Holdt had made lots of calls to Mitch Goldberg, here in town. According to Moe, he also made lots of calls to a 201 number right across the river from Manhattan, and that number was also registered to a Mitch Goldberg."

"You mean Mitch had two phones?" he asked.

"No," I said. "It turns out that there's another guy named Mitch Goldberg, although he calls himself 'Mitchell,' and he lives in New Jersey. But Jack Holdt was calling both of them."

"That's pretty strange," said Danny.

"That's what I thought," I said. "But then it occurred to me that the two Goldbergs are probably related, and they were probably both in whatever crooked drug deal this was that Senator Adler was running. That's why Holdt was calling both of them. One is up here, and one is in New Jersey, right across the river from Manhattan. I'll bet the drugs come in down there - probably though Newark Airport, and the New Jersey Goldberg runs them up here to the Connecticut Goldberg. It's only a fifteen-minute drive to Newark Airport for the Goldberg in Hoboken, New Jersey, so it all works very nicely."

"Did you talk to the Mitch Goldberg in New Jersey?" asked Danny.

"No," I confided. "He wasn't there. But I talked to his neighbor."

"How do you know it's not the same Mitch Goldberg?" he asked.

"The New Jersey Goldberg is a professional dancer. The neighbor said that he's my size and very athletic. That's not the same Goldberg as the barber that was murdered up here," I said.

"You're right," Danny said. "They're probably related. I'll bet the one in New Jersey is a nephew, or something like that."

"That's what I thought," I said.

"I wonder whether the one in New Jersey knows that his uncle got whacked?" Detective Danny speculated. "If he doesn't, maybe someone should tell him, so that he watches his back."

"Somehow, I don't think that the Goldberg hit was professionally done though," I speculated too.

"Why not?" Detective Danny asked. "It was nearly the same as the Holdt hit."

"No, it wasn't," I said. "Holdt was sitting in the driver's seat in his car. Whoever did the hit was sitting in the passenger's seat, and made a very clean shot. And then he made Holdt and the car disappear. Goldberg was sitting - or was put - into the back seat of his car. So he wasn't driving it. If it had been a professional hit, why would they put the car back there?"

"They had to put the car somewhere," Detective Danny said. "What's wrong with there?"

"Nothing," I said. "But why would they leave the engine running?"

"Who knows?" Detective Danny asked. "Maybe they didn't bother to shut it off and leave prints. If anything, I'd say that professionals didn't do the Holdt hit."

"Why not?" I asked.

"Why would they bother to make his car disappear?" Detective Danny asked.

"Maybe they didn't," I said.

"Then who did?" asked Danny.

"I don't know. From my point of view, maybe the cops did it. Maybe it was your buddy Detective Dorian," I said.

"Why would he do that?" asked Danny.

"I don't know," I said. "How is it that the cops don't seem to know anything about the Holdt murder? Why is it that Senator Adler didn't seem to believe the cops, and came to me?"

"Adler went to you because I gave him your name," Detective Danny pointed out. "Why would I do that if I was in on the murder?"

"You wouldn't," I responded. "I didn't mean that 'all the cops' were in on it. But what if it was just a few of them? What if it was the cop that had just cleaned up the Mitch Goldberg murder? What if it was that maggot Detective Dorian?"

"Detective Dorian's a maggot?" asked Detective Danny. "You've got a point there. Especially after you pointed out the pink socks that he was wearing. And all this time, I had thought you said 'faggot.' Are you serious?"

"I'm not sure," I said. "But something about Detective Dorian rubs me the wrong way. And it wasn't just his socks: those were the 'faggot' part, but those don't bother me. Much."

"You should probably find the other Goldberg and try to talk to him," Detective Danny suggested. "He might know something else that hasn't occurred to any of us."

"You're right, I should," I acknowledged. "On a later date. I've some other things that I need to do here first."

And then I added, "Have a nice evening with Dottie."

That night, Carol and I had a nice dinner. It was devoid of juliennes, brunoises, and batonnets, and I did the dishes without cutting my fingers. It was the beginning of a lovely evening.

Since I appreciated her so much, I even acquiesced to watching one of those romance movies on TV that women seem to enjoy so much. They're even less credible than the detective movies, but you don't actually have to pay attention, or think too hard. And no one gets shot.

It was the usual story: a plain-looking, albeit wholesome, single American woman is traveling in Europe. On a train, she meets a handsome, and wealthy, and romantic French count. On a boat, she meets a handsome, and wealthy, and romantic Italian prince. And while riding on an elephant, she meets a handsome, and wealthy, and romantic Egyptian king. All of them wear pink socks. And all of them instantly fall in love with her because she does normal stupid American-girl things.

Unlike real men, they all understand her feelings for the others, and they all respect each other's feelings for her. And they all respect each other. At this point, you realize that the director didn't really need to make them all wear pink socks. Some things are made pretty clear by the way people act. At least this way, she wouldn't have to sleep with any of them.

Well the woman doesn't know what to do. She's never met men like this before: men who don't have other girlfriends, men who smell better than their girlfriends would if they had other girlfriends, men who pick up the tabs without worrying about insulting women, men who hold doors (and I don't mean the guys in uniforms with their hands out, looking for tips) without acting superior to women, men who do what their mothers tell them to, you get the idea - women's fantasies masquerading as men, but wearing pink socks.

Then, because she's an un-worldly American, each man teaches her about his culture so that she can be sophisticated.

The Italian takes her on a gondola ride with a gondolier who sings some Italian-American songs like "*That's Amore!*", and who shows her his culinary prowess by making fettuccini Alfredo (the Italian equivalent of Mac 'n Cheese). The Frenchman takes her to the Eiffel Tower, and we learn that the French word for "Chinese" (*Chinois*) is pronounced the same as the Mandarin word for "Frog" (chin-wah). And the Egyptian smokes a kind of Egyptian cigarette that smells like camel-dung, and he takes her to The Luxor in Las Vegas where he shows her how to lose money by playing baccarat with some drunks.

So now she's worldly, although still a virgin, that is, at least with these guys, but not with her last real boyfriend, who was a pig.

I've always found it helpful to tune these movies out, and to not listen too hard. If you're a real man and you said half the nonsense these fantasy men say, your woman would suspect that you wore pink socks when no one was looking. And while she likes watching it in a movie, she'd actually be revolted by a real man who actually said any of this. That's why they call it "women's pornography."

But I did start to notice that the woman character always told the truth. She was always direct and honest about her feelings for the other men, about the fact that she liked to chew gum, the fact that she couldn't cook worth a damn and hated housework, the fact that she didn't have any money because her last boyfriend (the one that was a pig that she wasn't a virgin with) stole it all, that she didn't like to wear deodorant, that she hated putting on the dresses and shoes that made her look presentable, and so on.

This made the men love her even more - because she was so honest: they weren't used to women who were so honest. Maybe, they thought, it was "an American thing."

Maybe they needed to get out a little more.

And not only was she honest, but the Italian prince was honest too. I'm sure that he told her that he was gay. He didn't have to tell us, you could tell just by watching his mannerisms; Prince *Travone*, I think his name was. He then removes all doubt by mincing around while singing "*Volare*" for us.

The other two - the count and the king - you weren't as sure about. You started to think that maybe their pink socks were just a masquerade. Then we catch both of them in lots of lies. We find out that the Egyptian king actually has a harem at home, and has sex with camels, and the French count is a pervert that makes a sport of scoring innocent women on trains by talking lots of bullshit with a phony French accent. And both of them have shoe fetishes.

So in the end, the wholesome, truth-telling, American girl runs off into the sunset with the wholesome, truth-telling, gay, Italian prince to live in wedded bliss as the band plays "*That's Amore!*". They'll live in a big palace with a big staff that will do all of the cooking and cleaning for her, and she won't have to sleep with him. And the two lying perverts will continue their false lives of shoe fetishism, and will occasionally score uninteresting, plain looking American girls - just like most losers do.

Like I said, the movie was women's porn. But it did make me start to think of the Tweedles. Suppose I had a vacuous, plain-looking, gum-chewing, lazy American bimbo together with the Three Stooges, and I wanted to know which road went to the city. All I'd have to do is to ask one of them what a different one of them would say that a different one of them would say that a different one of them would say. Then I'd go to the beach. And you never know: if you went to the beach, you just might actually see a girl who's pretty there. In the city too. Both would sure beat this movie.

As the movie was ending, I saw a car go up Dottie's driveway. This time I knew it was Danny dropping her off. I hoped that they'd had a good time.

Day 10

A Secret Code and the Department Stores

I went downtown to talk to Moe. I parked in a lot across the street from the police station, and hoped that I wouldn't get a ticket. I had motion-sensitive cameras in my car. If I did get a ticket, at least I'd know who put it there.

I went into the station, and Tonya was there to check me in. So I checked her out as she was checking me in.

She had changed her hairstyle. Today all of her hair was orange, and she had formed a pair of "wispies" with her hair, one on each side of her head. She looked kind of like a Martian. She was wearing heavy makeup: orange lipstick to match her hair, and thick eyeliner. She had on a light green blouse with a short orange skirt and black fishnet stockings. Maybe she was a Martian leprechaun.

While Tonya did put together some strange combinations, she had a way of pulling them off. Martian leprechaun or not, she did make good eye-candy. I think she's in the wrong business. While very daring, she makes it work. She'd be better in fashion than working as a cop.

She smiled. "It's Mickey Mouse!" she said, and giggled.

"Is that what the two wispies are supposed to be? Ears? I thought you were a Martian, not Mickey Mouse," I said.

She looked confused, and then she giggled again. "No, *you're* Mickey Mouse!" she said. "I remember you."

"You're pretty smart," I said. "You have that '*je ne sais quoi*' about you."

"What's that?" she asked.

"I don't know," I said.

"Then why do you say it?" she asked.

"*Je ne sais quoi*," I responded.

"You're weird," she said. "But funny. I like you."

"Really?" I asked. "Have we met?"

She laughed again. "Why are you here again?" she asked.

"I wanted to talk to Moe," I said.

"I'll buzz him. I'm sure he's in," she said, and she hit a button.

Moe came out to the front desk, and looked surprised to see me. Moe doesn't wear a uniform. He just wears old clothes that are wrinkled, and that look like they've had plenty of food spilled on them. He's also one of the few cops that wears real shoes. True, they're old and worn, but they're real shoes. And pink socks aren't his style. I don't think that pink socks would occur to him.

Like Detective Danny and Detective Dorian, Moe is also a detective, but not a street-type. Moe is better with letters and numbers and computers and stuff like that. That's why he spends most of his time at the police station, and not out on the street. At least that's what Danny told me.

"I'm sorry that I couldn't stay for poker that night," I said. "Danny was telling me that Dorian plays really well. It's probably best that I didn't stay."

Moe made a face at the mention of Detective Dorian. "Yes, he really cleaned up," he said.

I chuckled. "I figured he would. But I actually dropped by to ask about numbers that might have been in Mitch Goldberg's book."

"Good," he said. "I'd rather talk about that than about poker."

"That's because it's just Earth poker," I responded.

This time Moe chuckled. "I liked the number stuff that you laid on us. It's amazing that those idiots believed you. Uranus poker? I'll have to remember that one. That's a real ball-twister. Come on back to my office, and we'll talk."

We went to Moe's office, and it was a mess. Kind of like my office, except this was in an older building. I sensed that Moe worked the same way that I did. He had lots of papers and books spread around on a side table, and a few empty coffee cups too. And there were numbers and symbols in a grid on his computer screen.

"What about Goldberg's book?" Moe asked.

"Well I assume that it had Holdt's number in it," I said. "But I found that in addition to Jack Holdt calling Mitch Goldberg up here, there's another Mitch Goldberg in New Jersey that Jack Holdt was calling too. I have his number; it's in the 201 area code. I wonder whether the Mitch Goldberg up here had Mitch Goldberg's number in New Jersey."

"It's funny that you mention that," said Moe. "There were some New Jersey numbers in his book, and I wondered why. On the other hand, the tristate region we're in is pretty small. I wouldn't be surprised if some California drugs didn't come in through Newark Airport."

"That's exactly what I thought," I said. "So I figured that the Mitch Goldberg up here might have some New Jersey numbers in his book. But the big surprise is that Holdt was connected to a guy named Mitch Goldberg in New Jersey as well as to the Mitch Goldberg that was murdered up here. This is the New Jersey number," I said, and I gave him my notebook with Mitchell Goldberg's number written on the top of the page.

Moe took a minute to look through his notes. "Nope. That number's not in here," he said.

"Actually, I'm not too surprised," I told Moe. "It's a safe bet that the two Goldbergs were related; probably an uncle and nephew. They probably knew each other's numbers, or had them programmed into their phones. There's no reason that Mitch Goldberg would encode his nephew's number into his little booklet."

"Yeah," said Moe. "He wouldn't do that. Especially if they were family and they talked a lot. Family members aren't a big secret, and you wouldn't encode their phone numbers in any special way."

"Well that's kind of what I was expecting," I said, "but I thought I'd ask anyway. You never know what'll turn up."

I left the police station, waved to Tonya on the way out, and found a parking ticket on my car.

When I got home, I took a run and a shower, and then I called Senator Adler, left a message, and he called me back on an unmarked line.

"Have you solved the case?" he asked.

"It's not I who haven't solved this particular case," I responded, putting on my politician's voice. "I've done everything possible to solve this case. But it's my opponent who has been standing in the way of this case being solved. Everyone wants this case solved except for my opponent!"

"What are you talking about?" he asked.

"Nothing," I said. "You were talking like a politician, and expected immediate results. So I talked like a politician and told you that I'm doing my best, but need some more information."

"That's talking like a politician?" he asked. "What do you need to know?"

"You had said that you'd have Holdt's email records looked at to see if we could find the user ID of the woman that he came out here to see. And I wanted to know if you found anything," I said.

"Yes, I told one of my people to call you. He didn't?" Adler asked.

"Nope. We must have missed each other," I said. "What did you find?" I asked.

"There's an email address that Holdt exchanged lots of notes with over the last six months," he said. "I have it written down here. It's a gmail address that's spelled 'megamalthea.' It makes no sense to me. Do you think that 'meg' is short for 'Meghan,' and that 'Amalthea' is her last name? I never heard of anyone named 'Amalthea.' Or do you think that it's 'mega-malthea,' where 'mega' means big, and 'malthea' has some special meaning to whoever made it up? I know that they both sound far-fetched."

"Usually people use some form of their name, although I can't see it here," I said. "I think 'Meghan-something' sounds like the best bet, but I couldn't tell you what the 'something' is. 'Amalthea' could be her last name, or at least part of it. I'll have one of the detectives see if he can find a name like that. I wish we had an IP address. Your people should have that."

"I'll ask them," he said, and we both hung up.

The next thing that I wanted to do was to follow through on my images at the mall, so I hopped in my car and headed over there to see whether I could talk to the department store managers.

First I went into Macy's, and I asked to see the store manager.

"Is there some kind of problem, sir?" I was asked.

"No, I just want to see the store manager," I said.

"Are you sure there's no kind of a problem, sir?"

"No, I just want to see the store manager," I repeated.

"But sir, if there's some kind of a problem . . ."

"Can I just see the store manager?" I asked.

Then a security guard came over and asked me if there was some kind of a problem, and I told him that I was looking for the store manager.

He looked like he was thinking of calling for some back-up, so I said "I have some questions that I need to ask about the images that were being shown on your windows the other night."

He asked me if I was a lawyer, and I guessed that the right answer was "Yes." So I said "Yes."

He immediately pointed to a staircase in one of the corners of the store, and said "up on the next level," and then he immediately took off.

I went to the staircase, went up a level and found the store manager's office. I knocked.

"Come in," said a female voice, so I opened the door.

"Are you looking for the exit?" she asked.

"No," I said. "I was looking for the store manager."

"Oh," she said, looking surprised. "That's me. Is there some kind of a problem?"

"I'm here to talk about the images that appeared on your windows the other night . . . ," I started to say.

But she cut me off: "If you're a lawyer, I'm not the one to talk to. I can give you the number of . . . ," so I cut her off too.

"I'm the one that made those images appear," I said.

She looked at me like maybe I was crazy, and I could see her eyes dart to the red "Security" button next to her phone. I knew she was thinking about how quickly I might lunge at her if she reached for it.

"I see," she said. "And can you always make images appear if you think about it?" she asked, as if trying to calm a crazy person down.

"No," I said. "I have special equipment. I'm a scientist by trade, and I created a new technology that can project images as if they are appearing within a sheet of glass. It's really not as hard as it sounds.

Although glass is an amorphous liquid, it's not liquescent at anything close to room temperature, which viewed in a different way means that its time constants are very long. So any specific set of Jacobian transformations on a particular surface is essentially static. What this means is that . . ."

I could see her eyes drifting over to the "Security" button again, so I stopped explaining.

"What I'm getting at is that I have a way of projecting advertisements that will appear within your store windows, and will subliminally attract customers to come in and buy whatever products you're interested in moving," I said, explaining the use of the technology at a more pragmatic level.

I continued: "Since the projected images comprise light, you can see them clearly at night, which is hardly subliminal. These would be a standard way of advertising products. But during the day, when there's lots of ambient light, the images become subliminal. This means that you'd be projecting products that all customers would see without being aware that they were seeing them. This is a new technology that would enable subliminal advertising to boost your sales without the customers being aware that you were using it."

She stopped looking at the "Security" button, and I could see a glimmer of interest.

"I intend to market this new technology to your competitors as well," I continued, "so if you chose not to use it, it would put you at a competitive disadvantage."

She looked surprised. "You're trying to use this new technology to make money, aren't you?" she asked in an accusatory way.

"Why do you work here? And do they pay you to work here?" I asked.

"Well yes," she continued, "but that's different."

"And if the store sells things to people, then the store is taking money from those people. Isn't that right?" I asked.

"Well yes," she continued, "but that's different too."

"I get it now," I said. "If the store takes money from the people, and you take money from the store, then that's good. But if an outsider makes more money for the store, and takes some of that money, then that's bad. How is that different?" I asked.

"Because in the case of an outsider," she said, "the motivation is greed."

"You mean that you don't work here because you're greedy?" I asked.

"No, I work here because I need the money," she explained.

"And why do you need the money?" I asked.

"Because all of the people that sell me services are greedy," she explained.

"Isn't capitalism great?" I asked.

"Capitalism is all about corporate greed," she said. "Individuals aren't greedy; individuals are good people. Individuals make money because they have to. And they have to because the corporations are greedy."

"You should be a teacher," I said. "You've explained it perfectly." She looked pleased.

"I'll tell you what," she said. "I'll call my bosses in corporate, and tell them about your new subliminal advertising technology. If you give me your contact information, I'll have them to call you. I'm not authorized to buy things like this, but they are, and I'm sure that they'll be interested. I can see how this new technology will help us all make more money."

"That's *greed!*" I said, under my breath.

I visited the other department stores at the mall, and had similar exchanges. I was hopeful that at least one of them would have the capital to try this out.

After spending most of the afternoon in meetings with each of the department store managers, I went home a little tired, so I pulled a couple of shots of espresso, and played with the userid "megamalthea" for a while using the internet.

In Greek mythology, "Amalthea" was the foster-mother of Zeus, who was the king of the gods. It's also the third moon of Jupiter, which was named for the mother of Zeus. And Amalthea orbits Jupiter at a distance of 2.54 times the radius of Jupiter. This happens to be the number of centimeters in an inch. What could these clues all mean? And could they change the way that poker was played on Jupiter?

Could Holdt's girlfriend have been named "Meghan" and something to do with Jupiter? Was there something having to do with a metric conversion in her name? This was quite a puzzle. So I took my espresso upstairs to the lab to play with the GBM (Golf-Ball Mortar) just to take my mind off of megamalthea, hoping that this puzzle would fall into place when I looked at it again.

It was late afternoon, and as sometimes happens late in the afternoon, one of the parties of golfers was drunk. I had gotten the drunks into a fight with the party ahead of them by accidentally firing a long ball onto the green when the sober party was doing their putts. It was an accident; I hadn't meant to shoot that ball, I was just watching the putting up close and I hit the wrong button. Naturally, the people that were putting assumed that the ball had come from the drunks, and some name-calling started. This got the drunks angry. Then the phone rang.

I picked up the phone and it was Pete Fletcher. He said, "when are you coming to the High School again? I think it would be good if you could explain your answer to the problem to the students. Many of them don't see why you'd need quadruplets."

I thought about the romance movie I had seen last night with the plain-looking, gum-chewing American bimbo together with the Three Stooges, and realized that I was generalizing the problem by using four people, and that Pete was primarily interested in the case in which there were exactly two roads.

"You don't need quadruplets if there are only two roads," I said, "but you do need to remember to flip the answer. The reason I said you'd need quadruplets is when there are more than two roads."

"Yes, I think it would be good if you could come in and explain that to the students," he said. "And again, the problem with quadruplets is that there are so few of them. I think that using twins with two roads is more practical."

"But if there are only two roads, you don't even need twins," I told him. "All you need is one Tweedle. And there are billions of Tweedles, so the problem is even easier than what Carroll said."

"Speaking of Carol, how is she?" asked Pete.

"Not Carol. We're talking about Louie Carroll," I told him.

"Who's he?" asked Pete.

"He's some guy. Never mind," I answered.

"But how can you do it with just one Tweedle?" asked Pete.

"Suppose you've got one guy named Tweedle. He doesn't have a twin. Or maybe he does, but we don't need his brother for this. Let's say that in any single conversation with Tweedle, either everything he says is true, or everything he says is false. There are two roads leaving town, and only one goes to the city. What would you ask Tweedle, assuming that he had no brothers or sisters?" I posed the question.

"Gee. If I ask Tweedle which road goes to the city, and he points to one, I don't know whether he's lying or whether he's telling the truth," said Pete.

"Here's the trick," I explained. "What you do is point to one of the two roads, and ask him whether he would say that he would say that the road went to the city."

"What do you mean 'whether he'd say' that the road went to the city?" asked Peter. "What would that prove?"

"You weren't listening," I said. "What I said was to ask him 'whether he'd say that he'd say' that the road went to the city? Hear the difference?"

"That makes no sense," said Pete. "I can see that if Tweedle is telling the truth, you're golden. But what if he's lying? And what do you mean by 'whether you'd say whether you'd say'? That makes no sense."

"Think about it," I said. "If he always lies, then he would say that the wrong road went to the city. But we're asking him whether he would say this, and he'll lie. So he'll tell us that he would not say that the wrong road went to the city. In other words, he'll reverse his own lie. Make sense?"

"I think I see," said Pete.

"And to boot, we don't need to reverse the answer. If he speaks the truth, he'll point to the right road, and if he lies, he'll point the right road. We don't even have to remember to reverse the answer. It's much better with a single Tweedle," I explained. "And there are many more single Tweedles than twins."

"I like this answer better than Carroll's," Pete said. "Let me try it with the students."

It was my turn to cook tonight. And as my culinary repertoire has grown and I've learned to take it more seriously, it's become almost like sex - in fact I've been thinking of having a mirror put on the ceiling over the dining room table to make dinner even more exciting.

Tonight it would be basics. I'd wanted to use up the fennel that I hadn't used in the cioppino, so I decided to make pasta con sarde - good peasant food and nothing fancy, although the flavors are hardly subtle, and there's a little work involved. And I'd be making a desert that was very simple and very elegant, which I'd chosen deliberately to set a stark contrast with the pasta. Zabaglione: a simple yet exquisite and decadent mixture of egg yolks and marsala; its only shortcoming is that it's actually legal.

Carol came in and poured a couple of glasses of wine and brought them to the island in the kitchen where she sat so that we could catch up on the day's events while I cooked. She put the glasses of wine down in front of her.

"Would you like some wine?" she asked me.

"Thanks," I said. "That's nice of you to ask. And sure, I'll have a couple of glasses of wine too."

She only gave me one, however one was enough to get me started, so I took her through the parts of my day relating to the case.

I told her that Moe hadn't found Mitchell Goldberg's number (New Jersey) in Mitch Goldberg's coded book, but that this wouldn't be surprising assuming that they were related. I told her that I had gone to the police station to talk to Moe, and had gotten a parking ticket and a photo of the man who gave it to me. I was trying to think of a form of justice that was sufficiently poetic, but so far was out of rhymes.

I tried a limerick: "I saw an obvious dim-bulb, who . . ." and I couldn't think of a rhyme. "What rhymes with 'dim-bulb?'" I asked.

"Lots of words rhyme with 'dim-bulb,'" she said. "There's . . . uhhh..."

"There once was an obvious dim-bulb, who . . . uhhh..." I replied.

Carol said, "I think you should try to meet with the Goldberg in New Jersey in person just to see whether he seems savvy to all of this, or whether he's not knowingly tied in."

"That rhymes with 'dim-bulb?'" I asked. "How? And the meter is all wrong."

"No, I've given up on that," she said. "I was just saying that you should probably go meet the Goldberg guy in New Jersey, and try to get a feeling for how he fits in."

"Well we know that Jack Holdt had made frequent phone calls to him, so it's pretty obvious that he's tied into this," I said. "Nonetheless, you're right. I'll put that on my list of things to do. After all, maybe he can think of something that rhymes with 'dim-bulb.'"

Then I told Carol about my various meetings with the store managers at the department stores at the mall, and that I had learned that any business run by others is all about "greed," but that once you can convince a store or an individual that they'll make more money too, then they want a piece of the action although they're purely driven by beneficence. So by selling them the technology, I was being greedy. But if they could use the technology to get people to buy more things from them, then it was charitable of them to use it.

I would have to try this reasoning with Mr. Fletcher's class, and see if the students thought that it made sense.

I also asked whether she had any insights into the user-ID "megamalthea," which was used by Jack Holdt. Whoever we could attach it to was Holdt's girlfriend, and maybe his fiancé. I was sure that it was a clever encoding, and that either her name was Meghan-something, or she was doing a large "mega" thing having something to do with Jupiter.

"Jupiter?" asked Carol. "What's that have to do with Jupiter?"

"Apparently, 'Amalthea' is the third moon of Jupiter," I explained.

"Aren't they the ones with the five suits of cards?" she asked jokingly.

"Five suits of cards?" I asked. "I hadn't heard that before."

"Did you realize that 'Amal' is George Clooney's wife?" she asked.

"I don't think that Holdt was in Mrs. Clooney's league, and I doubt that she was his type. But since you've mentioned people in theater, you did cause me to remember something. There's an opera by Menotti named 'Amahl and the Night Visitors,' and it's performed in a 'theater.' So maybe Holdt's girlfriend starred in a production of it, as in 'Amal-thea,'" I suggested.

"Amahl and the Night Visitors?" she asked skeptically. "Do you really think that someone would be so excited about this role that they'd make a user-ID out of it, and tack 'Mega' on the front of it? Amahl and the Night Visitors? I doubt it."

"You're right, they wouldn't," I said.

"Maybe you should send them an email, and see whether they respond," she suggested.

"Why didn't I think of that?" I asked. "What would I say in the email?"

"Maybe you should tell them that you're a friend of Jack Holdt's and you've been trying to contact him," she said.

"I'll have to think about that," I said. "What if they know that he's dead?"

"They'd probably tell you the bad news," she said.

"But what if it's not a girlfriend?" I asked. "What if it's the person that killed Holdt and made him disappear? They might feel obliged to make me disappear too."

"Then invite them over for some zabaglione, and maybe they'll change their mind," she said.

Carol always gives me unique insights.

Day 11

Dagwood and the Kryptonite

After breakfast, I called Mitchell Goldberg's number in New Jersey, and got an answering machine: "Hello, I'm unable to come to the phone right now. Please leave your name and number and I'll call you back."

I didn't leave my name or number. Although I'm sure he could look up the number if he was interested, I doubted that he'd be interested.

I poured myself another cup of coffee and my phone rang. It was Detective Danny.

"Hi Mick," Detective Danny said. "We found the license plates that were missing from Mitch Goldberg's car."

"That solves part of the mystery. Where did you find them?" I asked.

"A parking ticket was issued to a car having those plates. It was illegally parked, and the car was stolen. We don't know who stole it," Detective Danny said. "It's not unusual for car thieves to swipe plates and put them on stolen cars. That way, no one's looking for a car having those plates. It usually takes the person without the plates a few days to realize that their plates are missing, so they don't call it in. Whoever stole the plates is probably just a car thief with no connection to Goldberg."

"So that's a dead end?" I asked. "His plates were stolen by a random car thief who just needed some plates?"

"I'm afraid so," Detective Danny said. "That's a dead end."

"It's quite a coincidence that the car that Holdt was in was also missing its plates," I said.

"That's probably not a coincidence," Detective Danny said, "but we don't know. Those plates haven't turned up yet."

"Actually, you don't know that, because we don't know whose car it was," I said. "It's my hunch that the car belonged to - and still belongs to - Detective Dorian's friend, Dagwood, the rich guy with the six-car garage who lives on the Long Island Sound. Is there any way that you guys can bring that car in for a forensic exam?"

"I don't see how. On what grounds would we seize the car?" Detective Danny asked. "And what kind of forensics would we be looking for? Holdt has disappeared. Even if we found blood in the car, we don't have a sample of Holdt's blood, so there wouldn't be anything that we could compare it to. About all we could do is prove that the car used to be yellow. And we already know that."

"You could probably seize it on the legal technicality that he hasn't yet reported painting the car a new color," I said.

"And what would we find?" Detective Danny asked. "That he painted the car a new color?"

"Yes, I guess that's about it," I admitted. "But it's possible that Holdt left other things in the car."

"Like what?" Detective Danny asked.

"I have no idea," I said. "Maybe his gym bag. I saw that in the car when I saw him in the car on the day of the murder. Maybe you could get a DNA sample from something in his gym bag, and if there were any blood spots in the car, you could match the DNA from the blood to the DNA from the gym bag."

"But if we found a gym bag in the car, how do we know that it's Holdt's?" asked Detective Danny. "It could be anybody's gym bag. Again, without DNA that we know is Holdt's, it makes no difference whether we find a DNA sample. It could be Dagwood's DNA, or the DNA of anyone else who's been in his car. And even if it was Holdt's, there are no formal complaints that anything has happened to him. So what if it's Holdt's?"

"So I guess that until Holdt's body turns up, a physical investigation is pointless," I said.

"Pretty much," Detective Danny said. "There's no real reason to seize Dagwood's car, and I don't think we'd learn anything useful if we did."

"What if we seized Dagwood?" I wondered. "Maybe he would be forthcoming."

"On what grounds?" asked Detective Danny.

"I'm not thinking of seizing him in a legal sense," I said.

"I don't want to hear it," said Detective Danny.

"You're right," I said. "You don't."

"There's another thing that's pretty suspicious," said Detective Danny. "I think it's strange that Dagwood had Stu bring over a backhoe to dig such a big hole for Dottie's flower garden. Most people wouldn't dig a hole like that just to plant some flowers. There's probably something buried in that hole."

"Wouldn't that be pretty obvious?" I asked. "And what about Stu? Would that mean that he's in on it?"

"Don't worry about Stu," Danny said. "Don't you remember him from High School?"

"No, I don't. Did we know him?" I asked.

"Maybe you didn't. He was two years behind us, but he's our age. I dealt with him a few times. The guy is trash, and he's not that bright, but at least he's running a successful garden center," Danny said.

"What do you mean by 'trash?'" I asked.

"It's how the people on his side of town grew up. For example, he's on his third wife, but he still has the same in-laws," he said.

"Some people like their in-laws. Maybe if you find good in-laws, you should try to keep them," I said. "Good in-laws can be hard to come by."

"At any rate, I think that Dagwood could easily have used Stu's services without telling Stu what the real story was," Detective Danny explained.

You're right about that," I said. "Well I'll go see Dagwood this afternoon to see what I can learn. Bye."

———————————

I called Mitchell Goldberg's number in New Jersey again. This time someone answered: "Hello," he said, "who's speaking?" he asked. That was *tres*[5] European.

"You are," I answered.

———————————

[5]   "Very" in French, and several other European languages.

"Hello?" he said again. "Who's this?"

"Hello," I said. "I've been trying to reach Mr. Goldberg, and I was given this number. Is he there please?" I asked.

"Yes, I'm Mr. Goldberg," he said. "Did my agent give you this number?" he asked.

He was pretty smart. Since he's never home, why would he leave his home number with an agent? Either that, or he was pretty stupid, and didn't know that he had answered his home phone. Or stupider still, maybe he did know that he was on his home phone, and that really *is* the number that he gave to his agent.

"No, actually it's a little more complicated than that," I said.

I heard silence. He wasn't biting. Smart? Or stupid?

"Actually, I'm a detective, and I'm not sure whether I have the right Mr. Goldberg," I fibbed. "I'm in Connecticut, and I'm investigating a case involving a drug ring, and I was told that the ring had been looking for someone named Mitch Goldberg. We don't think that Mitch Goldberg's involved, but we're worried about his safety. I saw that this number was listed under 'M. Goldberg', so I called. I think that the Goldberg that they want is up here in Connecticut, but we're not at all far away, and thought I'd check all 'M. Goldbergs' in the region. I realize that it's a common name. Have you noticed anyone strange in your neighborhood? And does 'M' stand for 'Mitch?'"

There was a pause. "Actually, it stands for 'Mitchell,'" he said.

This was the guy that Jack Holdt had been calling, so he was tied into this somehow. I couldn't gamble on him being too stupid.

"So this isn't 'Mitch Goldberg?'" I asked.

"It's 'Mitchell Goldberg,'" he said.

I took a gamble: "Sounds like I've got the wrong Goldberg. Sorry for bothering you then."

"Some of my friends call me 'Mitch,'" he said. "But I use 'Mitchell' professionally."

"Professionally?" I asked. "What do you do?"

"I'm a dancer," he said.

"You mean like on Broadway?" I asked.

"No. I'm with the ballet," he replied.

"You mean *THE* ballet? As in 'Lincoln Center?'" I asked.

"Exactly," he said.

"Do you know a Mitch Goldberg in Connecticut?" I asked.

"Yes, I do," he said. "But I'm sure that there are several. I have an uncle named Mitch in Connecticut. I'm told that I was named after him."

I was starting to get nervous about spilling too much information, and was a little surprised that he was telling me as much as he was over the phone.

"Look, I don't know who you are, and I've no idea about drug rings," Mitchell said. "I'm with the ballet, and that's pretty much it. And I've an uncle named Mitch. So I don't know who you're looking for, but good luck," he said. "I've nothing more to tell you."

"Do you think that your uncle could be in any danger?" I asked. And then I took a gamble: "Isn't he a barber?"

There was a long pause. "How did you know that?" he asked.

"Just a lucky guess," I said. "Look, I'm going to be in the city tomorrow, and I'll be over on the West side. Maybe we could get together and talk in person when you're on a break."

"Why in person?" he asked.

"There are a number of things that are best not to discuss on the phone. Lots of phones are tapped. And I'd like to show you a picture to see whether we're talking about the same guy," I explained.

"Tomorrow I'll have a long break starting at around noon," he said. "We could meet somewhere near Lincoln Center if you're in the neighborhood then."

"I'll arrange to be," I said. "Let's meet across the street at Cafe Fiorello and have lunch. I'll pick up the tab; it'll be on my client."

"I thought you said you were a police detective," he said.

"No, I just said that I'm 'a detective,'" I responded. "I'm a private detective."

"How will I recognize you?" he asked.

"Is your picture on the Lincoln Center website?" I asked.

"Yes, it is," he said.

"Then I'll recognize you," I said. "See you tomorrow."

I hung up, and called Detective Danny.

"Danny, can you get me a picture of Mitch Goldberg?" I asked.

"Yeah, I'm sure that they'll have one at the hair salon at the mall. I'll swing by there and ask them for a copy," he said.

"I need it by morning," I said. "I'm going into the city to meet with the other Mitch Goldberg, and I want to see if he knows the Mitch Goldberg that was murdered up here. So I'll need a photo."

"I'm sure that I'll be able to get you one," he said.

"Great," I replied. "Bye," I said, and I hung up.

I drove across town to meet Carol for lunch. She'd been out shopping, and I was hoping it had been a success. While I'm never sure what "success" means when it comes to Carol's shopping, I can tell when it happens because she's in a good mood.

I did use The Fingers a lot on the way across town, which doesn't exactly lift my mood, but it palliates it. And when I got there, Carol was in a good mood, which lifts my mood. We had agreed to meet at a place near where Interstate 95 runs, because I had brought a Geiger counter with me, and was planning to visit Dagwood's house later this afternoon. I thought I'd take a short trip to the Long Island Sound this afternoon and drop in on him. I was sure he'd be happy to see me.

Since it was a nice day, Carol and I sat outside in their garden behind the restaurant since it was peaceful, and they had baffled the ambient noise with sound barriers and some baroque music. They also had a moderate herb garden that we could see from here, and they used the fresh herbs in their daily menus.

I was going to suggest sharing a split with her, but the main issue that we never seem to agree on is wine. She seems to like aromatic whites, and I go for heartier reds. Once in a while depending on what we're ordering, one or the other of us will cross over, but this is the exception rather than the rule. And when it comes to tastes in wine, I've found that it's a topic that's best to avoid. My advice would always be to stick to more neutral subjects, like sports and politics.

So we were seated. I ordered a cabernet, she ordered a chardonnay, we browsed today's menu, and then asked the waiter to bring us whatever he thought was especially good, hoping that the term "especially good" wasn't synonymous with "whatever's not moving."

I told Carol that Detective Danny reported that they had found the license plates from Mitch Goldberg's car, and that they had simply been stolen by a car thief to put on another car so that the police wouldn't see the plates of the car that was reported stolen. They didn't know who the car thief was, and didn't think that he had anything to do with Goldberg.

I explained that I had also suggested searching Dagwood's car, since I suspected that it was the car that I had seen Holdt's body in. But I also explained that Danny didn't see any point to doing this because there was no way to link it to Holdt without his DNA. And since we never found Holdt, and he came out here from California, we didn't have his DNA. Danny had a valid point.

"Why do you think that Dagwood's car was the one that Holdt was killed in?" she asked.

"How many yellow cars are there?" I asked. "And how many yellow cars disappear right after someone's murdered in them? And how many people paint their yellow cars blue right after dead people are seen sitting in them?"

"I'll admit that it's odd for someone to paint his car a different color," Carol allowed. "But still, do you think that Dottie's cousin Dagwood is tied to a murder?"

"I don't know," I admitted. "But I think it's strange that Dagwood brought the car to Dottie's house to paint it."

"Where else would he paint it?" she asked.

I told her that I'd learned that Dagwood was a wealthy man with a mansion on the Long Island Sound and a six-car garage.

"That's strange," Carol said. "Why would he bring it to Dottie's to paint it?"

"He wouldn't," I said. "He must have brought it there for another reason."

"Do you think that whatever the reason is was buried in Dottie's new garden?" she asked.

"That seems too obvious," I said.

"Obvious?" she asked. "I'm sure that Dagwood didn't know that you lived across the street," and she winked at me.

"Still," I said, "I would think that if Dagwood had some evidence that he wanted to get rid of, taking it out into the ocean would be a lot easier than burying it at Dottie's."

"That's true," she said. "But what do you think you'd find in the car?"

"I don't know," I said. "When I saw Jack Holdt in the front seat of the car, his old gym bag was in the back seat. Maybe his old gym bag is still in the car. It didn't look like the kind of thing that anyone would take great pains to protect. It was worn and dirty. It might be on the floor or in the trunk. It might hold some clues."

"An old gym bag?" she asked with surprise. "When I visited Dottie a couple of days after the murder, there was an old gym bag on the floor in her kitchen. She said that Dagwood had put it there, and that it had been in his car. She thought that it was Dagwood's."

"Dagwood's?" I asked. "Does he look like the kind of guy who carries real gear around in an old gym bag?"

"Maybe if it was burglary gear," she laughed.

"I'll bet that Dottie still has that old gym bag, and that it belonged to Jack Holdt," I said. "I'll bet that Danny could ask her for it if he was nice about it. After all, I'm going out to see Dagwood after lunch. I'll ask him if I can have it."

"Does he know that you're coming?" she asked. "And why would he tell Dottie to give it to you?"

"I'll ask him nicely," I said. "He might want to help us with the investigation if I'm nice enough."

I told her that I had called Mitchell Goldberg in New Jersey, and that I'd be meeting him for lunch across from Lincoln Center tomorrow.

"That's it?" Carol asked. "You mean you just called him and said 'Hi Mitchell, you don't know me, but would you like to meet me for such tomorrow at Lincoln Center?' and he said 'OK?'"

"No, there was more to it than that," I explained. "He's there during the day training, working on choreography, and practicing. I told him that I was a private detective that was looking into a dangerous situation involving a barber up here named Mitch Goldberg. Mitchell told me that his uncle's name is Mitch Goldberg and that he's a barber up here. I left him interested enough to talk to me. I said that I'd meet him at a restaurant across the street, and that I'd buy. He took me up on it."

"How are you going to know who he is?" she asked.

"He told me that his picture is on the American Ballet Theater website," I said, "so I found it, and know what he looks like."

"Did you say the 'American Ballet Theater?'" she asked.

"Yes," I said. "I told you that the other night."

"Do you mean 'AMerican bALlet THEAter' as in 'am-al-thea?'" she asked.

God, she was clever. "And his name is 'Mitchell Goldberg.' How much do you want to bet that his middle name is 'Egbert,' or something like that? 'MEG,' as in 'meg-amalthea.' You're good," I said; "the best."

———————

After lunch, I jumped on Interstate 95 and headed East while using my foghorn a lot, then cut off and went South to the Long Island Sound while using my foghorn a lot, took a left, used my foghorn, and found the address that Detective Danny had given me. I parked my car, and got out with the Geiger counter, which I turned on.

While mine has a digital readout, I had fixed up this Geiger counter so that I could produce audible clicks independent of the sensors, and regulate their rate using a dial on the back. I set the sound to give me a moderate click rate, and then I went up and rang the doorbell.

After several minutes, Dagwood answered the door. I both acted surprised to see that it was him, and I boosted the click rate when he stepped forward.

"What the hell?" he said. He looked both shocked and confused when he saw the Geiger counter and heard its rate go up.

"You're that guy, . . . that guy Dagwood!" I said, acting surprised. "You're the guy who was working on his car in Dottie's garage. I live across the street, and met you when you were coming down her driveway with that detective guy, that Detective Dorian guy."

He looked at me again, and said "Oh, right, I remember!" And then he pointed to the Geiger counter. "What the hell is that thing?" Dagwood asked.

I looked at my Geiger counter. "Oh, this?" I asked. "It's a special kind of Geiger counter. It's for measuring a special kind of radiation that comes from kryptonite."

"What's kryptonite?" Dagwood asked. "And what are you doing here?"

"I got here by following the Geiger counter," I said. "Some kryptonite landed on the earth in 1940. It's from outer space; it came from the planet Krypton. Some of the drug cartels use it for purifying celecoxib and metaxalone. But kryptonite can be very dangerous if it's not handled correctly."

"But why are you here?" he asked.

"The sensors picked up kryptonite when I was across the street at Dottie's," I explained. "She had an old gym bag that was radiating off the charts, and she thought it came from your car. So I just followed the sensors. Is your car here?"

"Yes," he said. "My car's in the garage. But why would my car have kryptonite in it?"

"I don't know," I said. "Did you lend it to anyone? Is it possible that someone used it for moving drugs, and you didn't know that that's what they were doing? Can we go see your car? I'd like to measure it."

"Sure, sure," he said. "Let's go out to the garage. It's in there."

We walked out to the garage, and when we entered, I turned the click rate up.

"The car must be heavily contaminated," I said. "I'd park it somewhere else if I were you."

"What does kryptonite do to you?" asked Dagwood.

"It causes impotence," I told him, "and it makes people delusional. It gives you an uncontrollable urge to dance. If music comes on, people who are infected can't stay seated. They have to dance, but then they can't have sex."

Dagwood looked very worried.

"Do you have another place that you can put this car?" I asked him.

Again, Dagwood looked very worried. "Yes," he said. "I'll find one."

"Also," I said, "Dottie still has your gym bag. As I told you, it was radiating off the charts, but I didn't want to take it or look inside without asking you. Is it OK if I take your gym bag to see why it's contaminated?"

"Yes, of course," he said. "It's not my gym bag anyway. Someone left it in the car. I don't know who it belongs to. You can have it."

"Then can you call Dottie and ask her to give it to me?" I asked. "I can't just go over to her house and take it."

"Yes, of course," Dagwood said. "I'll call her as soon as you leave, and ask her to give it to you."

"OK," I said. "I'll need to examine it. The sooner I get it, the better. I've got to go. I'm glad that I was able to track this kryptonite radiation down. The sooner I can contain it, the safer it will be for everyone. I'll go get the bag from Dottie."

"I'm glad you found this," he said. "I'd hate to think what would have happened if there was no one like you around who knew about kryptonite. Thanks," he said.

"No problem," I said. "I do things like this all the time. I'm a scientist. By the way, can I have your phone number in case I need to call you about anything I find in the gym bag?"

"Sure," he said, "I'll give it to you," and he did.

I got out of his beach neighborhood, found my way back to Interstate 95, and went home. When I got there, Jack Holdt's gym bag was on the floor in our foyer. Carol told me that Dottie had just brought it over.

"What happened?" Carol asked. "You simply asked Dagwood for the gym bag, and he sent Dottie over with it? What did you tell him?"

"Nothing, really," I said. "I just said that I'd like to have the bag, and it would be nice if he could have Dottie give it to me. And he said 'OK.'"

"As simple as that?" she asked. "He just said 'OK?' I'm amazed. Why would he do that?"

"I guess he doesn't like to dance," I said.

"Dance?" she asked. "What does the bag have to do with dancing?"

"It isn't the bag itself," I explained. "It's the kryptonite that's in the bag that makes you dance. This makes you irresistible to women, but the kryptonite makes you impotent. This is quite a dilemma for most men."

"But I'm sure that their girlfriends would love it," she said. "Imagine dancing all night! This kryptonite would make a great stocking stuffer. I could write the ad for them: 'Turn your man into a superman, and the two of you can dance all night!'"

I'd have to try that one out next time I visited the mall. I'm sure that as long as no one made a profit, it would be a great idea.

That night after dinner, I ran out to a local pub to meet with Danny and go through the case as I understood it so far. And by "case," I wasn't talking about the beer. I had a campari with soda, and left the case up to Danny. He was better at drinking those than I was.

Danny walked in, sat down to join me, and ordered a case of beer - or something like that. There was a bowl of nuts on our table, and lots of nuts at the other tables. Most of them were watching the game on TV. That makes for safe conversation, unlike varietal wines. That's why I had a campari with soda: it's not controversial, since no one likes it.

"You'll never guess what we found about an hour ago," Danny said.

"Don't tell me," I said. "Let me guess."

I went through the pantomime of concentration, being careful not to make it look too much like I was having a difficult bowel movement, because that's how it usually looks on TV game shows.

"They found a blue car that looked exactly like Dagwood's blue car, abandoned on the shoulder of Interstate 95," I said, with my hands on my forehead like Carnac the Magnificent.

I waved him off. "No, don't tell me," I said. "The plates were off of it, and it was found by Detective Dorian who just so happened to be coming back from Cos Cob when he saw it and thought that it looked suspicious, so he pulled over to investigate. And they have no idea who the owner is, because the serial numbers were scratched off the windshield."

Detective Danny looked amazed. "How did you know that?"

"I don't know," I said. "It was just a wild guess. So what did you find really?" I asked.

"That's exactly what we, I mean what Detective Dorian found," he said.

"I went out to visit Dagwood this afternoon, and I explained to him that the car was likely the source of something very important relating to the case. I thought that he might try to ditch it," I explained.

"By scratching the serial numbers off of it and leaving it abandoned on the Interstate?" he asked.

"Some people do strange things," I said, as the room erupted.

I guess something had happened in the game on TV. People in the bar were whistling and cheering. Maybe one of the players had been "pantsed;" I hadn't been paying attention.

And for those of you who don't follow sports, I recall from High School that "pantsing" was the act of sneaking up behind a player on the other team, and pulling his pants down when he wasn't expecting it. This usually made the spectators erupt like they just had.

"I thought you'd be interested to know that Holdt's gym bag was not found in the car," Detective Danny told me.

"I know. I have it," I informed him.

"What do you mean you have it?" Detective Danny asked.

"Dagwood had left Holdt's gym bag at Dottie's," I said, "and he asked Dottie to give it to me."

"Why would he do that?" asked Detective Danny.

"Because he's a nice guy," I said. "I told him that I'd find it helpful if I had the bag, and he said 'sure.' So he asked Dottie to give it to me, and she did."

"Just like that?" asked Detective Danny, clearly skeptical.

"Pretty much," I said. "When you ask nicely, people cooperate."

"And how did you know that Detective Dorian was the one that found the car?" Danny asked.

"Well Dagwood would need a ride," I explained. "You wouldn't expect him to drive it many miles away on the Interstate and walk home, would you? So, I assumed that Detective Dorian helped him drop the car off."

"Why would Detective Dorian do that?" Danny asked.

"Because he's wrapped up in this," I said. "I haven't quite figured out how he's wrapped up in it, but I'm sure that he is."

We watched the game for a couple of minutes and had some nuts. Everyone on the field had their pants back on.

"Did you get a picture of Mitch Goldberg for me?" I asked.

"Yes," Danny said. "I sent it to your phone. You mean to tell me that you actually connected with the Mitch Goldberg in New Jersey? And he's agreed to meet you for lunch tomorrow?" he asked, amazed.

"Well that was easy," I said. "I told him that I'd pick up the tab."

"What do you expect to get from that Mitch Goldberg?" he asked.

"I really don't know. It sounds like he's likely the nephew of the Mitch Goldberg up here, and we know that Jack Holdt was calling him about as much as he was calling his uncle. So my guess is that he's wrapped up in the crooked drug deal that was orchestrated by Senator Adler," I explained.

"So why would he talk to you?" Danny asked, reasonably.

"I'm not sure," I admitted. "Maybe I have a convincing tone when I'm talking on the telephone."

"Maybe you learned how to be convincing during all those years you spent at universities," Danny said.

"That has nothing to do with it," I responded. "Nothing worth knowing can be taught," I explained. "I'm also pretty sure that I know who's email address 'megamalthea' is."

"Really?" he asked. "How did you figure that one out?"

"I didn't," I said. "Carol was the one who saw it."

"Who's email address is it?" he asked.

"It depends on what Mitchell Goldberg's middle name is," I explained.

Detective Danny thought about this for a minute, and said "I don't get it."

"I'll give you a big hint," I said. "Suppose his middle initial is an E. Then the first three letters stand for 'Mitchell E. Goldberg.' Do you see it now?" I asked.

Detective Danny thought about it some more. "I've got 'meg.' But what the hell is 'amalthea?'" he asked.

"Mitchell E. Goldberg is a professional dancer at Lincoln Center," I explained.

Detective Danny thought some more. "I still don't get it," he said.

"Ever hear of the 'American Ballet Theater?'" I asked.

"No," he replied. "What's that?"

I was stunned for a minute. "That's the company that Mitchell Goldberg works for."

"Oh," he said. "Well that makes sense then. What do they do?" he asked.

"Who?" I asked in return.

"The company that Mitchell Goldberg works for," he said.

"They dance," I replied.

He stared at me for a minute. I think he was trying to figure out whether I was joking.

"And you're meeting him for lunch tomorrow?" Danny asked.

"Yes," I said. "I hope to learn a number of things."

"Are the two of you going dancing?" he asked.

"No," I said. "He does it for a living, and will be on his lunch break. And I only did it when I was single and was trying to get girls to like me. And I'm hardly in his league. Tomorrow we're just meeting for lunch. I hope to find out who Mitchell Goldberg is, and how he ties into this murder case. That's why I wanted the photo of Mitch Goldberg. I want to show it to him to see whether it's his uncle."

"What do you think you'll learn?" Danny asked.

"I don't know; maybe nothing," I said. "The puzzling thing is that if Mitchell Goldberg had something to hide, I don't think he'd have lunch with me. On the other hand, maybe he just wants to know how much I know, and then he'll play dumb."

"Or maybe he's just going to have lunch with you because you're picking up the tab," Danny said.

"That never hurts," I responded.

There were only two minutes left in the football game, and it was close. When it's close, the last two minutes usually can be wrapped up in forty-five minutes or less. This is when the teams' special players are used: their lawyers.

They stop the play every five or ten seconds, and then their lawyers come running out, and they argue for five or ten minutes. This is always the most exciting part of the game, although you don't get to hear the arguments. To the spectator, all you get to see is lots of gesticulating, pantomime, and occasionally a "Minister of Silly Walks" who picks up the ball and moves it in accordance with whichever lawyer won whatever the argument was.

I think that this is why most Europeans don't understand football: it's all of the lawyering. This is purely an American thing; you need to grow up here to really understand it.

On the other hand, Europeans watch soccer, which Americans don't understand. In soccer, the clock never stops, and the game only lasts an hour. Yet in that hour, the fans get piss-blind drunk, and frequently get into fistfights despite the fact that no one ever scores points. I guess you really need to be European to really understand that as well.

Danny ordered another beer, because he wanted to watch the last two minutes of the game, and those two minutes could take quite a while. As I've explained to those of you who don't understand football, this is the most exciting part.

I still had half of my campari and soda left, so I ordered a beer too. I figured I might as well drink something as long as I had come out to a pub.

Day 12

Mitchell Goldberg at Lincoln Center

In the morning, I went for my usual run, and I saw Dottie watering her flowers when I came up my driveway, so I stopped to thank her for having brought over the gym bag.

"Oh, that was no problem," said Dottie, and she smiled. "Dagwood made it sound like it was urgent that you get it, so I brought it down. Did you find what you were looking for?"

I hadn't even looked inside yet. I was sure that it would be the usual gym equipment that a serious lifter like Holdt would have. I didn't think there would be any surprises; I just wanted DNA samples in case we could ever find Holdt's body. This would tie the murder to Dagwood in a legal sense, and I was sure that it would make him more forthcoming.

"Yes, it had exactly what I was looking for," I said. And I wasn't lying; what I was looking for was just the gym bag. What was in it didn't really matter yet.

I noticed that Dottie had done her hair nicely, and was wearing a small amount of makeup.

"Your hair looks nice like that," I commented. "How are the flowers coming along?"

"Oh, thanks," she said. "These are perennials. There probably isn't more than another month left in the season before they go dormant, so I just wanted to give them a good start."

That made a lot of sense. Unfortunately, my hunch was that we would have to dig the flower bed up within the next week or two, since people would want to know what Dagwood had actually buried there. I didn't tell her this. Maybe she could talk her new boyfriend out of it.

"Did you and Danny have a nice evening the other night?" I asked. "He and I got together at the pub last night to watch the game, and he seemed more chipper than usual." I thought that "chipper" was sufficiently ambiguous, and that she'd fill in the blanks.

"Yes, we went into Stanford for a nice dinner," she said. "It was good to get out. I'd not been out for quite a while, and Danny seems like a very nice guy. I'm disappointed that I hadn't met him earlier."

"Yes, he is a nice guy," I said. "You two should go running together some morning. Speaking of which, I've an appointment down in the city, so I've got to be running along," making a bad pun that I was sure would gracefully give me an exit.

We waved goodbye, and I did my run. No cars followed me today. Since John Rogers had left town, this was getting to be a pattern.

I took a shower and had a light breakfast. I thought I'd drive into the city to meet Mitchell Goldberg, since driving is faster than the train once rush-hour is over. It's also less expensive, although I'd have to park my car in a garage which would cost about the same as the train.

And yes, if I cruise around in the Lincoln Center area, I can usually find a parking spot, but this isn't a good idea when you've got Connecticut plates. The parking cops are given quotas, so they usually ticket out-of-state plates even when they're legally parked. I've gotten several this way. The parking cops know that it's too much trouble for you to contest it, and it helps them meet their quota. So with Connecticut plates, I always park in a garage. And Lincoln Center has a nice one that's easy to get in and out of during the day, although when a show is on, it's a different story.

In Manhattan, I don't bother with The Fingers. There are too many people, and no one knows who you're giving The Fingers to. But I do use a special driving technique that's useful in the city. I weave back and forth sporadically. I don't change lanes; I just weave by a foot or so in each direction in a random pattern. This way, people assume that I'm on drugs, and the cabs don't crowd me in quite as much.

I had actually first learned to drive in Manhattan when I was a teenager. Back when I learned, everyone made big use of their horn; it was simply part of how you drove. Out of the New York City area, people think that honking your horn is a sign of "rudeness." When I first learned to drive, using your horn in Manhattan had nothing to do with being rude; it was simply a cautionary "hey man, I'm here" signal that you gave to other cars if you thought that the driver might not see you.

But today the police frown on the use of your horn, so I try not to use it when I'm in the city - as hard as that is.

I took the West Side Drive down to 79th Street, and then down Riverside to 72nd Street.

I'll admit that sometimes I'm reluctant to take Riverside - especially to 72nd, because it's residential, and pedestrians sometimes block intersections when the light's green.

Some Manhattan residents don't drive at all, never did, shouldn't, and they have no concept of what pains in the asses they can be while crossing intersections. I had to beep at one to get the hell out of the intersection. He was just standing there and the light was green.

He yelled at me not to "toot my horn!" so I yelled back at him that he could "toot my flute." Someday when robotics becomes better, it occurred to me that it wouldn't be a bad idea to have a pedestrian form of a Shit-Ninny. It could walk around the city and toot people's flutes. They'd be useful in shopping malls too: if you've ever seen "Dawn of the Dead," you've got the general idea.

I took 72nd Street over to Broadway, and Broadway down to Lincoln Center where I parked in the garage. It's much easier than taking the train.

I walked across Broadway to Cafe Fiorello, entered, and asked for a table with a view of the entrance. I told the Maitre D: "*Piacere signore, voglio un tavolo contro il muro, grazie[6],*" and was seated a little before noon at a table against the wall on the South side of the restaurant so that I could see everyone who came in the front door. I had looked up Mitchell Goldberg on the Lincoln Center website, so I knew roughly what he looked like, and was sure that I'd recognize him when he arrived.

At Cafe Fiorello they specialize in fresh antipasti, so it's a great place to meet people who might or might not have restrictions on what

---

[6]   Italian for "Please give me a table against the wall."

they'll eat. They have all kinds of grilled and marinated vegetables, onions and olives, artichokes, anchovies and sardines, and bruschetta and pestos; anyone can eat here.

Mitchell Goldberg walked in gracefully a little after noon. While I recognized him from his picture, he moved with the lightness and agility of a dancer, and my guess was that few of them ate here regularly, so I might have been able to guess it was he even without his picture. He was looking askance in all directions, so I gave him a wave, and motioned him over.

When he got to our table, I reached out my hand to shake, and said "Hi, I'm Mick."

He shook hands and sat down. "Mitchell," he said.

"Why don't we order first, and then I'll explain who I am and why I wanted to talk to you," I said.

"Good idea," he said, and shrugged out of his jacket, which he put on the back of his chair.

The waiter came by, and we gave him our orders. I got a bottle of mineral water and ordered antipasto, and Mitchell got a white wine, and ordered the same.

I took out my phone, and showed him the picture of Mitch Goldberg that Danny had sent me.

"This is the Mitch Goldberg that I was telling you about," I said. "Is this the same Mitch Goldberg that you said was your uncle?"

He looked briefly, and said "Yes, but I haven't seen him in a while. How is he?"

I put my phone back in its holster and said "The police told me that he was murdered."

He looked surprised. "How? And by who?" he asked, clearly taken aback. "I thought he was just a barber in a shopping mall up in Connecticut. Who would want to kill him?"

"I have no idea," I said in earnest. "That's part of the case that I'm working on. There were actually two murders, and I learned that your uncle was one of them, although I didn't see it. I knew him only slightly because he was the one that I always got to cut my hair."

The waiter came and served Mitchell his glass of wine, then opened the bottle of mineral water, poured some for each of us, and left it on the table.

"Really?" he asked. "When you went for a haircut, you always asked for my uncle Mitch?"

"Yes," I said. "I always enjoyed his style of conversation," I explained, without saying that it was because he didn't talk much.

"Yes," he said. "Uncle Mitch could be really funny when he wanted to be."

"Yes," I agreed, finding that hard to imagine, "he certainly could."

"How was he murdered?" he asked.

"The police told me that he'd been shot," I said.

"Was it an accident?" he asked. "Maybe he was hit by a stray bullet?" he asked, hopefully.

"No," I said. "The police told me it looked professional. It killed him instantly, and I'm sure that he never felt it, if that's any consolation."

"But who would want to kill him?" he asked. "He was a barber. Surely it was a mistake."

"Again, that's what I'm trying to figure out," I explained.

"You said that there were two murders," Mitchell said. "Were the two of them shot together, and have you figured out who the other guy was? I didn't know Uncle Mitch's friends, so I'm sure that the name wouldn't mean anything to me."

I pondered how to answer this, and the waiter came back with our antipasti. The server was very good here, because part of their business is quick turnover. I did a flourish with my table napkin to give me another couple of seconds, as I put it in my lap.

"That's actually one of the reasons that I wanted to talk to you," I said. "The two murders were not together, but I wanted to see whether you happened to know the second guy."

And of course, I knew that he knew the second guy, because the second guy - Jack Holdt - had called him - Mitchell Goldberg – quite a lot.

"Well I'm sure that I don't. Who was the second guy?" he asked.

"His name was Holdt," I said casually, and I watched his face carefully. I'm not sure why I did, because I'm bad at reading expressions. That's one of the reasons that I don't play poker.

Nonetheless, he looked very surprised, and he stopped chewing for a second.

"No, I don't know anyone in Connecticut with that name," Mitchell said. "It's not a name like Goldberg."

"He wasn't from Connecticut; he was from out of town," I said.

"I do happen to know someone with a similar sounding name, but it couldn't be the same guy," Mitchell said.

"How are you so sure?" I asked.

"Because I talked to him this morning, and he hadn't been murdered yet," Mitchell said.

So Mitchell was a comedian too. But was he a liar? I didn't know for sure, and I didn't want to tell him that I knew that he had talked to Holdt on the phone a lot.

We were close to finishing our lunch, and I wasn't feeling sure enough to push Mitchell in either direction yet, so I didn't let on that I was sure it was the same Holdt. So I made some small talk about the ballet, and tried not to sound too ignorant. I'm sure he was used to it.

When we'd finished our lunch, I thought I'd wrap up another loose end.

"Well Mitchell, this sounds like it's a dead end," I lied a little. "But just in case, it would be good if I had a way of getting a hold of you when something breaks. I'd prefer to let you know if we find the killers before you hear it on the news. And you're a hard guy to reach on the phone. Do you have an email address?"

"Sure," he said. He took out a business card and handed it to me. "It's on here."

"Thanks," I said, and nonchalantly slipped it into my shirt pocket resisting the urge to look at it, despite being very anxious to know whether Carol had been right.

We shook hands and did the usual "nice to meet you" exchange, and went our separate ways.

I eagerly pulled his business card out and looked. Sure enough, his middle name was "Edward," and his user ID was "megamalthea."

You could have knocked me over with a fender.

Driving home, I had to use The Fingers a lot. I went back up the Hudson River Parkway and cut over to Interstate 95 on the Cross Bronx Expressway when I got to the George Washington Bridge. That's an exit that frequently backs up. Part of the problem is that the bridge exits to New Jersey are both all-the-way-over on the left (to the upper level), and all-the-way-over on the right (to the lower level), while the exit for the Bronx is right in the middle.

This means that people headed to New Jersey who don't know that both exits exist might only see one of the "Exit To NJ" signs, and will try to completely cross the highway in either direction at the last second. I had three Fingers for that, and the big middle one went to the Bronx.

Despite learning to drive in New York City, my frustration there is that the people in the city don't know how to drive on highways.

They move way too slowly, hog lanes, and don't get the hell out of the way when you're going faster than they are. And for me, that's most of the time.

And in Connecticut, by the time you get to Greenwich, people drive like they own the god-damn road. The problem is that half of them probably do, so that's where The Fingers and the foghorn come in really handy.

I made it home. The drive to the city was much quicker and cheaper than taking the train, although I did have to pay to park my car, since parking is cheaper than a parking ticket. And the price to park in a garage is the same, regardless of your license plates. At least in smaller towns I could get a photo of whoever gave me the ticket. In New York City, what good would that do?

Speaking of which, I was still trying to come up with a limerick about the dim-bulb who gave me the parking ticket when I went downtown to talk to Moe the other day: "There once was an obvious dim-bulb, who . . ." I was stuck. Maybe if I could get the guy's name it would help.

I went inside, went to my espresso machine, and pulled a *doppio*, and then I called Detective Danny.

"Hello," he said. "What's up?"

"I went into the city and met with Mitchell Goldberg. It turns out that he's Mitch Goldberg's nephew," I told him. "He identified Mitch in the photo that you gave me."

"And what did he know about the case?" Danny asked.

"He pretended not to know anything," I said. "I told him that his uncle had been shot by a professional hitter, and he seemed surprised. At first he pretended to assume that maybe his uncle had been shot by mistake."

"And what about Holdt?" Danny asked.

"He claimed that he didn't know Holdt," I said. "Rather, he claimed that he didn't know this particular Holdt, but he knew another guy named Holdt that he had just spoken with, so the Holdt that he had spoken to couldn't have been the one that was hit."

"And you believed that?" asked Danny.

"Of course not," I said. "But he doesn't know that I know enough to know that he was lying. We know that the Holdt that was hit up here was Jack Holdt, and that Jack Holdt had called him on the phone and had sent him lots of email," I said.

"And how do we know that Jack Holdt sent him email?" Danny asked. "Did you get his user ID?"

"Yes, I did," I said, "and sure enough it was 'megamalthea.' Carol was right. But he didn't know that I knew that he and Holdt had exchanged lots of email, and I didn't tell him. If he's going to dig himself into a hole, I thought I'd let him. We can drop that information on him later, when we've got more evidence and we need him to cooperate."

"We might know that by tomorrow morning," Danny said. "I talked to Dottie this afternoon. She told me that she gave Carol the gym bag that you think is Holdt's."

"Yes, she did," I said. "She brought it over yesterday. And why will we know more about Holdt tomorrow morning?"

"I told Dottie that there's a police warrant to dig up her garden in the morning to see what's in the hole that was made with a commercial backhoe," Danny said. "The police thought it was unusual to put a garden in like this, and they think that Holdt might be buried under the garden. I explained this to her when I dropped by her house."

"You dropped by her house?" I asked. "That sounds serious."

He laughed. "I like Dottie," he said. "Of course she's upset about it getting her garden dug up, but when I explained the big mystery and the Holdt murder, she understood. In fact, she said if there's a dead guy in there, she wants him removed. But she was shocked when I told her this was possible. Because if Holdt is in there, it would mean that her cousin Dagwood put him there."

"Who got the warrant issued?" I asked.

"Detective Dorian did," Danny told me. "So he might not be wrapped up in this like you seem to think he is. All you know about Detective Dorian is that he's friends with Dagwood. Detective Dorian might be trustworthy."

"Are you talking about the Detective Dorian that's good friends with the Dagwood that would have been the one to bury Holdt under the garden? That Detective Dorian?" I asked. "You're right," I continued, "if Detective Dorian turns evidence on his friend Dagwood, then he's trustworthy."

"I didn't put it that way," Danny objected.

"I know," I said, "but that's the way it is. I still don't trust Detective Dorian."

"I guess we'll find out tomorrow then," said Danny.

"Somehow, I doubt it," I said. "I still don't see why anyone would have buried Holdt in Dottie's garden. Especially not Dagwood. He could have dumped him in the Long Island Sound."

"And I don't see why anyone would dig Dottie a garden using a professional backhoe," Danny said. "Holdt was a big guy. Getting him to the Long Island Sound might have been too hard for one person to do."

"But I don't see why a rich guy with a six-car garage on the Long Island Sound would repaint his car over at his cousin Dottie's," I said. "I still think that there's more to this. Maybe we'll find out tomorrow."

———————————

That night, I went through all of the new information with Carol. I told her about my lunch with Mitchell Goldberg across the street from Lincoln Center. I told her that I'd learned that he was Mitch Goldberg's nephew, and that he claimed that he didn't know that his uncle had been murdered. And I told her that Mitchell had lied about knowing Holdt.

While he did admit to knowing a guy named Holdt, he claimed that the Holdt that was murdered up here must have been a different Holdt. While I believe the part about the two Goldbergs, I don't believe that there were also two Holdts. After all, in the New York City area, how many Goldbergs do you know versus Holdts?

I was also pleased to tell her that Mitchell Goldberg's middle name was "Edward," hence his middle initial was "E," and that she was right about his user ID megamalthea: Mitchell E Goldberg, AMerican bALlet THEAter. I showed her his business card. She was right about that one.

We spent a few minutes speculating about Danny and Dottie, and whether it looked like a budding romance. I told her that I was surprised to see that Dottie is actually a pretty woman when she smiles and takes the trouble to make herself up a little. I think that both of them are good people, although they each have some quirks. Don't we all, except for me?

She wasn't entirely surprised when I said that the police were going to dig up Dottie's new garden. She thought that the way that Dagwood had put the new garden in - with help from his friend Stu - did seem unusual for flowers, and that she had suspected that they had buried something in there besides fertilizer. While it is a good idea to remove clay, this was extreme.

"But why would Dagwood bury someone there if he lived on the Long Island Sound?" she asked. "Wouldn't it be much less trouble to dump the body in the ocean with some blocks chained to it? The fish would take care of the evidence for good."

"That's exactly what I thought," I said. "But Danny raised the point that Holdt was quite large, and that Dagwood might not have been able to move him all by himself."

"But didn't he get his friend Stu to help him dig that hole?" she asked. "Couldn't the two of them have moved the body?"

"I went over to meet Stu, and he's not that swift," I explained. "While Dagwood was easily able to talk him into digging a big hole, Stu probably didn't think too hard about why he was digging it. Getting Stu to help him move a large dead body down to the coast would have been much harder to do without Stu figuring out that they were moving a large dead body. Maybe Dagwood simply buried him at Dottie's because Holdt was too difficult to move."

"But why would he use Dottie's garage to paint his car?" she asked. "Especially with his huge garage down on the sound?"

"Maybe it's the same problem," I said. "Maybe he couldn't move Holdt out of his car, and didn't want to drive down the Interstate with a big dead guy sitting in the front seat. So he took his car to Dottie's on local side streets, and fed her some nonsense about needing to use her garage to paint his car. And he offered to put in a garden in for her by way of thanks, figuring that he could get rid of Holdt right there."

"But wouldn't Dottie see Holdt sitting in his car, dead?" she asked.

"He probably still had Holdt sitting in the car when he brought it to Dottie's and put it in her garage, but he probably guessed that she wouldn't be curious enough to bother to go out and look. Why would she? The nonsense about the garden and the paint was all because he didn't want to drive out on the Interstate with a huge dead guy with a bullet hole in his head sitting in the passenger's seat," I explained. "The Interstate is always busy, and it's too easy to get pulled over."

Now that I was thinking about it, I thought it was likely that Holdt had been buried under Dottie's new garden. And it was pretty obvious that Dagwood did it. Holdt was murdered while sitting in his car, and Dagwood did a mysterious burial in the middle of the night over at Dottie's after telling her some nonsense about using a new kind of "night fertilizer."

While at first, I couldn't have imagined why he would have buried him here, it was simple: he didn't want to take his car out on the Interstate with a big dead guy named Holdt sitting in the passenger's seat. I was looking forward to tomorrow morning, to see what we'd dig up.

Day 13

What's Under Dottie's Garden?

In the morning, I had a quick breakfast and poured myself another cup of coffee to take up the driveway to see what the police had learned by digging up Dottie's new garden.

Detectives Danny and Dorian were there, as was Stu with one of his backhoes, and a few uniformed officers. I wondered whether any of them were one that gave me the parking ticket. I also wondered what the town had paid Stu to dig up the hole again.

Stu was making a lot of money out of this hole. Maybe he was in on whatever the scandal was: his scheme was to make lots of money by digging up the same hole as many times as he could.

The hole had already been dug up, and I didn't see Dottie's flowers. My hunch was that they hadn't bothered to remove them first, and had simply buried them under the dirt that they had excavated - none too carefully.

The hole was empty. And there wasn't anything lying on the ground near it. No bodies, no packages, and no "mystery nocturnal fertilizer" from California. At least we now knew that Dagwood had been lying about that one.

"It looks empty," I observed. ("Duh.") "You didn't find anything?" (Again, "Duh.")

"We don't know," said Detective Dorian.

"Duh?" I asked. "What's not to know?"

"Someone dug this up last night in the middle of the night," Detective Danny explained. "It was like this when we got here this morning."

"So I guess there was something in the hole," I said, "but now we don't know what."

"You should have been a police detective," said Detective Dorian.

"And you should have been a comedian," I responded. "Is it possible that there was nothing in the hole, but that someone wanted us to believe that there was?"

"You should have been a comedian," said Detective Dorian.

"And you should have been a police detective," I responded.

There were two obvious questions that I didn't raise in front of this crowd, both because they were obvious questions, and because their answers would likely implicate people that were standing here. First: Who knew that the police were going to dig this up this morning? Probably everyone here. And second: Is it likely that it had been dug up with one of Stu's backhoes? Probably.

"Stu, did you dig this up last night?" I asked him.

"Of course not. Why would I do that?" asked Stu. "You guys were going to pay me a lot to dig it up this morning."

"Because maybe you got paid more to dig it up last night," I said.

Stu pondered that, and then I could tell that it hit him. If he hadn't dug it up last night, he was clearly disappointed.

"No, I didn't dig it up last night," he said, and I could tell that he was thinking: "Darn!"

"Do you know whether any of your equipment was taken out last night?" I asked.

"I don't think so, but I'd have no way of knowing," he said. "But if someone took a backhoe, they would have needed the keys."

"Where do you keep the keys?" I asked him.

"In the backhoes," he said. "That way they don't get lost."

Maybe Stu should have been a comedian. Or better yet, a detective.

"So someone who knew that you guys would be digging this up this morning got a backhoe, came here in the middle of the night, dug it up, and took whatever was buried here. That's assuming that something was buried here," I said. "And if nothing was buried here,"

I continued, "then for some reason they wanted us to believe that something had been."

"Why would they bother to do that?" asked Detective Dorian.

"I can't imagine," I responded. "So something was probably buried here."

"It was probably the dead guy, Holdt," said Detective Dorian.

"So what happened to the body?" I asked him.

"Obviously, whoever dug him up moved him," he said.

"But how?" I asked. "With a backhoe? I doubt it. If they dug up Holdt's body, then they needed two vehicles: the backhoe, and another car or truck to put the body in to move it."

"So they had two vehicles," said Detective Dorian.

"That means that there were at least two of them," I said. "And at least one of them knew that we would be digging this up this morning."

The implication was obvious. Everyone looked at each other suspiciously. And so did I. I especially looked at the cops that I didn't know. I wondered whether one of them had given me the parking ticket.

I asked Detective Danny to come down to see me after they were done filling in the hole, and I walked back down my driveway with my empty coffee cup. On the one hand, I was disappointed that they didn't find anything this morning. But on the other hand, it meant that something incriminating had been moved, and that someone who was there this morning was in on it. And if it was Holdt's body that had been moved, then it took at least two people to move it.

I got myself another cup of coffee and called Dagwood while waiting for Danny to show up, since Dagwood had buried whatever it was that had been in the hole.

"Hello, this is Dagwood," he said, answering his phone.

"Dagwood," I responded, "this is Mickey Maux. I was over at your house the other day with the kryptonite detector."

"Yes," he said. "I remember you very well. What's up?"

"Someone came over to Dottie's house in the middle of the night, and dug up her new garden," I said. "I couldn't imagine who would do that, so I went over there with my detector, and sensed lots of kryptonite in the soil. Dottie told me that you had used a special kind of fertilizer that you got from California, and I'm guessing that it might have had kryptonite in it. If it came from California, chances are that it was imported from Mexico, and it might have been contaminated with kryptonite by one of the Mexican drug cartels."

There was a long pause, because this was a lot of bullshit to digest. "Really?" he replied.

"Yes," I said. "Do you have any more of that fertilizer that you got from California? Because if you do, you should probably dump it in the ocean."

"No I don't," he responded. "There was only the one batch that I had put into Dottie's garden. You said that someone dug it up?" he asked. "Who would do that?"

You would, I thought, although I didn't say so. "I can't imagine," I said. "Maybe they were jealous of her nice new garden, and just wanted to do something out of spite," I suggested.

"That sounds likely," Dagwood responded.

It does? Like hell. "But that seems like a lot of work for someone to do out of spite," I said. "Is it possible that anyone would think that you buried something in the hole besides the California fertilizer?"

"Bury something?" Dagwood asked. "Like what?"

"I've no idea," I said. "But the police think that whoever dug it up did it because they thought that something was in there."

"That's crazy," said Dagwood.

"Nonetheless," I responded, "I was going to come over again with my detector to see whether there are any residual traces of kryptonite in your garage from your handling of the Californian fertilizer."

"No, I don't think that you need to do that," he said, a little too quickly.

"Why?" I asked. "How do you know whether we got it all? I would have been satisfied until I found out about the contamination in the hole from whatever was in the Californian-Mexican fertilizer."

We both knew that "the fertilizer" was pure bullshit - which is always good fertilizer. But Dagwood was now in a position in which he couldn't tell me that there was no fertilizer, so he was trying to play along without making any mistakes. He was talking pure "fertilizer," a.k.a. bullshit.

"The fertilizer was in my car," he said. "I never took it out of my car until I brought it to Dottie's," he continued, "and I got rid of the car."

"You did?" I asked. "What happened to the car?"

"I left it out on the street with the keys in it, and it got stolen," he said, as if this was clever.

"Really?" I asked. "In Cos Cob? Stolen?"

"Yes," he said with a chuckle.

"Who would steal a beater like that in Cos Cob?" I thought, without saying so. "Is he really that stupid?" I wondered, again, without asking him.

"Wow," I said. "And I thought Cos Cob was safe. Nonetheless, I want to come over again with my detector and see whether it senses anything in your garage. This is dangerous stuff, and it's important to treat any areas that could have been exposed."

"Well I guess that it's important to be safe," he said, resignedly. "So you should probably come over and scan the area again."

It was clear that he wasn't looking forward to another visit. After all, he was probably very tired after being up all night digging a big hole.

My doorbell rang. Detective Danny was done supervising the filling in of the empty hole, and had come down to see me as I'd asked him to. I hoped that he hadn't gotten infected with any kryptonite.

"What's up?" asked Danny.

"I thought that you and I should go to Cos Cob, and pay a visit to Dagwood," I said. "I just got off the phone with him."

"And he agreed to see you?" Detective Danny asked, incredulously.

"Sure," I said. "Dagwood is very agreeable if you ask him the right way."

"I'll drive," he said, insistently.

"Actually, I'd prefer that," I said. "That way you can just turn your flashing lights on, and put the siren on, and people will get the hell out of the way. Most of them don't pay any attention to The Fingers or my foghorn. Maybe what I really need is a police car."

We walked down to Detective Danny's police car. "You'll have to sit in the back," he said.

"Really?" I asked. "And will I have to wear handcuffs? That will make me feel young again," and I got in the front, knowing that he'd been joking. I think.

We drove down to Cos Cob. Actually, driving in a police car isn't as good as I had imagined. The problem is that people see you coming in their rear-view mirrors, and they all slow down and do the speed limit. It pretty much made us do the speed limit as well. I think police cars would be better if they all had The Fingers on them. I'd think about how to propose this later.

We got to Dagwood's house, and went to the front door to ring the bell. I'd brought my Geiger counter with me, and had turned it on. No one answered, so we rang the bell again, and no one answered again.

We walked around back to his six-car garage. The garage was open, and Dagwood was coming back from his boat. Obviously, he'd been in his garage, and then had gone out to his boat. And he'd known that I was coming, although I'm sure that seeing Detective Danny was a surprise. Had he moved something from his garage to his boat? That was my bet.

"Hi guys," Dagwood yelled, waving with exaggerated nonchalance.

"Hi Dagwood," I yelled back emphatically while waving insouciantly in an attempt to mimic his poor acting. "I've brought my friend Danny with me, and my kryptonite detector. Is it OK if we look in your garage?"

I could see him hesitate, trying to figure out whether he would be waiving his Fifth-Amendment rights by merely saying "OK."

So he was very careful to ask, "*exactly* what are you looking for again?" as if he was merely being conversational, while stepping up his pace to reach us.

"Bullshit, and we've found it," I was tempted to say, but didn't. Instead I said, "Any traces of kryptonite."

Dagwood had reached us. "OK, let's see if there are any traces of kryptonite," he said, motioning us toward his garage.

When we went into the garage, I started modulating the Geiger counter so that it would beat fast, then slow, then fast, then slow, then fast again.

"That's strange," I said. "I've never seen it do this before."

"What's it mean?" asked Dagwood.

"What it would normally mean is that kryptonite had just been here *very recently*, and then it disappeared," I said, as if mystified. "That's very strange," I said, letting my gaze pointedly settle on his boat, which was floating out in his marina.

I could see the gears turning in his head as I continued to modulate the Geiger counter. "I wonder how that could have happened," I said pointedly, while continuing to stare at his boat. Dagwood looked very uncomfortable. I turned the Geiger counter off.

"By the way, have you met Detective Danny?" I asked.

Dagwood looked both suddenly started, and alarmed. Why had I introduced Detective Danny all of a sudden? Was Detective Danny there to arrest him?

"Detective Danny," I said, "I'd like you to meet Dagwood. He's Dottie's cousin. He's the one who's car was stolen."

They shook hands, Dagwood still looking uncertain.

"Well I'm not sure what to make of the reading," I said. "We know that kryptonite was in the garage when the car was here, but the car is gone now. Maybe the meter is just confused."

"That's probably what happened," Dagwood said. As if he would know. A kryptonite meter? More like a bullshit meter.

"What were you doing out on your boat?" I asked. "Were you lashing the jib boom to the mizzen mast?"

He didn't charge at me, swinging his fists. It was clear that this wasn't Newport, Rhode Island. He simply looked confused. "It's a motor boat," he said. "I was just stowing a few things."

"Do you think I should take the meter out on your boat and measure the radiation?" I asked.

"No, you don't need to do that," he said. "These were supplies that I got from the house," he said. "They weren't from the garage."

"Then why was your garage open?" I asked.

"I was just airing it out," Dagwood claimed.

"Dagwood," I said, "we have a warrant to search your boat." I fumbled in my pockets, and pulled out a sheet of paper with lots of printing on it. I had come prepared. "That's why I had this warrant prepared, and it's why I brought a police officer. We suspect that an illegal item was taken out of Dottie's garden last night, and that it was taken by you. Because your garage is already contaminated, I knew that you'd put it on your boat, where you could take it out into the sound and get rid of it if you had to."

I wanted to say "Book'em Danno," but instead, I said "Detective Danny, would you please check his boat? You know what we're looking for."

Luckily, Detective Danny didn't say "We do?," and Dagwood didn't ask to see the search warrant. And technically, it wasn't actually a warrant; it was a warranty. It said that if I had any trouble with the dishwasher that we'd bought last year, that the parts and labor would be covered.

We all went onto Dagwood's boat. Down in the cabin, the bilge was open, and there was a package that was sealed in plastic that was sticking out of it. The package was covered with dirt, like it had been dug up out of a deep hole. The package didn't quite fit all the way into the bilge, and it needed more manipulation, so Dagwood had not yet been able to cover it.

We must have shown up while he was trying to get it to fit, and he had had to come out to greet us. It probably never occurred to him that we'd have a warrant to search his boat. It hadn't occurred to me either.

I pulled the package out of the bilge, and this time I got to say: "Book'em Danno."

Detective Danny placed Dagwood under arrest, put handcuffs on him, and put him in the back seat of his cruiser. I wondered whether it made Dagwood feel young again.

We put the package in the trunk, and took Dagwood out of Cos Cob. We drove home, and put Dagwood in a holding cell downtown. Once the lab told us what was in the package, we would have some questions for Dagwood.

Of course, Detective Danny read him his Miranda Rights. And Since Miranda is a Spanish name, he read it to him in Spanish. *Bueno, si?*[7]

In the afternoon, I went to the High School to talk to Pete Fletcher's class about Carroll's Tweedle problem some more. I'm always enthusiastic about getting young minds to think and to develop.

I went through the usual nonsense to get into the High School.

I parked in the large lot in front of the visitor's entrance, and went in. I entered the main office, where the staff ignored me, so I did a loud "Ahem!" They looked at me like I was dirt, and they asked me to sign in. I told them that I was visiting Mr. Fletcher's class, and they pointed me in the right general direction.

I took an Ell, went up a couple of flights of stairs, and found Pete's science classroom. It was good to see Pete and his students again.

Last time, we'd been talking about a town that had two roads leaving it, with one going to the city, and the other to the beach. And we had the Tweedle brothers: Dee and Dumb - one always lies, and the other always tells the truth.

Pete reminded the students that last time I had suggested the more difficult case in which there were more than two roads leaving town.

---

7   Spanish for "That's good, isn't it?"

"Actually, having more than two roads doesn't make the problem that much more difficult," I told the students. "The really interesting cases are when there are less than two roads."

"What do you mean by less than two roads?" a student asked. "How can there be less than two roads? That doesn't make any sense."

"That's a great question," I said. "There are three ways to have less than two roads."

"How can there be three ways?" the student asked. "You said that there are less than two roads. The only way to have less than two roads is if there is exactly one road. But then there's really no question to ask." This was a bright student, and it was an opportunity for me to broaden him.

"Ah," I said, "I was hoping that someone would ask that. This is a great way for me to introduce another branch of mathematics called 'topology.'"

"What's topology?" the student asked.

"It's the stuff of geometric forms that remain invariant under certain sets of transformations," I said, "like bending and stretching - the way a road might run. There are actually two ways to have one road."

"There are?" he asked.

"Yes. There can be two distinctive roads - roads that go to different places, like one to the city, and one to the beach."

"Yes. That's the case that we've already solved," Pete reminded the class.

"But what if the two roads are the same road?" I asked the students.

"How can we have two roads that are the same?" the original student asked.

"Suppose that it's actually one road. Say it leaves town in one place, circles around, and then it comes back into town in another place. And it doesn't go anywhere else. Is that two roads?" I asked. "And especially, what if it crosses itself in one or more places before it comes back into town? Does that change the problem at all?"

The students thought about it.

"No, I guess it's only one road," one of the other students said. "But if you're in town, it looks like it's two roads."

"Exactly," I said, "That's topology. So now, how would you tell which Tweedle was Dee and which was Dumb?" I asked.

The class sat there in silence. They looked puzzled. Finally, one of them said: "We've no idea."

I gave them a hint. "Note that in this case, we don't really care about where the road - or roads - go, because we already know that the road - or roads - leave and then re-enter the town we're in. They both go here: both leave town, and both return to town. We know this. But what we don't know is which of the Tweedles is lying."

They thought about it some more. Then the bright student who had first asked about a single road finally saw the trick, and explained the answer to the rest of the class: "If the road leaves town and comes back another way, you could simply ask whether the road leaving comes back. Dumb would say no, and Dee would say yes."

"Exactly. It's actually very simple. The reason that no one saw it immediately was because you were all thinking too hard. That can happen a lot in mathematics. But that's the easiest of the three cases that I had wanted to talk about. Remember that I had said that there are three cases in which we have less than two roads leaving town? That was the first case."

I let them consider that for a minute before I continued. "Now let's consider the second case. Let's suppose that there is exactly one road that leaves town, and let's assume that it doesn't come back. And now you get to ask one of the Tweedles whether the road goes to the city."

The class thought for a long while. Finally, Pete said: "Hmmm . . . , I think we're stumped."

"Yes. This one is harder because it's completely subjective. What do we mean by the city? And when we ask if the road goes there - to the city, do we mean directly, or eventually? In this case, our questions are ambiguous, and Dee and Dumb could give any answers, because none of the answers are binary - none are really true or false. This situation leaves the realm of math, and ventures into a new domain; it's the domain of . . . 'politics,'" I explained.

The students looked mystified and amazed. They had thought that "politics" was easy. They had thought that politicians spoke in absolutes; in "truths." They thought about it for a while.

Finally, Pete spoke up. "OK, so those are the two cases in which there is one road leaving town. What's the third case?"

"This is the most interesting," I said. "The third case is when zero roads leave town."

The class looked baffled. Zero roads? What did that mean? It made no sense. They thought about it for a while, and I let them.

"What about the case when there are zero roads?" Pete asked. "Then how would you ask them whether it - the road that doesn't exist - went to the city?"

So I explained the final case. "This is a much more complex problem. We've talked about topology, and we've ventured into the domain of politics. We are now out of the realms of both mathematics and politics, and into a new domain. This new domain is called 'metaphysics.'"

"What's metaphysics?" one of the students finally asked.

"Well," I explained, "instead of a liar and a truth teller, let's assume that one is a solipsist, and the other a nihilist. We'll ask them whether a road that doesn't exist goes to the city."

They looked puzzled.

Finally, Pete asked, "And what would they say?"

I stared at them pondering the question for a good minute. And then I pondered it for another good minute. Finally, I concluded: "Exactly!"

And then I wanted to whet their appetites. "But having done this final case leads us to 'Adler's Problem.'"

"What's 'Adler's Problem?'" asked Pete.

"I'll save that for another time," I said. "It's always such a pleasure coming to talk to this smart class. I enjoyed seeing you all, but I have to go."

I left them to ponder the next pinnacle: Adler's Problem.

When I got home, Detective Danny called me. Now we had Dagwood, we had his car, and we had a large plastic-wrapped package that had been dug out of the hole at Dottie's. The lab was going through his car, and they had opened the package by mistake.

Apparently, the package had accidentally ripped open when they accidentally carried it past a sharp object that had been accidentally wedged into a doorway at the police station. Whoever put that object there and had wedged it in the doorway, and shouldn't have. They must have put the sharp object there accidentally, although it did spare them the trouble of getting a warrant.

The package contained lots of hard drugs. The car contained a small amount of dried blood, and almost nothing else; not even kryptonite. Dagwood must have cleaned it out nicely. While I already had Holdt's gym bag, the surprising thing was that the cops couldn't find lots of blood in the car. I would have thought that there would be more.

Was the hitter really that good? And even if he was, just moving a guy the size of Holdt in and out of the car would have made a mess.

The package of drugs was a lot smaller than Holdt, and Dagwood hadn't needed any help moving it. The question was why he had buried it, but the answer was fairly obvious: to hide it for a while.

He'd obviously stolen it, and wanted it to "disappear" until its rightful owner - Senator Adler, probably - decided that Dagwood didn't have it. That's exactly why he didn't want it at his house or on his boat. Adler's thugs would easily find it there if they showed up and searched his property. Especially if they'd beaten him up some. They wouldn't need a warrant. They wouldn't even need a warranty.

The only reason that he had dug it up last night was because he knew that the police were going to dig it up this morning. So he had to move it. It was small enough to move it himself, but he did need one of Stu's backhoes to dig it up. And as I'd learned this morning, getting one of Stu's backhoes in the middle of the night was easy. Stu's smart. He keeps the keys in them.

There were still a number of questions remaining, and I was sure that Dagwood would be volunteering lots of that information soon. A basic and immediate question was: Who told Dagwood that the police would be digging up Dottie's garden this morning? I had my bets, but this was a detail; it would implicate at least one of the cops.

But there were even bigger questions, and I wondered how many of those Dagwood could help us with. Why was Holdt in Dagwood's car in the first place? Who killed him? What had they done with his body? And how did they get the car out of there? Who killed Mitch Goldberg, and why? And why was Mitch Goldberg's car in the same place that Dagwood's car had been in?

And then of course, who was the cop that had given me a parking ticket? I didn't think that Dagwood could help me with that one.

"Do you want the gym bag?" I asked Detective Danny. "So that you can try to match the blood spots to whatever DNA you guys can find on Holdt's gym equipment?"

"No, we don't need it," Detective Danny said. "The DNA in the blood spots match Dagwood's. That's hardly surprising, since it was his car. But what do you think they did with Holdt's body?"

"Actually, I have a pretty good idea," I said. "I'll bet I can find it. But it would help if I could talk to Dagwood after I do."

I hung up the phone, and then I called Mitchell Goldberg in Hoboken, and got him in.

"Mitchell," I said, "This is Mickey Maux again. I've put a lot of work in on this case, and I know who killed your uncle."

"You do?" he asked. "Who did it? And why?"

"The 'why' is more complicated than I want to try to explain over the phone," I said. "And the 'who' is someone that you don't know, but it involved a double-cross against someone that you do know."

"But I don't know anyone up there but my uncle," he said.

"I'll come down to Hoboken tonight, and take you out to dinner," I offered. "It will be a long discussion, so dinner is appropriate, because it allows both pacing and digestion," I said, figuratively.

"I do have a night off," he said, "and I had intended to go out to dinner with my partner, since I seldom get nights off."

"I'll tell you what," I said. "You bring him, and I'll bring my wife. She's been helping me with this case, and we can make it a foursome. And if you're serious with him, your partner should hear some of these details."

We agreed to meet in Hoboken at the Trattoria Saporito on 4th Street and Washington, because the food's very good, and there's a big parking garage right around the corner.

When Carol got home, I told her that we were going down to New Jersey for dinner so that we could meet Mitchell Goldberg in person. While I had already met him, I explained that he would be bringing his partner who I thought should hear the story, and I thought it would be better if we made it a foursome. Carol is always good at picking up pieces of information that I miss, and I thought it would be a good idea if she met them too.

So we drove down through the city, and we took the West Side Drive down to the Lincoln Tunnel. Carol drove because she doesn't like the way that I drive. And she doesn't use her horn, and isn't aggressive enough, so it took longer than it should have, but I was careful not to comment, although it's an easy drive.

Once you're through the Lincoln Tunnel, it's only a five-minute jaunt to Sinatra Drive which runs right to 4th Street, although there are a couple of twists and turns along the way. And I brought a special gift with me to give to Mitchell Goldberg's partner.

On the drive down, I took Carol through my guesses as to who did the shootings and why, and explained why Mitchell was part of this, whether he wanted to be or not.

I was nearly certain that Dagwood had whacked Mitchell Goldberg's uncle Mitch, and he did it to steal the drugs that were sent here by Senator Adler. Inconspicuous as they come, Mitchell's uncle Mitch was in charge of distributing the drugs that Adler had delivered by some of his professional muscle. That muscle was Holdt, who I saw in Dagwood's car sitting there looking plenty dead too. But Holdt's body was never found. Now I was pretty sure where his body was.

The one thing that I didn't yet know was how Dagwood was able to tie into Senator Adler's organization.

We parked in a big garage on Hudson Street, walked up 3rd Street over to Washington, and crossed to go into Trattoria Saporito. Mitchell and his partner were already seated at a nicely laden four-top table by the window. Mitchell recognized me when we walked in. Carol and I walked over, and I shook hands with Mitchell, introduced Carol, and then shook hands with Mitchell's partner who looked much livelier than I had last remembered.

"I'm Mickey Maux," I said. "And I brought you your gym bag. You left it in the back of Dagwood's car when you took the train down here, and I thought you'd want it." I handed the gym bag to Mitchell Goldberg's partner, Jack Holdt, who looked quite surprised, but very glad to have his gym bag back.

"How did you know that it was my gym bag?" Jack asked. "And how do you know who I am?"

"Let's order some drinks first," I said. "We need to go through the events that I'm going to lay out slowly, and I'll need your help to fill in some details. It's easier to do when we're all relaxed."

I motioned to the waiter, we all ordered a round of drinks, and I helped Carol with her coat. I asked for an Italian chianti, just to keep things earthy. One of the great things about this place besides the food is that the tables in the back usually have armed mob guys, who are all packing heat, and are there enjoying the food. That makes the place extremely safe, since no one who knows the place would think of pulling anything funny in here.

The waiter brought us our drinks with some bread, and he took us through the evening's specialties. Then we resumed our discussion.

"I knew who you were because I saw you before. But you had your eyes closed," I said, "so you probably didn't get a good look at me. You were sitting in Dagwood's yellow car by a garbage Dumpster behind the supermarket, and you were playing dead. You were wearing a fake bullet wound - the kind of thing that you can buy in actor's supply stores."

"How did you know the bullet wound was fake?" he asked.

"Because you were wearing a brand-new sports-jacket," I said. "It had just gone on sale at Macy's. I don't know where you got yours, but it isn't the kind of thing you'd buy in California. It's a fall jacket - more for when the weather gets cool as it just has here. I'm sure you wouldn't have doused yourself with real blood just after arriving here and buying a new jacket. Also, your gym bag was in the back seat. It didn't match your new sports-jacket. I figured you'd left the gym bag there by accident. Either that, or you thought it would clash with your sports-jacket on the train ride down here."

"You can't be serious," Jack said. "You thought that the blood was fake because of my jacket?"

"Not entirely," I clarified. "The police lab scrubbed the car, and the only blood they found was the owner's," I said. "That's not unusual. Most people have traces of their own blood in their car. The owner of the car is a guy named Dagwood, who had been driving with you. If you'd actually been shot and had really bled, there's no way anyone could have gotten you out of that car without leaving blood stains all over the place. So I knew that the first shooting was a scam."

"The first shooting?" Jack asked. "Was there a second shooting?"

"Yes," I said. "The second shooting was real, and we all know about it. The victim was Mitch Goldberg, Mitchell's uncle."

"And who shot my uncle?" Mitchell asked.

"We'll get there," I said. "Jack was driving Dagwood's car, and Dagwood was in the passenger's seat."

"How did you know that?" asked Jack.

"Because the car had been hit by a Shit-Ninny. It was probably your Californian driving that caused that. What did you do?" I asked. "Did you break for a pedestrian or something like that?"

The waiter came by again, reminded us of the evening's specialties, and took our orders. I have a weakness for pasta al nero di seppia when it's offered, which it was, although I only get pasta as a first course. The nero di seppia is made with squid ink, which makes the noodles black, and it gives them a subtle flavoring that couples very nicely with simple sauces based on butter reductions. For a second course, I followed the pasta nero with braised sea bass in a black olive-based sauce, with some pesto on the side. Once again, it would be a black plating, which seemed appropriate for our main discussion, which would be about murder.

"As I was saying," I continued, "you were driving the car because Dagwood was holding the package of drugs. He had just gotten out of the car with the package to hide behind the garbage Dumpster when I came around the corner. The plan was for him to have the drugs nearby in case whoever the Connecticut dealer was - Mitch Goldberg in this case - tried to rob the delivery man - you in this case - and not pay. Jack here was sitting in the car without the drugs, so he couldn't be robbed. And Dagwood was hiding behind the Dumpster with the drugs that he'd produce after payment had been made. That's when I happened to arrive."

I let everyone ponder that while I tried to read the expression on Jack's face to see whether I was guessing correctly. I took a sip of my chianti, which was bracing, and I enjoyed the silence.

"You were anticipating the arrival of the Connecticut dealer - Mitch - when I showed up. You had your directional on for no particular reason - probably a California thing; after all, you had pulled over to the left, so why not use the directional? And you had your door open just because it was a nice autumn day, and you wanted to let some cool air in while you were sitting there. It was Dagwood who had warned you about me - probably after you got hit by the Shit-Ninny. I'm the one who made the Shit-Ninnies."

I paused to take another sip of my chianti, and I took a piece of bread with olive oil together with a tapenade that had come with the bread. The waiter also put down some amuse bouche for the table: some small polenta cakes with forest mushrooms. And then I continued.

"Dagwood recognized my car right away, because the roof has four Big Fingers on it. It didn't occur to me that my car was easy to identify until the police pointed it out, because people in the neighborhood behind the stores had also apparently recognized my car when I left the scene."

"Dagwood shouted to you to play dead, so you did. You're a pro. You likely had a fake bullet-wound sticker that you can get in most hobby shops, and all you did was to stick it on and sit still. Why did you play dead? It's because when people see a nicely dressed guy hanging around in a fancy yellow car behind a garbage Dumpster seemingly enjoying himself, it looks suspicious, and they might call the cops. But if it's a dead guy, they'll put the blinders on, and keep moving. I did a little of each. While I didn't really investigate, I did stop and take look. At a glance, you looked dead, but I didn't touch anything or examine the crime scene. And then I called the cops because I'm a dork."

The waiter brought our first course, and we paused to savor it somewhat. It would be truly criminal to make the dinner all business. This gave people time to replay my narrative as we ate. Jack didn't tell me that I was wrong about anything yet.

"So why do you think I left the scene?" Jack asked, as we were finishing our first course.

"You left the scene because I had stopped to investigate, and your best guess was that the cops were on the way. If the cops showed up and no one was there, they'd assume that it was a bogus call, and they wouldn't bother to look around. This made it safe for Dagwood to stay behind the Dumpster with the package of drugs. Without you there, there was nothing for anyone to see; no yellow car, no people, nothing but a garbage Dumpster - as it should be. If you'd been sitting there and the cops came, they would have asked you lots of questions. So you left the drug deal completely up to Dagwood."

Some servers came and cleared our plates from the table, swept off the breadcrumbs, and refilled our water. Having finished my chianti which I had chosen for its assertiveness to have with the more subtle pasta al nero di seppia, and feeling more confident in my version of what had likely happened the day of the murder, I ordered a viognier to go with my sea bass. I realized that this sounded a bit cavalier, but thought that a viognier would provide a surprisingly fruity contrast with the olives; I hoped that no one would notice if this seemed reckless of me.

"So I left, and so did you," I said to Jack. "This left Dagwood at the scene with the package of drugs, still hiding behind the garbage Dumpsters. That's when Mitchell's uncle showed up to get the package."

"Mitch knew that the exchange was to be at the Dumpsters behind the store, so he parked in about the same place that Jack had parked. He originally thought that he was early since no one was there, and then Dagwood emerged from behind the Dumpster holding the package of drugs, and he quickly got into the back seat of Mitch's car. There wouldn't have been enough room for both him and the package had he tried to get into the front seat, so he got in the back. And he got in on the passenger's side because he's probably right-handed, and he used his right hand to open the door."

"How do you know that he wasn't left-handed?" asked Mitchell, "or even ambidextrous?"

"I don't," I said. "Most people are right handed, so it's a guess. And very few people are ambidextrous, but I've often wished I was. In fact, I'd give my right arm to be ambidextrous."

They thought about that, and looked confused.

The waiter brought my viognier, and another glass of wine for Mitchell. I took a sip so that I could think about how it would go with sea bass and black olives. It's always helpful to imagine these things before the food actually arrives. I wasn't sure that it was quite right, but I thought that it would - at least - be interesting, and that I'd enjoy both.

"Because Dagwood had gotten into the back of the car, Mitch would have to get in the back too, to examine the package and to give Dagwood the money. So Mitch put his left directional on to make it obvious that he was parked there deliberately. Then he got out of the front driver's seat while leaving the driver's door open, since he wasn't going to be there for long, and he got into the back seat on the driver's side to look at the bundle and to pay Dagwood."

I paused to take another sip of wine, and to let this scenario seep in. Before, I had been describing what I thought had happened when Jack was there, so he could have refuted anything that I had said. But now I was describing what I supposed had happened after Jack and I had both left the scene. So it was all supposition, although I did my best to pretend that I was stating facts.

"Had Jack still been there, this would have been a simple trade; a business deal. But Dagwood is a greedy amateur with a big house and a big boat, and he thought that this was a big opportunity for him to make some more money by double-crossing everyone."

"After all, Senator Adler didn't know anything about Dagwood, and Jack didn't know very much. And Jack was supposedly going right back to California, so he probably didn't know anything about Mitch Goldberg either, so the name wouldn't register with him even if a murder were reported on the news. But Dagwood didn't know anything about Mitch's nephew Mitchell over here, and he didn't know that Jack wasn't going back to California, but instead would be moving to New Jersey with Mitchell. Dagwood didn't know of any connection between Jack and Mitch, but there was a very big one: Mitchell here," I said, gesturing toward Mitchell.

I took another pause, and had another taste of my wine, to reconsider how it would likely go with the sea bass. I started to think that maybe the viognier had been a mistake, but I was feeling daring tonight. I get that way when the wheels in my head turn.

"So Dagwood shot Mitch Goldberg for real, and then he stole the bundle of drugs. He shot Mitch in the right temple, and left him in the back seat with the driver's door open and the left directional on. Mitch slumped over into the seat, so you couldn't see him in the car unless you walked up to it and looked inside. Dagwood got out and simply ran the bundle over to Stu's Garden Center - about fifty yards away, where he put it under some bails of peat moss. If Stu saw him there moving the peat moss around, it would be no big deal. In fact, Dagwood was intending to go to Stu's Garden Center anyway so that Stu could give him a ride to the train station to pick up his car, which Jack was going to leave there."

"So when the police - Detective Dorian in this case - got to the crime scene, he found Mitch shot in the right temple, lying in the back seat of his car. The driver's door was open, the engine was running, and the left directional was on. And the car was missing its license plates because someone else just so happened to steal them from his car that same day. The theft of his plates was just a coincidence, and the police found his plates on a stolen car later. That had nothing to do with this drug transaction and murder."

"Speaking of license plates, Jack had taken the plates off of Dagwood's car and had left them in his trunk, just so that standers-by wouldn't have plates to ID the car with. Jack had borrowed a screwdriver at the gym to do this with. And Jack put the plates back on the car when he got to the train station. He knew that later that afternoon, Dagwood would simply go to the train station to get his car. And Stu drove Dagwood there to get it. Stu doesn't think very hard about what Dagwood asks him to do or why. Stu mostly does whatever Dagwood wants because Dagwood always picks up the bar tab whenever they go out to socialize."

The servers brought our main dishes out and served them. I tasted the pesto first just to imagine it with the viognier, and then I tasted the viognier. It hadn't been a mistake after all. This renewed my confidence in the narrative, and allowed me to relax a little more.

We dined and made some small talk so that we could enjoy our food without the undercurrent of tensions that I had brought to the table with the details of the crime. As we were finishing our dinners and folding down our silverware, I concluded my story.

"Dagwood assumed that Jack was taking the train to the city and would go to one of the airports. Instead, Jack took the PATH to Hoboken. But he forgot his gym bag in Dagwood's car. And Dagwood wanted to paint his car because his car had been seen by me, and possibly by others at what became the scene of the crime. And Dagwood wanted to hide the drugs for a while, just in case Senator Adler sent Jack back to look for him. But neither Adler nor Dagwood knew that Jack wasn't going back to California. So Jack has more-or-less dropped off of Senator Adler's radar screen. And most of the world thinks that Jack has disappeared. It's fine with me if we leave it that way."

"But because Dagwood wanted to hide the drugs, he buried them at his cousin's house. This way, if anyone - like Jack - showed up and searched Dagwood's property, they wouldn't find the drugs. So hiding the drugs at his cousin Dottie's house was perfect. No one would think to look for a package of drugs under a flower garden at his cousin Dottie's house. In fact, no one would likely connect Dagwood to Dottie at all, since they didn't have much to do with each other. So Dagwood made a false pretense of wanting to use Dottie's garage to paint his car, for which he would put in a flower garden, supposedly to thank her. He told her that he had to paint the car because he'd been hit by a Shit-Ninny, but in fact he thought it was important to change the color just in case people were looking for a yellow car."

The servers cleared our plates, re-cleaned the table, and we ordered espresso. I also asked for cannoli to share with Carol. I could see the two fitness guys - Jack and Mitchell - hide their grimaces. Before the cannoli arrived, I wrapped up my summary - at least the summary that I had been able to piece together so far.

"What Dagwood didn't know was that I live right across the street from Dottie, and I saw these mysterious comings and goings. After a while, it all fell into place, and it made sense."

I waited a few moments, and then I posed my question.

"The strange thing that I noticed is that the central character in all of these pieces of my story is Dagwood. Who is Dagwood? Where did he come from? Is he Senator Adler's main contact out here? I had thought that his main contact was Mitch Goldberg. If it's Dagwood, then why is it Dagwood that's doing all of the running around and all of the execution? The main contact doesn't usually do all the footwork. And why is it that he's driving around with Jack in order to meet with Mitch Goldberg? And why is it he that's double-crossing the senator? In other words, how does Dagwood connect to all of this? I don't understand his role, or who inserted him into this mess. Where did Dagwood come from, and who pulled him into this?"

Everyone looked confused, including Jack. "After all, Dagwood is a local Connecticut guy. If it's Mitch Goldberg that will be delivering the drugs to Jack - who came out here from California, how did Dagwood become a part of this, with no apparent connection to Mitch Goldberg?"

The waiter brought our espressos and left a bottle of anisette. He also brought my cannoli, and left some extra forks, which earned him disdainful glances from the two fitness guys.

Finally Jack said, "Dagwood was involved because I was told by Adler's main contact out here that Dagwood would accompany me and show me around."

"Main contact?" I asked. "Who is that?"

"The senator told me that his main contact out here is a guy that he trusted who would make sure that nothing went wrong. That guy met me at the station when I came up on the train. He brought Dagwood with him, and said that Dagwood would show me around, and would let me use his car. The two of them came to meet me at the station in Dagwood's car."

"What is his name?" I asked.

"He didn't tell me, but the senator said that he's actually tied to the cops, and that he'd make sure that the cops stayed out of it."

"What did he look like?" I asked.

"He was short like everyone else, although taller than you guys, but he was skinny," Jack explained. "I don't mean skinny in the sense that he's not built like me. I just mean that he just looked like an empty suit. Mitchell here isn't built like me either, but you can see his athletic lines, and you can see his strength when he moves. This guy didn't have that, although he took a lot of effort to move with precision, as if he was fit - almost pretending to be military. That struck me as strange. Most people who don't bother with fitness don't take the trouble to move like they're got a stick up their ass. This guy did that - as if it added some authority to some kind of imaginary stature that he held."

Jack thought some more. Then he added, "And he was dressed in a weird way. I was surprised that the Senator knew him."

"What do you mean by that? Dressed how?" I asked.

"He was wearing an expensive looking pinstriped suit," Jack continued, "but he had it accessorized all wrong. And he was wearing it with the wrong kind of shoes. It was like he was trying to dress like a gangster in a movie, but he didn't understand how to add all the odds and ends."

Carol laughed. "Odds and ends?" she asked. "Is that how men dress?"

"I meant accessories," Jack said. "Like his tie and his handkerchief matched exactly, and his socks were some strange color - not what you'd wear with pinstripes. He looked like a phony."

"I think I've got an idea who this is," I said. "Did he have a scar under his jawline?" I asked.

"I don't know," Jack said. "He's short like you guys, so I didn't see his jawline."

We finished our espressos, thanked each other for a nice evening, and I told them that I'd let them know whatever I found. I told Jack not to forget his gym bag, and he thanked me for bringing it down.

Carol and I left Trattoria Saporito, and walked back to the garage. It was a lovely evening.

Carol drove us home, again taking longer than she should have. I was patient, and did my best not to importune that she used her horn just a little bit.

On the drive home, Carol and I went through the entire story again, and she asked me who I thought the contact was that Jack had told us about. I told her that it fit the description of Detective Dorian, who I had never trusted.

We decided that tomorrow I would run through the whole thing with Danny, and that we'd figure out whether Detective Dorian was the connection. It also helped that Detective Danny had arrested Dagwood. I was sure that Dagwood would be willing to help us if I explained his situation to him clearly enough.

The trick here was that if Detective Dorian was our man, he was tied to Senator Adler, who was certain to want him eliminated. This would put Detective Dorian in a tough position. I'm sure that as a cop, he wouldn't want to go to jail either, although that would likely be the best way to protect himself from Adler.

"You seemed to have pieced together the entire thing," Carol said. "In fact, your piecing together of the facts was done almost too cleanly. I'm surprised that there aren't more loose ends. But there's one assertion that you made that you couldn't possibly have known."

"What's that?" I asked.

"At the beginning of your account, you said without hesitation that you knew that Jack had driven the car," Carol said. "How could you know that? Don't give me the nonsense about 'the Shit Ninny hitting their car because he drives like he's from California.' He might have bought that, but I don't."

"Ah, that piece," I said. "I used a special deductive technique that I often go to when I don't know the facts. It's an ancient technique, but few people know how to use it correctly."

"An ancient technique?" Carol asked. "What's that?"

"You might have noticed that I had tossed a coin on the drive down to Hoboken, when we were going through the tunnel," I said. "It came up heads, so I decided that Jack had been driving."

Carol looked surprised, and didn't say anything for a minute or two. "You tossed a coin?" she asked, incredulously. "How can you decide a fact by tossing a coin?"

"Well," I explained, "when you don't have anything else to go on, you should toss a coin. At least it gives you something."

"But you'll only be right half of the time," she stated.

"That's not true," I asserted. "I picked 'heads' because 'heads' has been right a little more than half the time. Otherwise I would have picked 'tails.'"

Carol shook her head, and didn't pursue this. And I didn't tell her to use the horn. It had been a lovely evening so far, and we both wanted to keep it that way.

When we got home, I noticed that Danny's car was parked behind Dottie's garage, and all of the lights were out. So I assumed that like Carol and me, Dottie and Danny had also had a lovely evening. I was looking forward to talking to him about the case in the morning, so it was nice to know that he was nearby.

Day 14

A Weapon is Found at Dagwood's

After having my coffee, I went for a run. I noticed that Danny's car was still parked behind Dottie's garage, and I wondered whether he was being paid overtime for that. I sent him a text to drop by before he left, and I took my run.

Again, no one followed me today.

I got home, took a shower, and poured another cup of coffee. The doorbell rang. It was Danny dropping by as I had asked, and he seemed eager to know what I had learned. I poured him a cup of coffee, and we sat at the island in the kitchen.

Carol came in and joined us so that we could go through our meeting with Mitchell and Jack together. I didn't bore him with my descriptions of the food since I didn't think he'd be that interested except for perhaps, the cannoli. While I'll admit that cannoli are inappropriate to have with the dinner that I'd eaten - kind of like having fortune cookies after a Chinese banquet, it was New Jersey. And in New Jersey, damn it, if you want cannoli, then have cannoli.

The big revelation last night was that we had found Jack Holdt. He was now living in Hoboken with Mitchell Goldberg, who was Mitch Goldberg's nephew. This resolved lots of the open-ended questions.

It seemed that Holdt had been professional muscle who had been working for Senator Adler, and had come to Connecticut to do a drug deal. Unknown to anyone including Senator Adler, Holdt was retiring; he was dropping completely out of site, and had moved to New Jersey to live with Mitchell Goldberg. He hadn't been murdered, and the police record hadn't made any note of him or his car, since I had been the only witness to both, and the police weren't sure that they believed me. No one had asked about Holdt except for Senator Adler. And the senator was from California, and couldn't talk directly to the police - it would look too suspicious, which it was.

So for all intents and purposes, Holdt had never had existed, still didn't exist, and no one was asking about him except for Adler. And Adler wouldn't persist because of who Adler was - a dirty senator, and because of why he wanted to know - a drug deal.

The police had the drugs. They had been recovered from Dagwood's boat after having been excavated from under a garden that Dagwood had put in across the street while painting his car a different color after being parked at the scene of a murder. And Jack Holdt had left the drugs with Dagwood, assuming that Dagwood was going to complete the transaction with Mitch Goldberg. Instead, Dagwood killed Mitch, and stole the drugs.

We certainly had Dagwood on stealing the drugs. But the murder allegation was currently supposition, and I couldn't prove it. Yet.

Detective Danny told me that Dagwood had posted bail, and was out. Since Dagwood had a lot of money, this hardly surprised me.

I suggested that we go pay Dagwood another visit, since he was now in quite a dilemma. Of course, I was sure that Dagwood would have been lawyered-up, and advised not to cooperate.

So our discussion would have to be an unofficial discussion in which we'd seek some agreement from Dagwood in exchange for things like his health. But instead of kryptonite, I thought that this time, Jack Holdt could join us. I thought that as a retired professional, Jack would be very good at convincing Dagwood to cooperate.

So I called Jack in Hoboken and got him in, and he agreed to take the PATH, and then the train from Grand Central Station over to Greenwich, where Detective Danny and I would pick him up at the train station.

This time I drove. We didn't want to show up at Dagwood's house in a police car, and thought that a standard civilian car would be more appropriate. True, I did have all of The Fingers, which I used quite a bit, and a loud foghorn which I used even more, but we made much better time than we had in the police car. Instead of slowing down when they saw the police car, people generally got the hell out of my way when I turned on the foghorn.

Once in a while, someone would give me the finger back; puny gestures compared to the four-foot The Finger that I'd given them.

We picked Jack up in Greenwich, where everyone drives like they own the road. We went through Greenwich and headed to Cos Cob. Once at a light, an irate man jumped out of his car and ran over to us, demanding that I get out of the car "to fight." I asked Jack to step out to see what the problem was, which he did, and the man quickly changed his mind for some reason.

I jumped on Interstate 95 and headed East while using my foghorn a lot, then cut off and went South to the Long Island Sound while using my foghorn a lot, took a left, used my foghorn, and we were at Dagwood's house in Cos Cob. I parked in front of Dagwood's house, and I had my car give Dagwood's house The Finger, which I left standing. I hoped that Dagwood would get the message.

We all got out, went to the front door, and rang the bell. I had Jack stand off to the side against the wall, where Dagwood wouldn't see him until he opened the door all the way. After ringing the bell again and again, Dagwood opened the storm door and gave us a look of disdain.

"My lawyer told me that I can't talk to you guys," he said.

"But we're not here on official business," I said. "This is a social call. We didn't come in a police car. We came in my car." I pointed to my car, which had the big four-foot Finger standing up and pointing at him.

"You see, I've learned a number of things about this case," I continued, "and I wanted to share those things with you. Depending on some of the details that I don't know, you could be in lots of trouble."

"But my lawyer told me not to talk to you," Dagwood repeated.

"Maybe I should have been clearer," I said. "The nature of that trouble that you're likely to be in has nothing to do with the law. It's a dimension that's orthogonal to whatever your lawyer wants to do in court. True, he could probably get 'He was Never Actually Convicted of Anything' inscribed on your tombstone. And how the tombstone got there would be illegal. But we're in another domain now. In this domain, talking to us can help you. Your lawyer can't."

"The only thing you've got me on is possession of drugs," Dagwood said. "And I didn't buy them from anyone, and I didn't sell them to anyone. All I did was to have them. My lawyer isn't even sure that this is a crime."

"Again, I'm not talking about crime in the legal sense of the word," I explained. "But the real crime was how you got them."

"How I got them?" Dagwood asked. "I found them. I was over at Stu's Garden Center, and took a walk behind the plaza up to where the supermarket is. And I saw this big bundle sitting there behind one of the Dumpsters. All I did was pick it up, and take it home."

Dagwood thought some more, and then embellished. "I didn't even know that it was drugs. I thought it was a large bag of rice that had been dropped outside the supermarket by mistake. All I did was to take this free bag of rice that was lying on the pavement. You mean there were actually drugs in there?" he asked smiling, like he was being clever.

Then he continued: "How would I have known that it was a package of drugs? I thought it was rice. I planted it in Dottie's garden because I saw an interesting article on the internet explaining how a big bag of rice makes excellent fertilizer to use with new flowerbeds."

"You should have been a lawyer," I said. "A crappy one, but a lawyer. The problem with your story is that I have a witness to the whole transaction - including the murder, that told me otherwise. He says you were the carrier and the murderer and the thief."

"And I have a fairy-godmother that says that you should talk to my lawyer," Dagwood replied.

"Perhaps you should invite your lawyer to join us," I suggested. "I've brought an old friend of mine with me. His name's Jack." I motioned to Jack to step out where Dagwood could see him.

"And after Jack's done with you, *your* name will be Jack-Shit," I explained. "Now if you think it would help some, Jack can break your legs for you while your lawyer advises you not to cooperate. But then we'd have to kill him, and he might charge you extra for that. I doubt that you could afford it."

I let that sink in for a minute. And I couldn't resist adding: "By the way, while we were driving over here, we heard on the radio that some terrorists hijacked a plane full of lawyers at Kennedy Airport. They're sitting on the runway now, and have threatened to release a lawyer every half-hour until their demands are met."

Dagwood looked confused; he wasn't sure whether I was serious.

"According to Jack," I continued, "you stole these drugs from him. He was merely carrying them. The drugs actually belong to a very important person in California. That person wants to know who stole them so that he can make an example out of that person. He thinks that it's important to make an example of that person so that other people who think about doing the same thing will reconsider. I don't think that your lawyer can do much to help you in this case."

It was obvious that Dagwood was shocked to see Jack Holdt. He had assumed that Jack went back to California, and therefore didn't know anything about what happened after he left the scene of the deal behind the supermarket. I could see it sinking in. Dagwood realized that he was in very serious trouble, and that it had nothing to do with lawyers.

Again, I suggested to Dagwood that he invite us all in so that we could sit down and have a frank discussion about what he knew, and what his options were.

We all sat down at the table in Dagwood's dining room so that we could lay out what we had, and see whether Dagwood could add anything. Dagwood already looked exhausted.

His dining room was very nicely furnished. There was a large oak dining table that seated eight people comfortably, with a six-foot tall china hutch against the wall between two windows on one side of the table, and a broad service cabinet against the wall on the other side of the table. The service cabinet had a mirrored top with about twenty bottles of liqueurs on it. In the corner was a small bar setup with a sink, a wine cabinet, and coffee service. A crystal chandelier hung above the dining table.

We sat at the table and I explained the facts to Dagwood.

"Jack drove your car to the drop point, and you took the drugs and hid behind a Dumpster with them. That's when I showed up. You stayed hidden and Jack played dead. I looked at the scene only briefly, and left. Then Jack took off, leaving you to complete the deal. You had both agreed that this was the best thing to do, just in case I called the cops, and the cops showed up. Jack couldn't be sitting there in a car that matched the description of the car that I'd given them - your car, by the way. Jack made the mistake of trusting you to complete the transaction. After all, the deal was simple: exchange the package for some cash. Jack didn't need to be there for this to happen. And as far as you knew, when Jack left the scene, he'd be gone for good."

I paused for a minute to allow everyone to digest this. I noticed that Jack was gave the occasional furtive glance toward the top of the tall china cabinet as if something was bothering him. I thought about Jack's puzzled glances, wasn't certain what they meant, and so I continued.

"But then Mitch Goldberg showed up with the cash, and you didn't complete the transaction as Jack had explained it to you. You thought that Jack was out of the picture, and that it would be easy to simply take money and then steal the drugs. So you took the money and killed Mitch Goldberg. Then you hid the drugs by burying them in the new garden that you had your friend Stu dig for you. This way, if anyone came to investigate you, there'd be no trace of the stolen drugs. You could simply dig them up at Dottie's and sell them later, after you were sure that no one was still looking for them."

"That's not exactly what happened," said Dagwood. "Yes, I admit that I got myself attached to this drug deal. But this deal was a first for me, and everything went wrong."

"Why would you get yourself attached to it?" I asked. "And how?"

"I know the main operator here in Connecticut," Dagwood explained. "He's tied to the senator back in California. Mitch Goldberg actually worked for him. Mitch was not the head of the operation; he merely did the legwork. But Mitch was getting old and careless. For example, the main guy learned that Mitch actually kept a small notebook full of names written in pen and pencil that used a very crude encoding that any High School kid could break. Maybe that's how it was done twenty years ago, but you can't do that today. The main guy was worried that Mitch would eventually screw up, ruin the operation, and get him busted. So he wanted someone younger than Mitch to do most of the ground work for him. I thought that I could do that. So he put me on this deal, and had me shadow Jack just to see how a pro works."

"And who is the main guy according to you?" I asked. I again noticed Jack staring at the top of the large china cabinet.

"I can't tell you," Dagwood said. "He'd kill me."

"But I thought you had a lawyer," I said. "Wouldn't your lawyer tell him that he wasn't allowed to kill you?"

I could see the lines of irony on his face. And I wondered what the hell Jack was staring at.

"At a minimum, you're going up for homicide," I explained. "And that's if you're lucky, because you might actually be safe in jail. The senator will be told that you're the one that robbed him, and he'll want to make an example of you. I think that jail would be a much better deal. In jail, people might beat the crap out of you once in a while, but they're probably not going to kill you unless you whine too much."

"But I didn't murder anyone," Dagwood whined with exasperation. "All I did was ride with Jack as a carrier, and the deal went bad. But I'm not the guy that killed Mitch Goldberg."

"Then how did Mitch Goldberg wind up dead?" I asked. "Jack had left the scene. Was it a suicide? You know, a case where the guy sitting in the back of a car shoots himself, but runs and hides the gun before the bullet reaches him, and then gets back in the car just in time . . . ?"

"No. Another guy came to help me after Jack took off," Dagwood whined again. "It's the guy I was telling you about: the main guy."

"Do you mean the main guy who doesn't exist? The one that you won't identify? That main guy?" I asked. "And Jack, isn't his whining starting to affect you the way it always does? Makes you homicidal the way the reports I've read say it does?"

"Yes, exactly," Dagwood and Jack both said with exasperation.

"Jack, are you looking at something?" I finally asked, still noticing his glances at the china cabinet.

"No, nothing," he said.

So I continued with Dagwood. "But Dagwood, that guy doesn't exist," I explained. "So I wouldn't try that story with a jury. It's not believable. I think you'd be better off with the story about how Mitch shot himself, but ran and hid the gun before the bullet reached him, and then got back in place just in time . . ."

Dagwood saw the futility of his position, and realized that he needed to cooperate, become a witness, incriminate himself, and so on. His life depended on it.

"The main guy that Senator Adler is connecting with is a guy named Detective Dorian," Dagwood exclaimed. "You met him out in front of your house when he came to pick me up at Dottie's. As you know, he's actually a police detective, so it gives him even better cover than Mitch had. He and I go back a-ways. I always thought he was very shrewd. I really don't want to turn evidence on him."

"You don't have to," I explained. "If you're the one that shot Mitch Goldberg, you can tell us, and it leaves Detective Dorian out of the equation. But then you'll go up for murder. If Detective Dorian's the one that shot him and you're willing to testify to that, it's flipping a coin. The jury might not believe you, since Detective Dorian's a cop. But if you flip a coin, choose 'heads.' It comes up a little more often than tails," I explained.

The last piece of advice confused him. He'd have to talk to Carol. I explained it to her on our drive home last night.

"No, that's exactly what happened," said Dagwood. "When Jack took off, I called Detective Dorian, and told him that the deal was going bad. I guess I panicked. Detective Dorian told me to stay behind the Dumpster and wait for Mitch to show up, and then do the deal with Mitch. So I did."

Dagwood paused for a minute to collect his recollections and to order them so that they made sense.

"When I was in the back seat of Mitch Goldberg's car trading the drugs for cash, Detective Dorian showed up in his police car with the lights flashing. He timed it nearly perfectly. My guess is that he followed Mitch over from the main mall, since he knew all the mechanics of the trade."

"He let Mitch drive behind the supermarket, where I was, he gave it a minute or two, and then he pulled up behind Mitch's car with his lights flashing. Mitch and I both froze. At first, I wasn't sure that it was Detective Dorian, so I thought we were busted. But then Detective Dorian got out of his car with his gun drawn, walked up to Mitch's car, came over to my side. He told me to get out, and he told Mitch to not move. I got out, and Detective Dorian reached into the car, took the bundle of drugs, and handed it to me. Then he reached back into the car and shot Mitch Goldberg." Dagwood looked frazzled, and stopped for a minute.

"Then what happened?" I asked, simply to prompt him to continue.

"Detective Dorian told me that I was now wrapped into the operation for good, and needed to keep my mouth shut, or I'd be going to jail for murder," Dagwood said. "He re-holstered his gun and told me that it was now a murder scene. He told me to take the drugs away from the scene, and he pocketed the money. He informed me that he was now there to do a murder investigation, and that I was the prime suspect as long as I continued to stand there, so from now on, I needed to do whatever he said."

"I guess this gave Detective Dorian an immediate and clean way to replace Mitch Goldberg, and to have a loyal servant," observed

Detective Danny. "He kills Mitch, and now has you in a position where he can frame you for it. He's holding all the cash, and it's now your problem to deal with the logistics of the drugs. This is actually very clever of Detective Dorian. And I thought he wasn't that bright."

"But how can we prove this?" I asked. "Detective Dorian will just say that he arrived at the scene and found Mitch Goldberg already dead. He'll say that no one else was there, but that we subsequently learned that Dagwood had stolen drugs from him, since he was found hiding them under Dottie's garden. The facts, as Detective Dorian will lay them out will make it clear that Dagwood killed Mitch Goldberg."

"But can't they trace the bullet to his police revolver?" Dagwood asked suddenly, as if this would be obvious proof that Detective Dorian had done it.

"Police revolver?" I asked. "Detective Dorian couldn't be that stupid. I'm sure that Detective Dorian must have used a stolen unregistered gun which he disposed of somewhere where we'll never find it. I'm sure we'll find that his police weapon was never fired, and is the wrong caliber. I think that Detective Dorian can frame you for it pretty easily, even if he's the actual killer."

We decided that we were done for now, and needed to probe Detective Dorian in a non-obvious way. So we got up to leave, and Jack walked over to the china cabinet. He reached up on top of the cabinet, and produced a gun that was lying up there. None of us had noticed it, but Jack - who was much taller - had seen a shape up there that bothered him. That's what he's been staring at. From the table, there was nothing to see. But he had noticed the end of a small cylinder protruding over the top of the cabinet. It was probably the murder weapon.

"Of course, we'll have to have this gun tested," I said to the room, "but I'll bet it's the murder weapon. This really isn't looking good for you," I said to Dagwood.

Dagwood looked shocked. "I didn't know that was up there," he proclaimed. "I never saw it before."

"I'll bet you have," I said. "It's probably the gun used to shoot Mitch Goldberg. You were there - whether you did the shooting or not. We'll know if this is the same gun very soon."

"But how did it get there?" asked Dagwood.

"Duh," I said. "Someone put it there. But to tell you the truth, I doubt it was you. Of all the places you could have put a murder weapon, why would you put it on top of the china cabinet in your dining room? Why would you even have it in your house - with that big ocean out there? You're not that stupid. Someone is trying to frame you. Detective Dorian? Does he ever come here?" I asked.

"Yes, all the time," Dagwood admitted. "As you know, he and I are friends."

"So planting this gun would have been very easy for him," I said.

"Yes," Dagwood replied. "He could have easily put it there. He's been to my house a couple of times since the shooting."

"OK, then we'll take the gun with us, and do some lab tests," I replied. "In the meantime, don't tell anyone that we found a gun. Let's keep this quiet for the time being."

We left Dagwood's house. Detective Danny and I took Jack back to the train station, and then headed home. I had to use The Fingers a lot in Greenwich, and the foghorn a lot on the highway.

Once Detective Danny and I were alone in the car, I asked him a couple of questions. I had an idea how we could solve the case for good.

"Is it possible for you to test the rifling on this pistol barrel and match it - or not - to the bullet that they took out of Mitch Goldberg?" I asked.

"Yes, the lab can do that easily," Detective Danny said.

"I didn't ask if the lab could do it. I asked if you could do it, and do it quietly," I explained. "I don't want other cops knowing about the gun, or that you're testing it."

"Why's that?" Danny asked.

"I have an idea that I'd like to try if this is the murder weapon," I said. "I'll explain it later."

"OK, I can do this quietly in the lab," Detective Danny said. "I'm not as good as the lab technicians, but I can get the pattern and see if it matches. I'll just tell the lab guys that I'm playing around just to learn how to do what they do."

"Try to do it this afternoon," I said. "Again, I have an idea. I'd also like you to get a search warrant for the police to search Dagwood's house in the morning. Also, make sure that Detective Dorian doesn't know about it. I don't want him there to search the house, at least not at first."

"OK, I can do that too," Danny said. "What will we be searching for?" he asked.

"This gun," I replied.

"But we have it," Danny said. "It's not in Dagwood's house. The formal search won't find it."

"I know," I said. "That's the point. Trust me on this one."

"Anything else?" Detective Danny asked.

"Yes," I said. "But only if this is the gun that was used to shoot Mitch Goldberg."

"So what do I need to do if this is the murder weapon?" Detective Danny asked.

"I'll need you to get me Detective Dorian's gun," I said.

"I can't do that," Detective Danny said. "How could I possibly get Detective Dorian's gun?"

"Does he wear it?" I asked.

"Not often," Danny admitted. "He usually leaves it in his locker."

"Well if this gun that we took from Dagwood's house is that gun that was used to murder Mitch Goldberg, then I want to look at Detective Dorian's gun," I said. "I just want to examine it. If you can get it for me tonight, I'll have it back to you early in the morning. You can return it to his locker, and he'll never know that it was missing."

"What good would that do?" Danny asked. "The police revolver is a 357-magnum. This gun here is a 22-caliber. They're not at all the same, and they don't shoot the same bullets."

"Just trust me on this," I said. "They're nearly the same."

"You obviously don't know much about guns," said Detective Danny.

"And assuming that this gun - the 22-caliber gun that we took from Dagwood's - matches the rifling on the bullet taken from Mitch Goldberg, I also will need that gun. I want to do a few simple tests, so I'll need both guns: the murder weapon, and Dagwood's revolver. I'll also need some rounds to fill each gun."

"What do you need the rounds for?" Detective Danny asked.

"I'll need them to do some tests," I replied, and I left it at that.

I dropped Detective Danny off at the police station with the gun that we'd taken from Dagwood's house, and I went home. I thought today went very well, probably because I did the driving.

My phone started ringing when I pulled into my driveway. It was Senator Adler, and he wanted to know the status.

"Don't worry senator," I said. "I've learned a lot about the case that had been unknown before, and I think that I've nearly got it solved. My hunch is that I might have some answers for you tomorrow. That depends on how several things turn out."

I hung up the phone, parked my car, and went inside.

Carol was in the kitchen, starting to get things out for dinner tonight. And for the first time, Dottie was there. Dottie was sitting at the island, and both of them were drinking coffee.

Dottie was made up very nicely, and was wearing a nice lacy blouse with some simple jewelry. She had curled her hair slightly, and it accented her features. She was actually a pretty woman when she put herself together.

I got myself an espresso, and I joined them.

"Good to see you Dottie," I said. "You should come by more often."

"Yes," she said. "I just came by to chat with Carol."

"What were you chatting about?" I asked.

"Clothes, mostly," Carol said. "Things you wouldn't understand. Dottie's trying a couple of new things with her outfits, and we were just exchanging ideas."

"New things with her outfits?" I asked. "Why's that?"

They both laughed.

"Where were you today?" Carol asked.

"Detective Danny and I took a ride down to Cos Cob to visit Dottie's cousin Dagwood," I said. "We just dropped in for a chat."

"Really?" Dottie asked. "And how's Danny doing?"

"He seems a little different lately," I said. "Happier. I think he's met someone that he likes."

"Really?" Dottie asked.

"Yeah," I said. "He just seems a little different; he's been even nicer than he usually is."

Carol and Dottie both laughed.

"Would you like me to help you with anything?" I asked Carol, thinking that perhaps I could cut something or clean something for her while she was doing other things.

"No, I think that I've got dinner under control," Carol said. "Actually, if you could run down stairs and bring up a few cans of stock, I'll need that."

I went down and got some stock. I didn't want to ask what she was making. When I came back up, Dottie was finishing her coffee, and said that she had to go.

"I hope you're not leaving just because I came home," I said.

"No, not at all," Dottie replied. "I've a date tonight, and I wanted to start getting ready."

A date tonight? That devil Danny didn't mention anything about it today. I guess that's how men are. On the other hand, women can be a little strange too. Dottie was going to "start getting ready?" How long would that take? Hours? I guess if it's an important date, then "hours" might be the right answer for a woman.

"Well it was very nice to see you Dottie," I said. "Please come by more often. You've cheered up our home."

Dottie laughed like she knew I was overdoing it with the compliments, said her goodbyes, and left. Once she was gone, I filled Carol in on what we had learned at Dottie's cousin's house that day.

I didn't want to discuss this with Dottie there, because no matter what else happened, her cousin Dagwood was in lots of trouble. He could go up for murder. Or, if he had been telling us the truth, he was still in trouble for a large drug transaction.

And even if he had been telling us the truth, he could still go up for murder. That would depend on whether we could prove that a cop - Detective Dorian - had done it. And that would be hard to do. After all, Detective Dorian had merely come to the murder scene "to investigate a murder that had taken place" based on a call that I had made to the police. No one could place him at the scene of the murder when it occurred except for Dagwood. And Dagwood would have big credibility problems, especially if he'd been framed for doing the shooting. After all, what was probably the murder weapon was found at his house.

Dagwood's main problem was that he was an amateur, and had stepped into lots of traps while working with some professionals. The real irony is that - assuming Dagwood had told us the truth - Detective Dorian had succeeded in cementing Dagwood into this mess by murdering Mitch Goldberg. And Dagwood was the obvious fall-guy for the murder.

Dagwood had been playing a little bit out of his league.

When Carol and I were about to sit for dinner, the doorbell rang, so I got it. I was expecting Danny, assuming that the gun that Jack had found at Dagwood's was the murder weapon, and I had assumed that it was.

Danny was dressed up nicely, so I invited him in, and shouted in to Carol to set another place in the dining room.

"Danny is all dressed up, and has come to join us for dinner," I shouted. "Can you put out another setting?"

"OK," Carol hollered back. "Joining us for dinner Danny? Is that why you're all dressed up?"

Danny looked a little embarrassed, and said, "Thanks, but actually I can't stay."

"You can't stay?" I asked. "Why not?"

"Because I have a date with Dottie," Danny said.

"Never mind, Carol," I shouted into the kitchen. "Danny says that he can't join us because he has a date."

We all laughed. Danny gave me a package, and said "The rifling matches. Here's Detective Dorian's revolver and the murder weapon."

"OK, thanks," I said.

"You do realize that these guns are not the same caliber, don't you?" Detective Danny asked.

"Caliber?" I asked. "What's that? I thought that guns were guns."

"But they're not interchangeable," said Detective Danny. "You can't fire 22-caliber bullets from the 357-magnum pistol, and you can't fire 357 rounds from the 22-caliber pistol. They won't even fit."

"They won't?" I asked. "Well I just want to do some tests. The tests shouldn't take long. In fact, I'll put Detective Dorian's gun back in the bag, and leave it behind the garage. I'm sure I'll be done with it before you're back from whatever you're doing this evening. You can pick it up behind my garage whenever you're done with your date."

"Are you leaving both guns?" Detective Danny asked.

"No," I replied, "just Detective Dorian's. That way, you can slip it back in his locker before he comes in tomorrow morning. He'll never know it was gone. But I'll keep the murder weapon for now."

"OK, I'll pick it up later tonight," Danny said.

"And you got the warrant?" I asked. "The search of Dagwood's house is scheduled for tomorrow morning?"

"Yes, that's all set," Danny said. "And Detective Dorian doesn't know about it. He went home early tonight. That's why I was able to get his gun in time for my date."

"Great," I said. "Then have a lovely evening. And don't do anything that I would."

"OK, got it," Danny said. "I'll have a lovely evening. And don't forget to leave Detective Dorian's gun behind the garage."

"Don't worry about it," I said. "It'll be there."

Danny left to go pick up Dottie, and I sat down for dinner with Carol.

After dinner, I did the dishes, and then went downstairs to my shop in the cellar with the two guns. There was a little bit of work that I needed to do.

When I was done, I put Detective Dorian's gun back in the bag, left the bag behind the garage, and joined Carol in the family room to watch the news with her.

"How did the gun tests work out?" Carol asked.

"Great," I responded. "Everything fit together, just like I was hoping it would."

Day 15

The Murder Weapon

In the morning, Detective Danny came by and picked me up. Because this was official police business, we wanted to go to Dagwood's house in a police car. So it took a lot longer for us to get to Cos Cob. Traffic slowed down when they saw us coming, so we were stuck doing the speed limit.

I had brought the 22-caliber pistol with me, and had wrapped it up carefully so that it wouldn't be apparent. When we got to Dagwood's in Cos Cob, two other police cars were waiting for us.

We served Dagwood with the search warrant, went in, and started a methodical search of his house. Dagwood wanted to know what we were looking for.

"The murder weapon," I told him.

"But yesterday, . . ." he started to protest, and I cut him off.

"You should stay silent," I said. "Stay silent, and don't say anything."

"But yesterday, . . ." he started to say again, and I cut him off again.

"Button it," I said. "Trust me."

I had Detective Danny call Detective Dorian to tell him about the search and to invite him down to join us. "Tell Dorian that we think that the murder weapon is somewhere in Dagwood's house, and we're searching for it. He should come join us if he can."

We went through the house, searching each room methodically. As we finished each room, we put police tape across the doorway to indicate that the room was off the list. We also took lots of photos to show the specific areas that we'd searched. This included the insides of drawers, and of course, the top of the china cabinet in the dining room.

After the dining room had been taped off, and when all of the other police were in other areas of the house, I slipped back into the dining room, put the pistol that I'd brought with me on top of the china cabinet where we'd found it yesterday, and I slipped back out. No one saw me do it.

Sure enough, when we were nearly done, Detective Dorian showed up in a police car with all of his lights flashing. He must have turned them on so that he'd make much better time coming down here.

Detective Danny and I walked out onto the front steps as Detective Dorian pulled into the driveway and stopped. "Did you find the gun?" Detective Dorian asked us.

"What gun?" I asked.

"The murder weapon," Detective Dorian explained. "The gun that you got the warrant to search for. Good thinking, by the way. How did you come to realize that Dagwood was probably the guy who did it?"

"Dagwood was probably the guy who did it?" I asked. "That never occurred to me. I just thought we might find the gun here. I'm glad that you could join us."

"Well did you find the gun?" Detective Dorian asked again.

"No, not yet, unfortunately," I responded, "and we're almost done."

"Did you look carefully?" Detective Dorian asked.

"Yes, very carefully," I said. "If you'd like to help us finish, come on in. We're cordoned-off the rooms that we've finished searching."

"But how do you know that you didn't miss something?" Detective Dorian asked, as he brushed past us to get into the house.

He gave some cursory glances up the hall into the kitchen with the occasional furtive glance into the dining room. He saw that the dining room had been cordoned off, but the kitchen had not.

"Did you guys search the dining room?" he asked.

"Yes," I said. "That's why it's cordoned off."

"And you didn't find anything in there?" he asked.

"Nope," I responded.

He walked into the kitchen, and gave it a few more cursory glances. It was obvious that he wasn't interested in the kitchen.

"We didn't search the kitchen yet," I said. "Do you want to search it?"

"OK," he said, and he started opening drawers and cabinets to glance inside them, without looking seriously.

"Finding anything?" I asked.

"Nope," he responded.

We all searched the kitchen, this time more thoroughly than Detective Dorian had been doing. When we finished, I said: "It looks like kitchen is clean too."

Detective Dorian finally proclaimed, "I've a funny feeling about the dining room. Call it my 'Detective Instincts.' Any problem if I search it again?"

"No, please do," we both said.

Detective Dorian went into the dining room, quickly looked under the table and underneath the chairs, and again cursorily into the cabinets - all of the obvious places that we would have searched. Then he stepped up onto a chair, and looked on top of the china cabinet - as if this wouldn't have occurred to anyone who didn't have "Detective Instincts."

"Well, well," Detective Dorian proclaimed. "What have we here?" he said, reaching over and on top of the china cabinet while holding a handkerchief. Detective Dorian produced the pistol that I'd left there after I'd taken a photo of the top of the same china cabinet showing that is was barren. He had been careful to put his handkerchief over the pistol before picking it up so that he wouldn't add his fingerprints to it.

"What have you found?" I asked.

"The murder weapon," Detective Dorian proclaimed, holding out the pistol draped within his handkerchief.

"That can't be the murder weapon," I said.

Detective Dorian looked baffled. "What do you mean by that?" he asked.

"Why would Dagwood put a murder weapon on top of the china cabinet in his dining-room?" I asked. "That's too stupid. I can't imagine why he'd put it there."

Detective Dorian glared at me. "But here it is!" he exclaimed. "I've found it. Indeed, who would put a gun up there? Who knows why he stashed it there? I'm sure it's the murder weapon."

"No it isn't," I said. "What if I told you that I'm the one that put it there?"

He looked at me like I was an idiot. "I'd say that you're an idiot," he said. I always knew that Detective Dorian didn't like me. I think this was the last straw.

Detective Dorian repeated it for the other cops who had heard the commotion and had come down to see what was happening. "We've found the gun. We're going to take it down to the lab to do rifling tests to see whether this is the murder weapon. And I'll bet anything that it is. Arrest Dagwood," he directed, about his friend. What are friends for?

Dagwood looked very upset. He obviously suspected that I had staged this just to frame him for good. But he did look confused. Why had I taken the gun last night, and then returned it? Was it just so that I could get more cops to his house to be witnesses?

We took Dagwood back into custody, and the uniforms took the gun that Detective Dorian had found, and we all headed to the police station. The cops needed to book Dagwood again, and we needed to do ballistics tests on the gun.

At the police station, we put Dagwood in a cell, and then we headed downstairs to the range and the weapons lab to fire some test rounds.

First, the lab took the gun that was found at Dagwood's house, and dusted it for fingerprints. They found lots of them, and I was willing to bet that they were Dagwood's. In fact, I was sure of it, since I had him handle the weapon this morning before I'd put it on top of the china cabinet.

Then we went to do ballistics tests to see what the rifling pattern produced by this gun was. To do the testing on pistol rounds, a technician fires several rounds though a long tank of water. The water in the tank is able to slow the bullet down before it strikes the end of the tank so that the round isn't significantly distorted.

The lab can then look at the striations around the bullet itself to see whether the rifling imposed by the test-gun barrel was the same rifling that was on the round that was taken out of Mitch Goldberg. If the rifling matches sufficiently well, then this would provide strong evidence that the test-gun was the murder weapon, since it was the same gun barrel that must have produced those striations.

Note that while we'll get rifling patterns from any round, there can be some statistical variations, and in this case, the test medium is somewhat different. Nonetheless, if the lab can reproduce the rifling patterns on the bullet taken from Mitch Goldberg by using this gun, it's fairly conclusive that this gun is the murder weapon - especially given all of the circumstantial evidence, the people involved, and the fact that the gun was found at Dagwood's.

A technician took the gun that was taken from Dagwood's house, fired several rounds into the tank, and then collected them so that the lab could look at the striations. This is where I stepped in to introduce a new variable.

"Because there can be variations in rounds," I started, "we can't reproduce the rifling exactly. After all, a bullet is a piece of metal that comprises tiny metallic grains. It's malleable, so each bullet will distort itself a little differently as it travels through any medium. Also, the bullet that killed Mitch Goldberg went through flesh and hit some bone along the way, so it's certainly distorted in a different way than the ones that we're taking out of this water tank."

"So I want to get a rifling pattern from bullets out of a different gun," I said as I reached out and grabbed the gun that was protruding from Detective Dorian's holster. He tried to stop me.

"Wait a minute," Detective Dorian protested. "That's my gun. I didn't give you permission to use my gun."

"It doesn't really matter," I said. "I just need a second gun. Is there any particular reason why you don't want us to see the rifling pattern produced by your gun?"

This put him in an awkward situation, and he took a moment to respond while considering a good way to get out of giving us his gun.

"But my gun is a 357-magnum. It's not at all like the gun that was used to kill Mitch Goldberg," said Detective Dorian. "Using my gun for test rounds won't prove anything."

"Yes it will," I asserted. "I'm a scientist, and I know what I'm doing. I don't care if your gun is a 357-magnum. I just need a second rifling pattern. I can do everything that I need to do by using statistical methods."

He looked uncertain, but could no longer refuse outright.

"Well OK then," he said, relinquishing his pistol. "Fire some rounds with this," he added, handing his gun to the technician. "But I don't see what it will prove."

The technician took Detective Dorian's gun, and fired a few rounds into the tank.

"Make sure to label those two sets of volleys carefully," I said to the technician.

"You bet we will," the technician said. "We've got three rounds fired from each gun, and we did two volleys. Besides, the first set were shot from a 22-caliber pistol, and the second set were shot from a 357-magnum. It would be impossible to mix them up."

"Great," I said. "When will you have the patterns for us?" I asked.

"Later this afternoon," the technician said.

"Just to make sure that we make no mistakes, what are you labelling each set?" I asked.

"We're labelling them #1 and #2," the technician responded.

I thought about that for a minute. "That's very clever," I said. "How did you think of those names?" I asked.

The technician looked confused. "That's how we always label them," he said.

"And which one is #1?" I asked.

"The first one," the technician responded.

I made myself look confused. "I don't think I can remember that," I said. "Can you also write on #1 something like 'Dagwood murder weapon,' and on #2 'Detective Dorian test rounds?' That would help me a lot."

"Sure," the technician replied, and he walked away shaking his head.

Because it was going to be a while, all of us decided to take a break, and to come back to the station later in the afternoon for the final results. Detective Danny and I took off to our favorite coffee shop downtown, Holy Moly.

Danny and I got a table at Holy Moly, our favorite coffee shop downtown, and I stood in line to get us both some coffee, while Danny held the table. I joined Danny at the table after the barista made our coffees.

"What was the point of having the search done this morning?" Detective Danny asked. "We already had the murder weapon."

"I wanted to see how quickly Detective Dorian would find it," I said. "We didn't find it at all - not that we were looking for it. Jack found it because he's extra tall, and has an eye for things like that."

"I'm sure we would have found it had we searched the place," Detective Danny said.

"Of course," I responded. "But on top of a china cabinet? Who would bother to hide a weapon on top of a china cabinet? If that was really Dagwood's gun, I would have expected him to have taken it out onto the Long Island Sound and to have dumped it in the ocean if he was smart. Or if he wasn't smart, to simply stash it in his dresser or bedroom closet. But on top of a china cabinet in the dining room? Only someone who had no reason to ever go into the bedroom would do that - and I don't think that Dagwood and Detective Dorian swing that way. So I don't think that Dagwood ever put that gun there, and I don't think that it's the murder weapon."

"If it wasn't the murder weapon, why was it hidden at all?" Detective Danny asked.

"It was hidden so that we'd think it was the murder weapon," I explained.

"Well they're doing rifling tests on it now," Detective Danny said. "So we'll know shortly."

"I looked at the gun last night," I said. "I don't think that the gun they have is the one that was used to murder Mitch Goldberg."

"So where is the murder weapon?" Detective Danny asked.

"I think that they're running tests now that will show who the killer is," I said.

Detective Danny thought about that. "That's pretty cryptic," he said.

"Yes, it is," I replied.

As we sat there in silence, the High School teacher Pete Fletcher happened to walk in, and I asked him to join us. First Pete got a cup of coffee, and then he sat down with us. I introduced Danny and Pete to each other.

"A math teacher?" Danny asked. "I was never any good at math."

"Math isn't actually hard," Pete explained. "You just have to reason about most problems, and they'll make sense. The key to math is reasoning and consistency. It has very little to do with juggling numbers. That's what accountants do, and I can't do that either."

"Really?" Danny asked. "Well I'm pretty good at reasoning, but was never good at math. Do you have an example?"

"Mick here came to the school and taught the kids about a very famous math problem called the 'Tweedle Problem,'" Pete said.

"The 'Tweedle problem?'" Danny asked. "I never heard of it."

"Yes," Pete said, putting on a scholarly tone. "It was done by a famous mathematician named Louie Carroll. They wrote a well-known song about him called 'Louie, Louie.'"

"I know the song very well from the old days," said Danny. "That was about a mathematician? I never knew that. What's the 'Tweedle Problem?'"

"There are four Tweedles," Pete said. "Their names are Dee, Dumb, Duh!, and Doo-Doo."

"Dee, Dumb, Duh!, and Doo-doo?" Danny asked. "And you said that this is math?"

"Yes," Pete said. "This is serious math. Let's assume that two of them always lie, and that the other two always tell the truth."

"Which two lie, and which two tell the truth?" asked Danny.

"Ah!" Pete said. "That's where the math comes in. We don't know. When you talk to one of them, you know which one of them it is; that is, you know whether it's Dee, Dumb, Duh!, or Doo-Doo. But you don't know whether he's lying or telling the truth. But what you also know is that if he's lying, then he'll always lie, and if he's telling the truth, then he'll always tell the truth."

"But that's not like real life," Detective Danny explained. "Real people don't always lie or always tell the truth. Real people do both."

"Yes," I said, "but some real people tend to tell the truth, and some tend to lie, so this is a math problem that's almost like real life. But there's another important detail here. We also know that among the four Tweedles, exactly two of them lie, and exactly two of them tell the truth."

"That's too confusing," Detective Danny said. "And those are stupid names. 'Dee, Dumb, Duh!, and Doo-Doo?' He picked stupid names like that, and they wrote a song about him? 'Louie, Louie?' I don't believe it. That sounds like bullshit."

"Yes, that's all true," said Pete the science teacher. "So let's say that two of the Tweedles always lie and that the other two always tell the truth. What question would you ask one of them so that from whatever answer he gave you, you could infer the truth about something?"

"Well since you don't know whether the answer will be the truth or whether it will be a lie," Detective Danny said immediately, "the question you'd ask one of them would have to be about the answer that you could expect from a different one of them."

"You see?" I said. "That's the entire puzzle, and you got it right away. Most people can't see this that quickly. You would be good at math if you just played with it a little."

"But that's still a stupid question," Detective Danny said, "and it doesn't reflect real life, and their names are stupid."

"OK, then let me give you a real problem," I said. "Let me give you a problem from real life." I thought for just a minute.

"Well let's hear it," Detective Danny said. "I'm ready for a real problem."

So, I posed a real problem. "Instead of 'Dee, Dumb, Duh!, and Doo-Doo,' let's say that the four real people are named 'Danny, Dottie, Dagwood, and Dorian.' Let's say that they all know each other, and that two of them - Dannie and Dottie - tend to be honest, and usually tell the truth, and the other two - Dagwood and Dorian - are hard to trust, and tend to lie a lot. If I picked one of them, say I pick Dottie, what question could I ask Dottie so that from her answer I could figure out who murdered Mitch Goldberg?"

"Ah!" Danny exclaimed. "Now that's a real question that I can relate to. This is what math is all about?" he asked. "I think I could actually be good at it."

Detective Danny took a napkin out of the napkin-holder and a pen out of his pocket, and he started jotting things down on the napkin. I could tell he was off in his own world, and was very focused - just like I get when I'm working on problems. Danny likely would be good at mathematics. He'd just need to learn some basics - probably the basics that many kids phase out when they're in High School.

Detective Danny was working away diligently.

While Danny worked away, Pete said, "Well I'm ready to hear about the last problem that you mentioned. You've mentioned it a couple of times, but never told me what it was."

"The last problem?" I asked. "I don't remember. Which one was that?"

"You said that it was called 'Adler's Problem,'" Pete said.

"Oh yes - 'Adler's Problem' is a gem," I responded. "It might be too advanced for a High School class, but I'll explain it to you here. It's the kind of thing that's perfect for a coffee shop."

"So what is 'Adler's Problem?'" asked Pete.

I took a deep breath, and explained: "Alfred Adler was one of the founders of what we now call psychology. He was a contemporary of both Carl Jung and Sigmund Freud."

I thought for a minute, to arrange my thoughts, and then continued: "Alfred Adler believed that a person's behavior is motivated by an innate desire to achieve superiority. On the other hand, Carl Jung, who founded the school of analytical psychology postulated the process of what he called 'individuation,' by which he meant 'the process of integrating the conscious with the unconscious while maintaining conscious autonomy.' And Sigmund Freud founded the school of psychoanalysis, and is best known for his theories about the unconscious mind, and principally the unconscious mind's main defense mechanism, which he called 'repression.' Freud felt that repression was built in, and that it was a natural defense mechanism that all people had. This was in contrast to Adler's belief that that all people innately strove for personal superiority."

I paused to collect my thoughts. Pete looked a little confused, but then he urged me on. "OK, but what's 'Adler's Problem?'" he asked.

So I continued to explain: "Well one day, Adler, Jung, and Freud were standing in a circle - actually it was a triangle - on campus. They were enjoying the sun, and talking about psychology," I said. And then, all at once, Carl Jung excitedly exclaimed: 'Sigmund! Sigmund!'"

After another moment, I continued: "Carl Jung grabbed Sigmund Freud's sleeve and shook it in alarm. 'Sigmund!' he exclaimed again. Freud looked at Jung and said: 'What's the matter Carl?' And Jung said: 'I hate to tell you this, but Adler is peeing on your shoe!' Sigmund Freud looked down at his shoe, and saw that this was true, and that Adler was peeing on it."

"And then what happened?" asked Pete, clearly drawn in.

"Freud looked calmly at Jung, and said: 'That's Adler's problem.'"

We finished our coffee, and Detective Danny drove us back to the police station so that we could all learn the results of the ballistics tests. We figured that the lab would be done by now, and we'd find whether the gun was the one that was used to kill Mitch Goldberg.

On the way back, Detective Danny, who was driving, said "I figured it out."

"You figured what out?" I asked.

"I figured out what question I'd ask Dottie to figure out who killed Mitch Goldberg," he said.

"What would you ask her?" I asked.

"I'd ask Dottie whether she'd ask me to figure it out," Danny said. "And then I'd beat the crap out of Dagwood until he agreed to turn evidence on that prick Detective Dorian. And if that didn't work, then I'd beat the crap out of Detective Dorian."

"See?" I asked him. "You'd be a natural as a mathematician. A little practical thought, and you've solved the problem." I sang "Louie, Louie" the rest of the way back to the station.

We went downstairs to the range and police lab, and there was a big argument in progress. Detective Dorian and a couple of other officers had beaten us there, and the technician was explaining that something went wrong with the tests, and that he'd have to repeat them.

"What could go wrong with a simple ballistics test?" Detective Dorian was demanding to know. "We were all here when it was done. You fired a few rounds through the water chamber. What else is there?"

"Something's wrong," the technician was trying to explain. "I'm not sure how it got screwed up, but the samples we got from your gun can't be correct. We need to repeat the tests."

"I don't even see the point of firing test rounds from my gun, and I objected to this in the first place," Detective Dorian was stating angrily. "There is no reason to take tests from my gun. It's only Mickey Maux here who wanted them, and no one else understands the point. Again, it's a 357-magnum, and the murder weapon was a 22-caliber pistol."

"Well somehow, we got the samples mixed up," the technician was trying to explain. "So we need to repeat the tests."

Detective Dorian was reluctant to give them his gun again, so Detective Danny called the chief, and the chief came down and instructed Detective Dorian to turn it over.

"One thing that we did do was to analyze the fingerprints that we took from the 22-caliber pistol," the technician said. "They're Dagwood's prints. They're all over the gun. I understand that you're holding him upstairs."

"That's correct," Detective Danny said. "It's reassuring to know that we got the right guy, and that his prints are on the murder weapon."

Actually, I wasn't at all surprised, since I had asked Dagwood to handle the gun a lot before I placed it up on top of the china cabinet this morning. I thought that it would be important to tie this gun to him, just in case there were any mistakes made.

"You're sure that those are Dagwood's fingerprints on the 22-caliber pistol?" I asked.

"Positive," the technician said. "They're all over it. But we will need to repeat the ballistics tests."

"What went wrong?" I asked.

"I don't know," the technician said. "Somehow we're missing the 357-magnum test-round firings. I'm not sure what happened to them. They probably got moved by someone who came in to clean up, and we'll find them tomorrow. But we need to repeat the firings. I'll do this tonight, and for sure we'll have the results in the morning."

So the final results would have to wait until tomorrow morning. We all left the lab, and I left the police station. The one positive thing that came of this is that on the way out, I recognized the cop whose pictures I had who wrote me a ticket the other day. He was getting into his personal car to go home. It was a nice red Toyota.

So I snapped a shot of his plates, and sent it to the Shit-Ninny control station. Every dark cloud has a silver lining.

I went home and started to make dinner. I thought that Carol and I could go to the Cineplex tonight to see a good movie. Rather, we'd each see a good movie. One of man's greatest inventions is the Cineplex. It was obviously invented by married people for use by married people.

When people are single and dating, they have to go to the same movies together. And to impress their dates, they have to pretend that they're enjoying whatever movie they've agreed to see. So sometimes a dating couple will go to see a woman's love-story movie, and the man will pretend that he's having a good time trying not to barf while having no idea what's going on in the movie, and sometimes the same couple will go to see a man's shoot-'em-up movie, and the woman will try to keep her eyes open and pretend that she's finding all of the blood and guts exciting.

Once you're married, you don't have to do this. You can go to the theater together. The wife can go see the "love-love kiss-kiss" movie, and the husband can go see the "bang-bang shoot-em-up" movie. The two of you can meet in the lobby at the end of the movies, and then you can go out for a drink, both having enjoyed your movies. And over your drinks, you can talk about other things.

I had found a good man's movie that I had wanted to see.

It was about a bunch of weird looking science guys who had hijacked a moon-vehicle from NASA that was loaded with machine guns and rockets. They were going to destroy the world and kill everyone in order to stop people from causing global warming. This was because they were worried that global warming would destroy the world and kill everyone. They were working in cahoots with an evil, shape-changing space alien. And there was a group that was trying to stop them. This was a bunch of bearded, tattooed tough-guys with lots of body-piercings who rode motorcycles, and who had bazookas that fired nuclear warheads. They wanted to kill the weird-looking science guys because they wanted global warming to continue because they wanted to destroy the world first by shooting everyone. And then there was a large tribe of flesh-eating zombies who drove around in garbage trucks and school busses, and who wanted to save the world so that they could continue to eat human flesh. You get the idea - a great-sounding movie. I never understood why women didn't like these.

And I knew that there was a good woman's movie that Carol had wanted to see.

It was about a typical, plain-looking American girl who meets three very wealthy and very handsome gay guys - each with a different kind of accent - while she's riding on trains through Europe. All of them love her, but don't want to have sex with her. In the end, she marries one of them, and the other two marry each other. I never understood why women liked movies like this. I guess you have to be a woman to enjoy these.

Carol and I had dinner, went to the movies, and then went out for a nightcap in a local nightspot with nice lighting. We got a small table by the front window that had a small lit candle in a holder on the center of the table. There was soft background music playing, and we could hear chatter coming from the large bar-lounge in the center of the room. Lots of middle-aged people were there, trying not to pick each other up.

The waitress brought us a couple of "mystery martinis" that were red and delicious. When I was younger, I would have been embarrassed to be seen with a pretty red drink in a funny glass sitting in front of me. I was also thinking that this wouldn't work for our hero in any detective movie either. What was in it? I probably didn't want to know. It looked like a girlie-drink.

"How was your movie?" I asked Carol.

"Great," she said. "They fell in love and got married in the end."

"Really?" I asked. "Gee, that must have been a surprise. I wish I'd seen it."

"Maybe next time," Carol said. "And how was your movie?" she asked.

"Great," I said. "They killed the bad guys and saved the world in the end."

"Really?" she asked. "Gee, that must have been a surprise. I wish I'd seen it."

"Maybe next time," I said. "We should go out to see movies like this more often."

"So what happened with the case today?" Carol asked. "Was the gun that they found at Dagwood's house Dagwood's gun? And was it the murder weapon?"

"No," I said, "but they don't know that yet."

"Then how do you know it?" she asked.

"Because I'm the one that provided it," I answered. "It's our gun."

"Is it that small pistol from that collection that you have downstairs?" Carol asked.

"Yes, that's the one," I said. "I'll see if I can get it back when the case is over."

"So how did they leave things if that was the wrong pistol?" she asked.

"They were going to re-do the tests. The lab guys have probably already done them," I said, "and we'll see what they found in the morning."

"Won't they just find that the gun doesn't match?" Carol asked.

"Not at all," I replied. "I think that they'll find that it matches quite nicely."

"How can that be?" Carol asked.

"It's just simple mathematics," I said. "I've transposed the logic of Louie Carroll's Tweedle paradox, and I've turned it into what will be a modern version of 'Adler's Problem.'"

"What's Louie Carroll's Tweedle paradox?" she asked.

"Do you know the song 'Louie, Louie?'" I asked.

"Of course," she said.

"Well that's the gist of what I did," I said. "We'll see if it works in the morning."

We finished our mystery martinis and went home. On the way out, I noticed that all of the middle-aged bar patrons were still having a great evening, because no one had picked anyone up yet.

Day 16

Adler's Problem

In the morning I got up early, took my run, had a light breakfast, and headed downtown. I wanted to know what the police lab had found with their second set of tests, and was eager to see if this would provide the final answers to this perplexing case.

When I got to the police station and parked my car, I immediately saw an ostentatious sign. There was a nice red Toyota parked near me. It was the one that I'd seen yesterday that belonged to the cop that had given me the ticket. It had been hit with numerous paintballs. I knew that it was going to be a great day.

Detective Danny had set up a meeting in the conference room on the main floor so that we could review the findings. He'd even had coffee brought in, so I served myself a cup. There was a conference table with chairs around it, and more chairs along one wall in case there were too many people - which there were. There was also a projector in the front of the room that one of the lab guys was connecting to his computer. We were going to see some pictures.

Of course Danny was there, and so was Detective Dorian, as was the chief. This was a clear sign that this case had developed momentum, probably because the lab had had problems with their first set of tests, and because Detective Dorian had been reluctant to allow them to test his gun. There were also a few other officers that I recognized from yesterday, but I didn't know their names.

But the big surprise was that Senator Adler was there with a private secretary, an attorney, and a personal bodyguard. I was quite surprised to see an out-of-state senator, let alone *any* senator sitting in on an investigation. So I asked Detective Danny what was going on, and why the senator was there.

Detective Danny told me that the senator was told by someone that the case "had been solved," so he flew out from California because he had personal interest in knowing what had happened to his bodyguard, Jack Holdt. No one had told him that his bodyguard was just fine, had secretly retired, and was living in the nice part of New Jersey.

I wondered how the senator had even known that the case had reached a breaking point, since I hadn't told him. Someone else must have told him. It certainly couldn't have been the chief, because today could prove embarrassing, and I was sure that the chief was too low-level to call the senator anyway, so it must have been Detective Dorian. After all, I'd learned that Detective Dorian worked for the senator.

"Hello senator," I said, walking over to shake his hand. "I'm surprised to see you here."

"Hi Maux," he replied. "I was told that you might have solved the case, so I wanted to be here when it broke. And I especially wanted to make sure that certain confidential information is not released by the police," he said, gesturing at his attorney, "depending on what that information is, if you understand my meaning." He stared directly at me to make sure that I got his drift.

"Of course, senator," I replied, "and I'm glad that you were able to join us."

I sat down at a chair in the front of the room, which Detective Danny had reserved for me. He knew that I'd want to look closely at the evidence, and ask lots of questions.

The guy from the lab started by introducing himself as "Officer Stevens" and then projected an image of the bullet that had been removed from Mitch Goldberg. There were several shots of it so that we could see the rifling pattern. And yes, since the bullet had gone into Mitch Goldberg, it was distorted.

Officer Stevens explained what the images were and what they showed, just in case anyone in the room - like the senator - didn't understand what they were looking at.

Officer Stevens then told us that he was going to show the patterns from the rounds fired from the 22-caliber pistol that Detective Dorian had found at Dagwood's house. I could see that both Detective Dorian and the senator appeared very interested.

The technician explained that there were actually two sets of firings done, because the lab had been confused by the results of the first set. So he showed us six riflings; three from each set of firings. They all looked very similar.

"I don't see what the problem with the first set of firings was," said Detective Dorian. "Can you please explain why you had to redo them?"

"I'll answer that question with the pictures that I have coming up," Stevens explained. "You're right that for this gun, both sets of firings produced very similar results. The same was true of the two sets of firings done with the other gun."

"You mean the two sets of firings done with the 357-magnum?" Detective Dorian asked.

"I'll get to that," said Officer Stevens. "Give me a couple of minutes."

"I just want to understand why you thought that you needed to repeat the tests," said Detective Dorian.

"That wasn't up to me," said Officer Stevens. "Someone higher up asked that we repeat the tests," he said, glancing at the chief. "We wanted to make sure that they were correct, because they seemed puzzling at first."

"What was puzzling?" asked Detective Dorian. "If I look at the riflings on these six rounds - the ones fired by Dagwood's gun - they have the same riflings as on the bullet taken from Goldberg."

"All riflings are similar to some extent," explained Officer Stevens. "When I was new at this, I would have said that they looked the same. But since I've been studying rifling patterns for quite some time now, I can see a few distinct differences. Let me point them out."

Officer Stevens went through the images that we'd seen again, and pointed out some subtle distortions that were clearly different. Since I'd never studied rifling patterns, I wouldn't have known what to look for, but after Stevens went through the pictures again and pointed to several things, it was clear that they were different.

"The gun that fired the six test rounds was not the same gun that was used to murder the subject," Officer Stevens concluded. "The murder weapon was a different gun. I'm not sure where you got this gun that we tested, but this ain't it."

Detective Dorian looked very surprised. I wasn't surprised at all, since the test gun was mine. I had substituted it the night before.

"On the other hand," Officer Stevens continued, "the next gun was a puzzle. The next gun is the reason that we had to repeat the tests. We thought that we'd made a mistake, and then we examined the gun. It was no mistake. Whoever did this was very clever."

Detective Dorian looked very confused. Maybe it was because Officer Stevens had said that the gun's owner - Dorian - was "very clever."

"Why was Detective Dorian's gun a puzzle?" I asked. "It's just a 357-magnum; a standard police pistol. What's puzzling about it?"

Officer Stevens paused for a minute, and then projected the rounds fired from Detective Dorian's gun. "The puzzle was that these aren't 357-rounds. They're 22-caliber rounds as well. Yesterday we thought that somehow, we'd made a mistake, and had tested the 22-caliber pistol twice by accident. So we ran the tests again, and found that it was no mistake."

"What do you mean by 'it was no mistake?'" asked the chief. "A 357-round is 357 mils, and a 22-caliber round is 220 mils. How could a 357-magnum pistol fire 22-caliber bullets?"

"Because someone who was very clever doctored the murder weapon," Officer Stevens answered.

"What do you mean by 'doctored the murder weapon?'" asked the chief. "'Doctored?' How? And what makes it the murder weapon?"

"We know it's the murder weapon because of the rifling patterns," Officer Stevens answered. Stevens put up pictures showing the 22-caliber rounds fired from Detective Dorian's 357-magnum, and the 22-caliber round taken from the victim, Mitch Goldberg.

"The rifling patterns are virtually identical," Officer Stevens continued. He then pointed out all of the little distortions in the patterns, and showed how those were nearly identical to the patterns in the round taken from Mitch Goldberg.

"I think that there's no question that this is the murder weapon. I would testify to that any day," concluded Officer Stevens, a senior lab technician, and an expert on rifling patterns.

"But that makes no sense," said Detective Dorian, talking to Officer Stevens as if Stevens didn't understand the basics. "My gun is a 357-magnum. It can't fire 22-caliber bullets."

"You mean it couldn't when it was new," the technician said. "But someone modified it. Probably so that no one would find the real murder weapon. And even if they did find it, someone modified it so that no one would suspect that the weapon that they were holding was the murder weapon. This 357-magnum pistol is the murder weapon, but it was modified so that it would fire 22-caliber bullets."

"That's not possible," said the chief. "A 357-magnum couldn't possibly fire 22-caliber bullets. And it wouldn't be safe to even try it."

"That's what we thought at first," said Officer Stevens. "But then we examined the gun. Someone took a 22-caliber gun barrel and machined it down so that it would fit into the 357-caliber gun barrel - which had been bored-out to accommodate the 22-caliber barrel. Then they slid the 22-caliber barrel down into the 357 barrel, and they made the 357-magnum pistol into a 22-caliber pistol. It was very clever, and I never would have thought to even look for this. But after two sets of tests we knew that there was something strange about this gun. There's no question that it's the murder weapon."

"But it's a revolver," Detective Dorian said. "The 357 chambers can't hold 22-caliber rounds."

"That's a much simpler problem," Officer Stevens, the senior technician, said. "All they did was to wrap the cartridges with electrical tape. True, it makes them harder to pull out, but it makes the 22-caliber rounds fit. Electrical tape is about 10 mils thick. Whoever did this ran electrical tape around each of the cartridges about six times so that they fit. The 22-caliber rounds with electrical tape wrapped around them fit smoothly into the 357 chambers."

"That means that Detective Dorian is the one that murdered Mitch Goldberg," I said.

Detective Dorian exploded: "That's crazy!" he shouted. "I did not use this gun to shoot Mitch Goldberg. Mitch Goldberg was shot with the pistol that we found at Dagwood's. The lab obviously made a mistake, and their explanation isn't credible. They need to re-examine these weapons."

"But they already did re-examine them," I said. "And they figured out that Mitch Goldberg was murdered with your gun."

Detective Dorian exploded again. "But that's not my gun!" he shouted.

"It isn't?" I asked. "But we took it from you yesterday down in the lab. What do you mean 'it isn't your gun?' Who's is it? You were carrying it."

"I mean . . ." he shouted, but wasn't sure where to take it, so he just started babbling.

"You're under arrest," said the chief. "We'll figure all this out. But in the meantime, I'm going to have to arrest you."

Detective Dorian pulled himself together, and continued to argue. "But we've already arrested Dagwood for the murder, and we found the murder weapon at his house."

"Correction," I offered. "You're the one that found that weapon at his house. We searched his house before you got there, and we didn't find it. You're the one that found it."

"That's because you guys did a sloppy job of searching for it," Detective Dorian replied.

"That's not true," I countered, pulling out my phone, pulling up the photos, and scrolling to the one showing the top of the china cabinet at Dagwood's house. I showed everyone the photo. We searched Dagwood's house before Detective Dorian showed up, and I took lots of pictures. Here is a picture of the top of the china cabinet - where Detective Dorian claims to have found Dagwood's gun - before Detective Dorian got there. There's no gun here. Then Detective Dorian shows up and finds a gun here? It's pretty obvious that he planted it."

"I did not!" Detective Dorian started shouting again. "The gun was up there when I looked! You guys just did a sloppy job."

"But here's a picture of the top of the china cabinet before you arrived," I countered. "There's nothing up there. How is it that a gun materialized right after you showed up? We had that room cordoned off after we searched it. To me, it's pretty clear that you brought the gun with you and you planted it there."

"I didn't plant the gun!" Detective Dorian yelled. "I found it there. I didn't bring it with me."

Everyone was looking at Detective Dorian like he was nuts.

"And it isn't even the murder weapon," I continued. "It failed the rifling tests. Do you think that the lab guys are stupid or something? You're the one who was carrying the murder weapon. Why did you plant a bogus gun at Dagwood's house? Were you trying to frame him or something?"

"But I'm a cop!" Detective Dorian continued. "I'm one of you guys. I didn't do it. We've already got Dagwood under arrest, and he's the one that had the drugs, so he's the murderer. It's obvious that he shot Mitch Goldberg, since we caught him with the drugs. He buried them at his cousin's house and then was trying to hide them on his boat."

"But Dagwood said that you're the one that shot Mitch Goldberg. And you're the one that had the murder weapon," I added.

"I wasn't even there," Detective Dorian said. "I was responding to a call. Someone reported a murder, and I was sent to investigate."

"I was the one that reported the murder," I said. "But I didn't see Dagwood there." I neglected to mention that it was a different murder, and that it wasn't a murder. I didn't want to tell Senator Adler things that he didn't need to know.

"That's because the murder had already happened, and Dagwood had left," Detective Dorian argued. It was clear that we were mixing up the two murder scenes, which was fine with me.

"How do you know that Dagwood did it if he had left?" I asked.

"Because when I got there, I saw him in the car with Mitch Goldberg," Detective Dorian said. "They were doing a drug deal, and I went to stop it."

"I thought that the murder had already happened and that Dagwood had already left," I said. "I thought that you were sent there to investigate a murder that had already happened, and now you're telling us that when you got there, you saw Dagwood doing a drug deal with Mitch Goldberg. So it sounds like you actually got there before there was a murder. How could you have been responding to a call about a murder that had already happened if it didn't happen until after you got there?"

He didn't know how to explain his way out of that one, so he brought up my first visit to the police station. "But you reported a different murder. I was responding to that murder."

"A different murder?" I asked, and tried to look confused. "What murder was that?"

"The other murder," he said.

"What other murder?" I asked.

Again, everyone looked at Detective Dorian like he was nuts.

"To me," I continued, "it looks like you went behind the store to do a drug deal with Mitch Goldberg and Dagwood. The only murder was Mitch Goldberg's. And Dagwood says that you did it."

"No," Detective Dorian corrected me. "The drug deal had nothing to do with me. It was just Mitch Goldberg and Dagwood, and the guy from California."

"A guy from California?" I asked. "Who's that?"

"The guy from California, who brought the drugs," Detective Dorian said.

"What guy from California?" I repeated. "I thought you just said that when you got there, it was just Mitch and Dagwood. There was a big package of drugs, but there was no guy from California. So apparently, Mitch and Dagwood were doing a drug deal, and there was a guy from California that wasn't there, and then you showed up."

"Yes," he said. "And I saw them with a big package of drugs."

"Well it seems that Dagwood left the scene with the big package of drugs," I said. "Didn't you try to stop him?"

He wasn't sure what to say. "Well I was going to, but he ran, and I had to deal with the murder."

"So you witnessed the murder?" I asked.

"Yes," Detective Dorian continued. "Dagwood shot Mitch Goldberg, and then he ran down the alley with the drugs."

"But it sounds like he shot him with your gun," I said. "How did he do that? And why didn't you call for backup? And why didn't you report the murder since you witnessed it and knew who did it? And why didn't you report the drugs?"

I let the room sit in silence for a minute, and then I continued.

"I'll tell you why," I said. "It's because you're the one that's dealing the drugs. And you've got a great cover as a police detective. Dagwood admitted that he was doing a drug deal, but he claims that you showed up at the scene and murdered Mitch Goldberg, then took off with the money. I'm fairly handy with computers, and I saw some very large cash deposits made to your bank account following this deal. The deal went bad. But you left with the cash, Dagwood left with the drugs, and one of you shot Mitch Goldberg using your gun."

"Dagwood shot Mitch Goldberg," Detective Dorian said.

"Why would he do that?" I asked. "He'd just bought lots of drugs from him."

"He did it so that he could keep the money," Detective Dorian said.

"But he didn't keep the money," I said. "You're the one that took the money."

"Don't accuse me of stealing the money," Detective Dorian said, and I noticed that he glanced at Senator Adler who looked pretty angry, although he was making an effort to look disinterested.

"Dagwood had nothing to gain by shooting Mitch Goldberg," I said. "He was doing a drug deal. It was nearly done. Dagwood gave

Goldberg a big package of drugs, and Goldberg gave Dagwood a big package of money. The deal was done. Then you showed up. You shot Mitch Goldberg, stole the money, and let Dagwood take off with the drugs. And you didn't report anything except that you had found Mitch Goldberg murdered. And Dagwood told us that you're the one that shot him, and that he was an eye-witness."

"But you can't believe Dagwood," Detective Dorian argued. "He's a low-life drug dealer."

"Well he is a low-life," I said, "but a rich low-life. And he's not a drug dealer. This was his first 'deal,' and he's obviously an amateur. He was trying out a new profession, and he's not good at it. Dagwood is a doofus. But he doesn't shoot people. He doesn't have the stomach for it. But I can tell that you do."

"How can you tell?" Detective Dorian asked defiantly. "What gives you the magical power to know who can do what?"

"I can just sense these things," I replied. "I first suspected you when I saw you wearing pink socks and brown shoes with a blue pinstriped suit," I said, and people that were in range looked at Detective Dorian's feet. "But when the lethal bullet matched your gun, that's what did it for me."

I could see Detective Dorian getting angry. "That wasn't my gun!" he shouted.

"Yes it was," I said. "We took it from you, and the lab showed that it's the murder weapon. Why did you shoot him?" I asked. "He was a relatively inoffensive barber who wasn't physically intimidating in the least. Why did you have to shoot him? Just to steal the senator's money?" I asked, shifting my gaze to the senator, who looked startled.

"Dorian, you should keep your mouth shut!" exclaimed the senator.

Suddenly, Detective Dorian looked very angry. It was clear that Detective Dorian's anger was directed at the senator, because it was clear that Detective Dorian was screwed, and he didn't appreciate Senator Adler's interjection.

"I didn't steal the senator's money!" Detective Dorian exclaimed. "That was my payment for eliminating Mitch Goldberg. The senator directed it, and that was my payment."

Senator Adler's lawyer jumped up and objected strenuously, for whatever good that did him.

And I got up and left strenuously, for whatever good that did me. I was done here, so I figured that the rest of it would have to be worked out by the lawyers. And I also felt that I had earned the money that the senator had given me. I hoped that he was happy with my work.

Since I was done at the police station, I got in my car and went to Holy Moly's to get a latte. I was able to get a nice table in the corner, and I'd brought my computer so that I could play some chess. When I was about ten minutes into my game, Detective Danny showed up.

"I thought I'd find you here," Danny said. "You left a real mess back at the station."

"I did?" I asked. "All I did was to solve the case. As to who's actually guilty, that will have to be sorted out by the lawyers, and that could take them years. Criminal law is like football, and the lawyers are like the refs, umps, and field judges in the game. I'm now out of the loop. The 'official play' is over, and the rest is up to the lawyers. They'll argue the details."

Detective Danny got in line to get some coffee, and I continued my chess game. Once he had his coffee, he came back and joined me.

"While they served the senator's attorney with some legal mumbo jumbo, they didn't exactly arrest him," Danny confessed. "That would have been awkward. But his attorney is going to have a lot of homework to do, and Senator Adler will likely be charged later."

"But doesn't that depend entirely on Dorian's story?" I asked.

"Well that's obviously the problem," Danny allowed. "And Detective Dorian is a police officer."

"That just throws another wrench into it," I said. "As a cop, Detective Dorian will just say that he'd been framed, that he didn't really do it, that this was all hearsay based on testimony from Dagwood, and that Dagwood is just a flakey drug dealer that made this up to try to pin it on him because he's the detective that was in the process of nailing Dagwood, and so on."

"But what about Detective Dorian's allegation made against Senator Adler?" Danny asked.

"He'll just say that he mis-spoke and that everyone misunderstood him," I said. "And the senator's attorney will claim that there's nothing tying the senator to any of this, and that this is all a setup by crooked cops, and that he's not even from around here, and so on."

"I think you're right," Danny said. "The entire case is circumstantial. It's a big complicated web of supposed facts - about half of them lies - that were put together by people who are impossible to trust. Without that one piece of physical evidence that we got by pure luck, I don't think we'd be able to prove anything. We probably couldn't even have served indictments on these guys. A local police detective and a senator from California? But with the physical evidence that we lucked into, I think we can even get some convictions."

"What physical evidence?" I asked.

"That gun," Danny said. "That was almost too clever for me to believe. And I never would have guessed that Detective Dorian was that clever. He's obviously smarter than I thought. I don't think it would have occurred to anyone but Dorian to put a 22-caliber pistol barrel into a 357-magnum. Why would anyone do that? The irony is that this is what's going to hang him. Dorian obviously went to a lot of trouble to doctor that murder weapon. I don't think any jury would believe that he was innocent after seeing all the trouble that he went to in order to make that thing."

"Yes, you're right," I said. "I don't see how he can argue that an obfuscation as elaborate as that one was done for no reason. That was obviously done by someone who was clever. Who'd-a thunk that Dorian was that smart?"

"And just to think that we found it in the eleventh hour, and by pure chance," Danny said. "You just happened to ask for his gun so that we could compare the rounds fired from the gun taken from Dagwood's house with another gun. And that gun turned out to be the murder weapon. Who'd-a thunk it?"

"Well he was standing there, and he had a gun," I said. "So I guess it was just pure luck that I chose his gun."

"But I also want to know how were you able to figure out that Dorian did the shooting, and not Dagwood. Tell me how you knew that," Detective Danny said.

"Actually, you're the one that figured that out for me," I said.

"I am?" Danny asked, incredulously. "How did I do that?"

"It was your solution to the famous 'Tweedle Problem' that you worked out here at Holy Moly's yesterday," I said. "I think you had a brilliant solution for a real version of the problem: the 'Tweedle Problem' put into the real world, where people don't always lie or always tell the truth. You solved it, and it inspired me. So I used your solution to solve the case today."

"You did?" he asked. "I don't remember what my solution was, exactly."

"Well it had something to do with you and Dottie making a little whoopee," I said, "but I don't remember the specifics of that. And then you said that you'd beat the crap out of Dagwood and Detective Dorian until one of them flipped on the other. So I beat up Dagwood yesterday, and he started leveling with me. So then I beat up Detective Dorian this morning, and he broke. You're the one that solved this."

"You're right about that," Detective Danny allowed. "But the thing that happened this morning that really surprised me is that we've now got Senator Adler on the hook too: as a big drug-dealing mastermind. I never expected that. And whether or not Senator Adler ever gets convicted or goes to jail, his career as a senator is over. He's screwed either way."

"Well," I said musingly, and I took the last swallow of my latte, "that's Adler's problem."

Printed in the United States
By Bookmasters